Praise for Just Like A Dame

"PI stories are hot at the moment, and this is a great addition to the genre. While it's normally a genre I avoid, this is mixed with chick-lit and boisterous good humor to create a laugh-out-loud funny book with sizzling chemistry between its two leads, fantastic dialogue and riotous – and very hot – sex scenes. The romance is genuine and that's what really makes this book a winner. Don't miss it."

--Enchanted Ramblings

"If you want something funny and hot to take with you to the beach, this is the book you need! The action is non-stop, as is the dialog. The slapstick comedy is so well done that I laughed from cover to cover. ...it is obvious that opposites do attract in this story, because it has some of the hottest male/female sex scenes I've seen recently."

--Fallen Angel Reviews

"... a witty tale of Love at first sight. Ms. Dobbs perfectly blended the hot sex scenes with some serious, and other times hilarious moments in between. Max and Angel steamed up the pages as seamlessly as they nearly brought me to tears with laughter during their little spats. ... an enjoyable read filled with hot sex, comedic relief and a great romance."

--Joyfully Reviewed

"...a sexy romp enlivened by wit and charm. Ms. Dobbs, here is a very jazzed and very grateful reviewer saying thank you for filling her reading hours with pleasure and laughter!"

--JERR (Just Erotic Romance Reviews)

"...a fast moving, character driven story about two people who are instantly attracted to each other, but because of their attitudes about gender can be easily split apart. A big plus is that the author includes scenes from Max's hardboiled detective books. This is the perfect way for his alter ego to surface and for the reader to see the vet's creative mindset. The idea of pairing a feminist with a chauvinist balances the attraction with potential conflict."

--Gotta Write Network

"If you like a story with mucho erotica, this is the one for you! Scattered throughout this book are extremely naughty scenes. One finishes, you recover, and another one begins. It does have a plot to it too, I promise! ...Giggles abounded for me while reading this. ... Funny, quirky, and quite rude for my l'il eyes – if you enjoy a bit of the ol' saucy stuff, go buy this book!"

--Ellis Reviews

Just Like A Dame

By Daisy Dexter Dobbs

A Samhain Publishing, Ltd. publication.

Samhain Publishing, Ltd.
2932 Ross Clark Circle, #384
Dothan, AL 36301

Just Like A Dame
Copyright © 2006 by Daisy Dexter Dobbs
Cover by Scott Carpenter
Print ISBN: 1-59998-210-2
Digital ISBN: 1-59998-019-3
www.samhainpublishing.com

First Samhain Publishing, Ltd. electronic publication: April 2006
First Samhain Publishing, Ltd. print publication: July 2006

Dedication

To Mike and Jen. My never-ending source of comedic inspiration.

Prologue

Emerging from the blackness she comes to me, bathed in a light so radiant I'm forced to shield my vision. Like a glorious avenging angel, the beauty's eyes flash and her wings spread as she brandishes her terrible swift sword. I lay motionless on my bed, rendered inert by the unbearable carnal itch that only she can scratch. Even as I watch the gleaming blade of her sword glint, I sense that she hasn't come to slay me. On the contrary, her mission is one of consummate pleasure...pure, intense and profound.

Her approach slow and deliberate, the angel extends the long blade toward my groin, purses her lips and then blows the merest whisper of breath down its length, straight to my rigid, naked cock. It feels as if she has touched me, wrapped her fingers around my girth and caressed me. As if entranced, she watches as my flesh responds, bobbing and rising to remarkable heights under her scrutiny. Parting her lips again, she sends another rush of warm breath wafting over my primed cock, cloaking me with pleasure. And then she licks her lips and moans while her wings flutter gently. Her impassioned utterance resonates in my ears and speaks to me of a famished angel eager to savor my potent male essence. I'll make sure that she is sated, and then some.

Her gown, all but transparent, perfectly flaunts her generous breasts and glistening pussy. The angel's arousal is evidenced in her puckered nipples and the juices shimmering on her pale thighs. Upon sheathing her sword in the white leather scabbard anchored across her back, her fingers travel from her throat to her breasts where they linger a moment and then all the way down her belly to her cunt.

I've never seen a sight quite so luscious as this exquisite ethereal being touching herself. My body tenses in heady anticipation of exploring those same places with my hands, my mouth and my cock…and then ramming hard into her pussy, impaling her.

She's close now. So near that her musky scent of desire pervades my senses like a powerful drug. Every fiber of my being tingles with lust and my cock jerks impatiently as she reaches the side of my bed, fingering the mattress a hairsbreadth from my hip. She gazes down at my erect cock and then into my eyes with unveiled longing.

Our physical union is imminent.

I am about to fuck an angel…

Chapter One

Roused from his deliciously erotic dream by the incessant pounding and ringing at his front door, Max Wiley growled a few choice obscenities, grabbed the baseball bat from under his bed and blindly charged down the stairs with his dog, Spill, at his heels. Some sonuvabitch was going to have hell to pay for jerking him out of his dream just as he was about to sink himself into that sweet, angelic pussy.

Peering out the window he spied an attractive blonde, barefoot and clad only in a long, white nightgown, banging on his door with one hand and applying staccato bursts to the doorbell with the other. With her wild mass of flaxen curls creating an airy halo, she resembled the glorious angel in his dream...minus the wings and terrible swift sword. His mind still wrapped in a fog, Max wondered for a moment if he was still dreaming. The continued racket at the door, combined with Spill's raucous barks and growls, instantly dissolved that theory. He shook his head briskly, gave it a good whack with the heel of his hand and took another look. Yup. There really was a gorgeous, nearly naked woman battering against his door. He cracked open the door and stumbled back as the frantic woman burst in.

"Oh my God, I've killed him. *I've killed Henry!*"

"Huh?" Max had been up late working on the latest manuscript in his Jack Clyde, Private Detective hardboiled crime mystery series, which was already a week overdue. He'd only fallen asleep about an hour ago and was foggy as hell.

"I didn't mean to do it," she screeched, which had the little beagle snarling. "It was an accident!"

Battling back from the clutches of passion-laced sleep, Max scratched his head with one hand and his chest with the other as he bellowed a cavernous yawn. "Lady, what in the world are you talking about?"

"*Please.*" She fisted the sleeve of Max's T-shirt and yanked. "You've got to come with me right away."

His dog-brain deciphering that his owner was being attacked, Spill immediately morphed into his fierce guard dog mode, clamping his teeth on the hem of the woman's gown and shaking it back and forth wildly.

"Easy, boy," Max said, gently easing Spill away with the tip of the baseball bat. "It's okay." Standing firm as the woman continued to tug, he gaped at the wild-eyed vision standing on his doorstep. "Do you have any idea what time it is?"

Drop-jawed, the woman flailed her arms through the air. "What do you mean, *do I know what time it is*? Of course I know what time it is. It's three o'clock in the morning. How can you even ask me something like that after what I just told you?" She seized Max's T-shirt again, wrenching it. "I think he's dead. Come on, hurry up. You've got to see if there's anything you can do."

"Whoa, wait a minute. Slow down..." Max struggled to clear his thoughts. Gorgeous or not, the woman was either a murderer or a nut case—or both—and prancing out into the night with her probably wasn't a good idea. "Do you mind telling me just exactly what you're talking about and who you are?"

Rolling her eyes skyward, she emitted an impatient huff. "Angel."

Max's eyes widened and he looked again for any sign of a sword or, perhaps, a pair of concealed wings.

"Angel Brewster. I live a few doors down from you. I think I may have just killed Henry. He's just lying there, not moving...well, he was sort of twitching and writhing at first, but he's not anymore. I can't tell if he's breathing or not." She looked up at Max who stood silently befuddled. "Well, what are you waiting for? Come on. We need to hurry." She resumed her yanking. Spill fastened himself to her nightgown again, low on his haunches and growling as he bravely battled the billowy white material.

Domestic abuse, Max reasoned as he nudged Spill away. The angel and her husband had some sort of argument that had escalated into a battle and she slew the guy with her sword...piercing, slicing, hacking... Max winced. Maybe she caught him fucking his secretary...or maybe the bastard was a wife beater...

"Did he hurt you?" he asked as his gaze roved over her pale skin, in search of injuries. "Any bruises or broken bones?"

Angel looked at him as if he had two heads. "Of course not. Henry knows how much I love him. I've always seen to his needs. Why would he want to hurt his mistress?"

"Ah, so you're Henry's mistress."

"Yes."

Max nodded knowingly. Clearly a case of BDSM gone terribly awry. On the other hand, maybe the guy told her that it was finished, that she was history and he was going back to his homely, rich wife after she'd given him an ultimatum. Of course, maybe Angel had just gotten tired of the guy and found herself a new, richer sugar daddy. Max quickly appraised her form, backlit from the dim streetlamp. He felt his cock stir as he eyed the full, sensuous curves. So much like the heavenly being in his dream. Too much. A saucy scenario whisked through his mind as he noted her angelic white gown. Yeah, it would fit perfectly as the opener for his next Jack Clyde novel...

She was full and round with milky-white skin spilling out over a white leather bustier, a scrap of silky white panties and legs that wouldn't quit. It wasn't the cool, dank night air that shot a shiver up the blonde's spine, it was a bad case of nerves and murderous intentions. She told Henry she wanted to try a new sex game and the poor shmoe believed her because she had that fuck-me look written all over her. Yeah, she was an angel with a body made for sin and she knew just how to use it. Henry was built like a bull moose, with hands as big as a couple of hams, but the promise of pussy had his dick doing the thinking for him tonight. The big lug willingly let her secure him to the white satin-covered bed with a pair of white fur-lined cuffs. Angel worked him into a passionate lather by doing a slow striptease, and then taunted him with her little white leather whip as she rode him to a screaming orgasm...

Max shifted as his erection bloomed. That was the trouble with creating provocative scenes for his books. His head knew it was just make believe, but his dumb dick never got the message right.

In the afterglow, the little vixen withdrew her mighty sword from its white-leather sheath and slaughtered him. When she was finished, Henry looked like a slab of bloody bacon. The blonde obviously became flummoxed when things got ugly and gory. That's when she donned her innocent-looking white dress and came banging on the office door of Jack Clyde, Private Detective. My door. She had the face of a wide-eyed innocent and a larcenous heart, and from the minute I laid eyes on her I was hooked...

"Are you listening to me?" Angel all but shrieked. Max realized he'd completely missed what she'd said while he'd been busy envisioning the deliciously deadly scene.

She waved an outstretched finger toward the baseball bat. "Unless you plan to beat me over the head with that thing, will you please put it down? It makes me nervous."

After a long moment's hesitation, Max dropped the bat to the thick-pile carpet, speaking calmly as he led the agitated woman to a ladder-back chair in the foyer. "All right, listen, Ms. Brewster, why don't you just sit down here and try to calm yourself while I call the police."

Angel's head snapped up and she stiffened. "The police? Why do you have to call the police? Do they actually arrest people for things like this?"

Slanting her an incredulous look, Max did his best not to telegraph the fact that he thought the sexy blonde had more than a few screws loose. Exerting maximum effort to maintain his calm manner, he said, "Well...let's just say that the police usually like to be notified when a woman butchers her lover." Forcing a reassuring smile, he gingerly sidled over to the small table under the entryway mirror, picked up his cell phone and began punching in a number.

"*What!?*" Angel screeched as she vaulted from the chair, clawing at Max's cell phone until she succeeded in flipping the cover closed. "Where did you get a gruesome idea like that? In the first place, you idiot, Henry's not my lover. He's my—"

"Husband?" Max broke in. "Doesn't matter. I'm afraid it's still a case for the police, ma'am." He flipped open the phone again, only to have Angel snatch it from him and hurl it into the next room, leaving him drop-jawed and sputtering as Spill ran to retrieve it.

"Oh for heaven's sake." Angel growled in frustration. "If you'd been paying attention you would have heard me the first time. Henry's not my husband. He's my cocker spaniel!"

"Cocker spaniel?"

"That's what I said. Maybe I need to spell it out for you...C-O-C-K-E-R—"

"Wait a minute..." Max spoke in a deliberate, slow manner, as if speaking to a child. "You murdered your dog?"

Trilling an exasperated sigh, Angel said, "Well of course I didn't murder him—I mean, at least not in a premeditated way. I *poisoned* him." Slanting Max a look that clearly expressed the fact that she viewed him as feeble-minded, Angel rolled her eyes.

"Oh well, that's different," he said sarcastically as he bobbed his head up and down. Dropping the cell phone at Max's feet, Spill cocked his head up at the woman, first left and then right, seeming to share the same incredulity as Max at the situation.

"You know," Angel said, balling her fists against her curvy hips, "I'm having a major crisis here, fighting to maintain my composure, and I really do not appreciate your sarcasm."

Furrowing her brows, she took a moment to scrutinize the man who stood before her. Max felt his cock stir as her gaze quickly scanned his face, across his chest, down to the plaid boxers covering his groin and back again.

Angel's tongue peeked out to swipe across her lips and she cleared her throat. "When you moved in last month, word around the neighborhood was that you're a veterinarian—so, what's the story?" she asked. "Are you or aren't you?"

"Yes, but—"

Raking her fingers through her jumbled curls and then grasping the sleeves of Max's shirt, Angel shook him. "Well then, for chrissakes, Dr. Wiley, will you please get your vet bag or whatever it is you need and follow me?" Her bottom lip began to tremble. Blinking lush lashes over her sea-blue eyes, a set of fat tears escaped and trailed down her cheeks. She gave Max a pleading look as she clung to his T-shirt. "I can't lose Henry, Doctor...I just can't."

Max was a goner. Hesitantly, he reached out and patted the woman's shoulders, surprised when, sobbing, she melted against his chest. The impact of her tears slammed into him with the force of a train. Separated only by the thin material of his T-shirt and her sleeveless cotton gown, he held her for a few minutes, enjoying the swell of her ample breasts heaving against his chest as she sobbed. Their bodies were pressed so closely Max could feel her heart hammering against him. She felt warm, soft and vulnerable in his arms. As he alternately stroked and patted her back, offering random murmurs of comfort, he remembered that she was stark naked underneath the gown—and he swallowed a rising groan.

It only got worse when her breasts started bouncing against his chest because she was...laughing?

"Mind telling me what's so funny?" Max said, stilling his comforting hand and convinced that the woman was a bona fide fruitcake.

"Your dog is licking my ankles," she said, tittering. "It tickles."

Unmistakably aroused, and painfully aware of his tenting shorts, Max cleared his throat. He reluctantly pulled back, holding the ivory-skinned beauty at arm's length before his overzealous cock burst clear through his shorts. "Yeah, he turns to mush when a woman cries."

Angel looked down at Spill and gasped. Max knew what was coming next.

"Oh, the poor little thing only has three legs." She squatted and caressed Spill's head in her hands, murmuring sympathetic baby talk to the beagle with the missing front leg as she massaged his ears. Max huffed a laugh as he watched his ferocious attack dog snuggle against Angel's leg, looking as downtrodden and pitiful as he possibly could while eagerly lapping up the attention.

"He manages just fine," Max said. "Don't you, boy?" He could have sworn that Spill's lip curled in disdain as the dog nestled deeper into the folds of Angel's gown. "Okay," he said to Angel, "just give me a minute to change and I'll be right back." He slapped his thigh. "Come on, Spill." The dog didn't budge.

Angel looked up at Max with those big watery eyes. "His name is Spill?"

"Yeah." When Angel drew the dog to her bosom Max actually found himself getting jealous. "Back in a minute," he said again.

Great job, ace, he silently chastised himself as he bolted upstairs. *Here you've got a half-crazed woman coming to you in a professional capacity and all you can think about is fondling her breasts and checking out her pussy. Nice, Wiley, real nice.* Scrambling into a pair of jeans and slipping a pair of worn, leather loafers over his bare feet, Max worked to tear his mind from his rowdy cock and lascivious thoughts and steer them to the situation at hand.

It wasn't easy...they didn't come much sexier than Angel Brewster. Those full, lush, womanly curves...that pouty mouth...skin as soft as a flower petal...hair like silken flax... As he grabbed his medical bag he paused and smiled, wondering if her pussy was as blonde as—

Shit! What the hell was he doing? Was he insane?

Instead of getting his libido under control, his cock was even more rigid now, pulsing hard against the denim, demanding to be appeased. Leaning his hands on the dresser, Max dropped his head and sucked in a deep breath, willing himself to rein in the raging testosterone. He glanced up at himself in the mirror, taking in his pained expression. Amazing how a respected and generally composed animal doctor could so quickly morph into a sex-obsessed animal himself.

After a few more deep breaths, he calmly strode down the stairs with medical bag in hand and, hopefully, a new handle on his carnal urges.

Chapter Two

Angel's townhouse was still, except for the faint sound of voices coming from the television. "Why don't you lead me to your cocker spaniel, Ms. Brewster, and tell me exactly what happened."

"Henry and I were up watching an old Cary Grant movie, *Arsenic and Old Lace* and—"

Max cringed. "Arsenic...is that where you got the idea to poison your dog?" What a pity. She was so young and attractive—and so completely whacko. The poor deluded dame was obviously in need of professional help.

There was that look again—the one where she eyed him as if he were sprouting horns. "Is that supposed to be some kind of a sick joke, *Doctor?* Because if it is, I don't find it funny in the least."

"No, of course not. I—"

"As I was saying before you interrupted me, Henry and I were watching TV and—"

"At three o'clock in the morning?"

Angel tsked. "Yes." Looking defiant, she crossed her arms over her chest. "Do you find that amusing for some reason, Dr. Wiley?"

Unaware that he was sporting a smile, Max banished it from his features. "Well, no, I just—"

"Good, then can we please get back to what's really important here?" She eyed Max warily. "In answer to your question about what happened, I was munching on some chocolate chips when Henry jumped up and grabbed the bag in his teeth, spilling the chips all over the floor. Before I could pick them all up, Henry had gobbled up quite a bit."

"Chocolate is highly toxic to dogs," Max said.

"Well, of course it is." Angel threw her arms into the air, letting them slap against her sides as they fell. "Don't you think I know that? I mean, if I didn't know that, then why on earth would I be telling you that I *poisoned* my poor little dog?"

Max offered a cautious smile. "Sorry. Most dog owners aren't aware of the hazards of chocolate." Doing his best to remember that this woman was highly stressed about her pet, Max still found it difficult to deal with Angel Brewster's defensive, belligerent attitude at three in the morning.

"Well I'm not most dog owners, Dr. Wiley." She transmitted a steely glare Max's way. "I am a very responsible pet owner. Henry is the most important thing to me in the whole world. I would never have purposely given chocolate to my dog." Huffing a disgusted sigh, she mumbled something under her breath.

"I didn't mean to suggest that you did, Ms. Brewster." Max's professional tone and insipid smile barely covered his growing impatience. The fact that the attractive Ms. Brewster seemed to think he was some sort of an imbecile grated on his nerves. If the times didn't dictate such a high measure of political correctness, and he were, say, a private eye like Jack Clyde instead of the neighborhood pet doctor, Max might be tempted to grab the luscious blonde by the shoulders, shake some much needed sense into her, and smoosh a grapefruit into her gorgeous kisser, just the way Cagney had done to Mae Clark in

The Public Enemy. Then he'd pull her firmly against him and watch those big baby blues of hers go wide as he rammed his iron-hard cock into her silky depths—or maybe he'd fuck her first, *then* smoosh her with the grapefruit.

The unlikely scenario brought a devilish smile to his lips. Once he'd had his way with her he'd cast the lusty, busty broad aside, letting her drop to the floor in a quivering mass, right next to Henry, and he'd walk out the door and out of her life forever. Max's smile increased—along with the size of his erection.

Angel trilled an exasperated sigh. "Well, are you going to take a look at Henry or are you just going to stand there with that great big stupid grin on your face?"

A narrow-eyed glare replaced Max's grin. Trouble. That's what happened when he let his dick do his thinking for him. "Lead the way." Nope, he didn't care how beautiful Angel Brewster was, or how big her eyes were, or how much he longed to jiggle those full round tits of hers in his hands—this was a dame he most definitely did *not* want to get tangled up with. Now, if only he could get his testosterone driven anatomy to agree with him. Glancing down at his burgeoning arousal he groaned.

As they entered the family room, Angel pointed to a spot on the floor in front of the television. "There he is. There's my poor Henry." She slapped her hands against her cheeks and whimpered.

Max went to the little cocker spaniel's side and began to examine the motionless dog. He glanced back at Angel. "What exactly happened after he ingested the chocolate?"

"Well, he...he..." Angel's bottom lip trembled again. "Henry began to race around the room in circles. Then he dropped and started to go into some sort of convulsions. After that he just got real still and I couldn't tell if he was even breathing. That's when I came over to get you."

"Semisweet or milk chocolate?" Max asked, lifting the lids of Henry's eyes to check them. "How big was the bag—is there any chocolate left?"

"For heaven's sake, Dr. Wiley, how can you even think about munching on candy when my little dog is sprawled out there on the floor, either dead or dying?"

"Lord, give me strength," Max mumbled under his breath as he chuckled softly. "I need to know the type of chocolate, Ms. Brewster," he said her name through clenched teeth, "because it's the theobromine in chocolate that makes it toxic. The concentration of theobromine varies with the formulation of the chocolate. Because of the added ingredients, milk chocolate has less than semisweet, and semisweet has less than unsweetened chocolate."

Angel flinched. "Oh," she said sheepishly. "I'm sorry. Milk chocolate." Padding over to one of the end tables, she turned on a lamp. "Here's a little more light for you." She offered a self-effacing smile.

"That's good—the fact that it was milk chocolate, I mean." Max smiled warmly, not altogether sorry to see the lovely Ms. Brewster flustered and apologetic. "I wanted to know if there was any chocolate left so I could get an idea how much Henry ingested."

"Oh," she said again with a tentative smile. "It was a small bag—six ounces, I think. I'd eaten nearly half the bag before Henry grabbed it."

"You ate half the bag?" Max restated absently as he felt Henry's belly.

Standing arms akimbo, Angel's features morphed into a frown. "Yes, I ate half the bag. So? I work out and eat a healthy, low-calorie vegetarian diet all week long. I allow myself a little chocolate once a week. Is that a crime?"

"I'm sorry, I didn't mean to sound accusatory. I just—"

"Uh-huh. You just thought you'd make an unwarranted comment about my weight, is that it?" Angel tapped her foot impatiently. "Just because I'm not one of those fashionably anorexic women who subsists on a diet of black coffee and lettuce leaves to suit our male-dominated society's skewed image of what a woman should look like doesn't mean that I'm not fit and healthy and quite satisfied with my appearance. In fact—"

"Jesus! Will you please *shut up!*" Damn, he'd never met a woman yet who didn't make things more complicated than they needed to be.

Angel's eyes widened in surprise. After an astonished gasp, her mouth snapped shut.

Max sucked in a deep breath. "For chrissakes, Ms. Brewster, I was simply calculating the amount Henry ate. That's all. I don't care what you weigh or what you eat or what your personal views are about the state of our society, male or female. All I care about is tending to your dog, okay?" He glanced back at Angel, swallowing hard as he noticed that the lamplight behind her silhouetted the lush, curvaceous nakedness beneath her cotton nightgown even better than the streetlamp had. No, she certainly wasn't anorexic. She was all woman. Big, bold, and beautiful. And infuriating as hell.

Averting his eyes from her deliciously backlit shape, he cleared his throat. Against his better judgment, Max allowed his gaze to return to her for just a moment before turning back to Henry. *Careful, Wiley—better rein in those libidinous thoughts of yours before you get in over your head with this nutty dame.* Of course, his traitorous cock wasn't interested in being safe or logical.

Drawing her bottom lip through her teeth, Angel relaxed her stance, letting her arms fall to their sides. "I'm sorry...I'm just terribly on edge. Jumping down people's throats isn't my usual style. Honest."

Max gave a half-smile, nodding in response as she lifted one shoulder in a contrite shrug. His eyes flew to Angel's breast as it shifted and he felt his cock jolt. Nope, uh-uh. This was no good. Regardless of her given name, this woman was no angel—she was some sort of devil-temptress whose magic was transforming him into a hedonistic lecher. Max engaged in a mighty struggle with his bewitched libido. *Must...tear...gaze...from...breasts...*

"I think Henry ate up most of what fell before I could stop him. Is...is he dead?"

Max snapped his gaze to her face and swallowed hard as Angel swiped at a new rush of tears with her fingers.

"No, he's still alive. Fortunately, he didn't ingest enough for it to be a deadly dose."

Angel threw her head back and breathed a colossal sigh of relief. "He's going to be okay then?" Rushing to Henry's side, she dropped to her knees and bent down to hug her dog.

"I think he'll be fine, but we should bring Henry in to my clinic for treatment just to be on the safe side."

"Can't you just give him whatever he needs here?"

Looking down into the most mesmerizing pair of eyes he'd ever seen, Max was acutely aware of the heat Angel's body radiated—not to mention the alluring fragrance of her delicate perfume combined with the faint, sweet aroma of chocolate on her breath. Intoxicating...bewitching...

She leaned over and stroked her fingers through the dog's fur, giving Max a delicious, partial view of her breasts. Tearing his gaze from their rhythmic rise and fall, he cleared his throat and reminded himself that, regardless of the unusual circumstances, this was still a business call and the curvy Angel Brewster was a client. Sucking in a deep breath, he chanced another glimpse at her translucent skin before shifting his attention to the furry patient and forcing himself into his professional mode.

"In a situation like this," Max said in his best doctor tone while fixing his gaze on Henry, "it's very important to support cardiovascular function, control electrolytes and arrhythmias, and the acid-base balance." *There, that wasn't so difficult.* He made a conscious effort to block Angel's enticing fragrance from his nostrils and blot the inviting depths of her eyes and those spectacular breasts from his thoughts.

Angel reached out and touched Max's shoulder. "He *is* going to be all right, isn't he, Dr. Wiley?" Her voice was soft and quivery.

Damn, he wished she hadn't touched him. He might have been all right if she just hadn't touched him.

No longer able to fight the urge, he gazed into her eyes again and smiled. She really was awfully sweet and seemed...*relatively* rational when she wasn't intent on playing the shrew. Angel shifted a bit and her nipples strained against the cotton. His fingers itched to reach out and pinch the rosy buds. To take them in his teeth and... Rising to his feet—the safest thing to do under the circumstances—Max exhaled the breath he'd been unaware he was holding and cleared his throat.

"Basically, Ms. Brewster, treatment for the ingestion of theobromine follows the same strategy as for caffeine overdose. Administration of an activated charcoal slurry is a major component of the treatment. While I'm able to stuff a whole lot into my trusty little medical bag, I'm afraid what I've got in here isn't going to do the trick."

Angel nodded. "All right, I understand. Just let me grab my house keys and we can go." She rose to her feet and disappeared around the corner, returning in less than a minute, jingling her key ring. "Okay, all ready."

A slow smile crept across Max's face. "Uh, don't you want to...I mean, shouldn't you..." He motioned to her nightgown with his outstretched finger.

Angel impatiently flapped her arms. "What?"

"Well, I just thought you might want to change your clothes, Ms. Brewster. Of course, if you're comfortable dressed like that, then far be it from me..."

Angel looked down at herself and gasped. "Oh my God. I'm wearing my nightgown!" Looking horrified, she slapped her hands across her chest.

"Ahem...yes. I couldn't help but notice." He broadcast a silly smile.

"I forgot. In all the commotion, I completely forgot." Breathing in an audible exclamation of dismay, Angel shot Max a venomous look. "Dr. Wiley! How could you?"

"What do you mean? How could I what?"

"Look at me," Angel bellowed. "That's what."

Now it was Max's turn to breathe an audible exclamation. "Well, excuse me for doing what any normal man would do when he's jarred out of a sound sleep at three in the morning by a beautiful, nearly naked woman."

"That's just the point—you're not just any normal man—you're a doctor! Doctors are not supposed to ogle."

"Ogle?" Max sputtered. "I was most definitely *not* ogling." He plowed his fingers through his hair, fighting back the wave of guilt that threatened to wash over him. Okay, so maybe he *was* ogling—just a little. Dammit, it wasn't his fault if she came banging on his door in the middle of the night looking like some luscious, bosomy angel. "So, in your opinion, doctors are

25

supposed to be immune to having normal urges. We're supposed to be above and beyond that nasty, humanistic sort of thing, huh?"

"Well, they certainly should be when they're acting in a professional capacity, *Doctor* Wiley." Angel enunciated his title with added emphasis. "Whether they're people doctors *or* pet doctors."

Releasing a string of choice expletives under his breath, Max swiped his hand over his face and rubbed his jaw. "Again, Ms. Brewster, may I remind you that these are not my normal business hours."

"Granted, but you're still a—" The sound of Henry emitting a low growl distracted Angel from her tirade. "He's making sounds. That's good, isn't it?" Without waiting for an answer, she went to Henry's side and knelt. "Aw, how's my poor little Henry, hmmm?" she said softly as she lovingly nuzzled her pet. "Don't you worry, sweetie, Dr. Wiley's going to take good care of you and make you all better." His eyes still closed, Henry uttered a little moan and plastered Angel's face with a generous lick.

Max smiled. "It's definitely a positive sign that he's responding to you. I'm sure Henry's going to be just fine, but we really do need to get him to the clinic now."

Repositioning her hands over her chest and transmitting a narrow-eyed glare, Angel rose. Max raised his hands as if to signal surrender, and turned away.

"I'm not looking," he said.

"Cross your heart?"

Max made the motion over his chest. "Cross my heart."

With that, Angel scooted across the room and dashed up the stairs.

Hearing her return a couple of minutes later, Max, his back still turned, said, "Well, is it safe?"

"Huh?"

"To look, I mean."

"Oh, yeah," Angel said. "It's safe to look now. I'm decent."

Max spun around and smiled. Gone was the airy, semi-transparent, little white cotton number, but in its place were a pair of jeans that hugged Angel's delectable curves, leaving little to the imagination. Max sensed a slow, appreciative smile crossing his face. The turquoise T-shirt stretched across her breasts was emblazoned with a pair of golden wings, perfectly highlighting the faint outline of her bra and a pert set of nipples that beckoned like berries waiting to be plucked and savored...

Uh-uh. Max shook his head. *Still not safe to look.*

Chapter Three

Having been open just a few months, Wiley Veterinary Clinic and Animal Hospital, just outside of downtown Portland, still smelled like fresh paint, with just a slight undertone of *eau de dog*. Its soft, muted earth tones and soothing choice of artwork and photos suggested a love of the outdoors. The waiting room felt comfortable and appealing rather than cold and clinical like so many veterinarian offices.

"This is really nice. Did, uh," Angel paused, looking down at her shoes, "your wife do the decorating?" Oh jeez...where did *that* come from? She groaned as soon as the stereotypical female question left her mouth. Her cronies at *Women's Wit and Wisdom* would have a field day if they heard their magazine's lead columnist sounding like a man-hungry moron.

"Nope," Max said as he carried the somewhat skittish Henry into one of the treatment rooms and set him on a table. "I'm not married. I've got to take all the blame myself." He grinned up at Angel and she felt herself melt. Damn, she'd clearly been without a man for too long.

Her cheeks growing warm, she shifted her gaze from Max's chiseled features and looked around the treatment room. "I especially like all the photos. The photographer did a great job capturing those dogs and cats in action."

"Glad you like them, they're mine. It's a hobby." He turned his attention to his patient. "Henry's heartbeat is becoming more normal. Seems he's got good recuperative powers." Upon further examination, Max turned to Angel, sporting a dimpled smile. "It's evident that he's well taken care of, Ms. Brewster."

Angel's whole demeanor brightened as she looked into his smile-crinkled eyes. "Thanks, Dr. Wiley." Gliding her fingers through Henry's silky rust coat, she added, "Please, call me Angel."

Nodding, Max broke into a full grin. "Okay, Angel—and no more of this Dr. Wiley stuff, either—it's Max."

"Max," she repeated softly as she looked up into those enticing eyes of his. Their gazes met and locked for a moment before he cleared his throat and returned his attention to Henry.

The neighborhood scuttlebutt was that Max Wiley was a hunk, but Angel certainly never expected the guy to come outfitted with a killer set of dimples, bourbon-hued eyes, thick, inky-black locks hanging over his brow, and the tall, lean musculature of an Adonis. At first, he did seem to be just a tad dopey—and awfully exasperating. Of course, with a body and face like that, who cared? In the midst of her angst over Henry's dilemma, she'd been determined to ignore the fact that the man was flat-out, drop-dead gorgeous. Instead, she'd found herself drooling over the striking, smart-mouthed stranger when her poor little puppy was clinging to the last vestiges of life. She slapped her hands up to her face and groaned at the painful memory of her wicked, demented, heartless, and revoltingly typical female behavior.

She'd become a disgrace to her long held feminist beliefs.

"Um...are you okay, Angel?"

"Huh?" She whipped her head up. "Oh, yeah...yes, I'm fine. Just, um, thinking about Henry. Thanks." She felt herself relax a bit when he smiled. Her gaze traveled to his tousled just-tumbled-out-of-bed hair, focusing on the lock dangling over his eye. Her hand rose involuntarily and she stilled it before reaching out to smooth back his hair. Her gaze found its way to his chest. Such a broad expanse of muscle. When she'd collapsed in tears against him earlier, she'd been amazed at the solid feel of his pecs. Eyeing Max's T-shirt, which was hopelessly stretched out of shape after all her tugging and yanking, it was clearly evident that he worked out. She could just imagine feathering her fingers over the sculpted peaks and valleys, trailing them from the planes of his chest down his abs...swirling a fingertip around his navel...and then venturing lower, investigating that big bulge under his jeans...

"—if you're not squeamish, that is."

"Hmm?" Drawing her concentration away from his inviting physique, Angel's eyes grew wide as she realized she hadn't been paying attention to what Max was saying. "I'm sorry...what was that?"

"That's okay, I understand." He gave a sympathetic nod and patted her shoulder. "You've got a lot on your mind."

"Oh, doctor...you have no idea." Looking skyward, Angel sucked in a deep breath, letting it out in a whoosh.

Max slanted her a bemused look. "Anyway, I was saying that I usually have one of my assistants give me a hand in these procedures. If you're not squeamish, I could use your help."

"Squeamish?" She huffed. "Just because I'm a woman you don't automatically have to assume that I have a weak stomach. Just tell me what to do." Angel knew she'd probably overreacted a bit when Max gave her an eye roll. Damn, she hadn't intended to be argumentative.

"Look, all I meant was—"

"I know." She held up her hand. "I'm sorry, really. You were just trying to be nice. Honestly, I didn't mean to be such a…well, to be so snippy." She gave an apologetic smile. "Henry's emergency has obviously rattled my nerves more than I realized."

"No problem," Max said. "It's perfectly understandable."

She hoped he really did feel that way. After all, here she was behaving like a lovelorn female one minute and Super-Bitch the next. It would be a miracle if the man didn't think she had a few screws loose.

Time passed quickly as Angel assisted—without putting her foot in her mouth even once as they worked side by side. Observing Max's caring, confident manner and skilled hands as he administered a cathartic and the activated charcoal slurry, then performed a gastric lavage, Angel found herself developing a sincere admiration for him. She'd also developed a definite warm spot that radiated deep into her belly, settling with a delicious quiver at her core—but it had nothing whatsoever to do with his professional ability, and everything to do with raw animal magnetism.

"The problem with dogs discovering milk chocolate," Max said as he worked on Henry, "is that they develop a liking for it. Since dogs don't seem to be as sensitive to bitter tastes as humans, they may then eat the more concentrated unsweetened baker's chocolate, which is highly toxic, if they get a chance." He lifted his gaze and smiled at Angel. Damn, he had a killer smile. "Or, they'll consume a toxic amount of milk or semisweet chocolate if they can get into an improperly stored supply."

"From now on, my chocolate cache will remain under lock and key. It will be consumed behind locked doors—or in my car." Angel beamed a wide grin.

"That about does it," Max said, stripping off his surgical gloves. "Poor little fella's going to be pretty tuckered out for the rest of the day. His insides will be a little sore, but other than that he should be just fine." He scooped Henry's limp, sedated body gently from the table. "I'm just going to secure him in one of these small caged areas so he doesn't hurt himself when he starts to come around."

With that completed, he removed his smock. Angel became mesmerized by the bunching and cording of his muscles as he moved. She studied his features. He looked tired and worn out, but handsome as hell. Who'd have thought that the neighborhood pet doctor would turn out to be such a delectable hunk? Or that a feminist magazine columnist would be thinking of him as a male sex object...as eye-candy?

Not that it mattered what she thought of him, of course. Theirs was going to be a purely professional relationship.

"You were great, Max. Thank you so much."

He grinned. She liked the fact that he smiled so easily and seemed to have a ready sense of humor. Oh yeah, Max Wiley was definitely someone she'd like to know better. *Much* better. Unfortunately she probably wouldn't get the chance. She hadn't exactly made a brilliant first impression. It was memorable all right, but for all the wrong reasons. She gave a wistful sigh at the thought of what might have been.

"Talk about great, what about you, Angel? You never even flinched. I couldn't have asked for a better assistant."

Angel removed her gloves, discarding them in the push-pedal trashcan. Then she shimmied out of her smock. "I've got news for you, doc. You know that pervasive percussion beat you heard while we were working?" Max slanted her a puzzled expression. "Well, those were my knees knocking together and my stomach doing flip-flops," she admitted.

Watching her poor little puppy go through the series of invasive treatment procedures affected Angel more than she thought it would, leaving her somewhat lightheaded. "As a matter of fact, if you don't mind," she said, steadying herself against a counter, "I think I'd like to sit down for a few minutes." Offering a weak smile, she mopped her hand across her brow and wobbled a bit.

Max was at her side in an instant, wrapping one arm around her waist and grasping her arm with the other hand to support her. "Hey, you look a little green. You all right?"

"Sure, just a little woozy. I'll be fine." Angel's knees buckled and Max scooped her into his arms. Carrying her into his private office, he deposited her on the buckskin-brown leather sofa, tucking a tapestry throw pillow beneath her head.

"Whew," Angel said, "this is really embarrassing. I'm usually not the fainthearted type."

"No...fainthearted you're definitely not. I can attest to that." He squatted next to the couch, offering a warm smile. "Too little sleep, a whole lot of worrying over your pet, and watching some none too pleasant procedures will do the trick every time. Whether you're male or female," Max added quickly in self-defense. Absently, he swept the stray tendrils of hair from her face with his fingers. Angel felt her heart lurch at his touch and she shivered.

"Your skin feels very cool," he said, smoothing a trail from her temple to her neck.

Was it her imagination or had his voice become husky?

And, was it her imagination or was every feminist cell in her body suddenly itching to hump the eye-candy?

"We need to warm you up," Max added.

Her pussy immediately dampened as a tantalizing swarm of heated images filled her mind. Oh yes...she could think of any number of ways for him to warm her up. For starters he could run those capable hands of his under her shirt and over her breasts and then—

"I was thinking about a nice, steamy cup of coffee," Max offered, snapping her out of her horny reverie and back to reality. "I've got my own trusty little coffeemaker right here, a bag of ground French roast beans, powdered creamer and packets of raw sugar. I do make a mean cuppa joe if I do say so myself."

Angel propped herself up on one elbow. "That's very kind of you, but I don't want to put you through any more trouble than I already have."

"Hey," he said, bouncing to his feet with the grace of an athlete. "I'm making some for myself anyway, so it's no trouble."

"Okay then. A good, strong cup of coffee sounds heavenly." She plopped back against the pillow and surveyed Max's office. Manly. Tasteful. Inviting—just like its owner. Her gaze fell on the small bookcase across the room and she chuckled.

"Mickey Spillane, Raymond Chandler," she read aloud from the book spines. "*The Big Kill. My Gun is Quick. The Big Sleep.* I spotted similar paperbacks out in the waiting room, too. Sheesh. Do you actually read that stuff, or do you just keep it around to anesthetize your patients' owners?" She wrinkled her nose as she snickered.

Max dropped the last measure of coffee grounds into the basket and turned to glance at the bookcase. "Hardboiled crime fiction? Uh...yeah," he said. "I read it. I take it you're not a fan of the genre." Flipping the switch on the coffeemaker, he returned to the couch, taking a seat next to Angel.

"Nope. Too sexist and clichéd for me," she said, doing her best to ignore the nudge of awareness that lodged deep in her belly with Max sitting so close. "Frankly, I thought all that sexist private dick stuff stopped being popular back in the forties or fifties."

"I wouldn't exactly call it sexist," Max said.

Angel's jaw dropped. "Oh, puhleeze. Dumb blondes, leggy dolls, ditzy dames, busty broads, hookers with hearts of gold, sinister floozies in trench coats and... And the woman's always guilty of something or other. I mean, honestly, Max, how can you possibly claim those books aren't sexist? The attitudes and actions of the male characters in those books exemplify the height of chauvinism."

"Well I—" Max began.

"Oh, good grief," Angel cut him off as something else in the bookcase caught her attention. "Here's a whole series featuring a private detective and his dog by Frank Coleman. Never heard of him. *Jack Clyde, Private Detective and his Crime-Busting Dog, Billy.*" Angel laughed. "Now that's absolutely hysterical."

"I don't see what's so damn funny about a man and his trusty sidekick dog solving crimes together," Max said, bristling. Angel noticed right away that she'd seemed to hit a nerve. "Frank Coleman is a newer author," Max added. "He's gaining quite a following with this series, actually."

With a quick inventory of the book titles, Angel noted that more than a dozen were by Coleman. After all Max had done for Henry after she'd practically dragged the poor man from his home in the middle of the night, she certainly shouldn't be discourteous—even if his taste in reading material sucked. She cleared her throat and smiled.

"I'm sorry. You've been very kind, Max. I certainly didn't mean to insult your reading preferences. By the number of his books there, I can see that you're a fan of the author. I, um, I guess you read Coleman because of the dog connection, you being a veterinarian and all, huh? That's logical. And reasonable. I mean, dogs are man's best friend, so I guess a private eye with a smart, helpful dog to sniff out evidence is appealing to male readers." Aware that, in the effort to smooth Max's ruffled feathers, she'd been babbling like a brainless twit, Angel clamped her mouth shut and broadened her smile, hoping it came across as sincere.

Max shrugged. "Don't worry about it. No offense taken."

As Max's lips hiked into a half-smile, an unbidden, inappropriate image of the good doctor, shirtless and sweating, flashed into Angel's mind. What was the matter with her for chrissakes? The guy offered her a fractional smile and her libido riots. She blinked hard and shivered.

"Cold?" Max asked, settling his hand on her forehead.

"No, uh..." *On fire is more like it.* "Thanks. I'm..." *Tongue-tied because I can't think straight when you touch me. Hot for your body. So horny my pussy is dripping with need.* Inching away from Max and straightening, Angel cleared her throat again. "Well, would you look at that," she said, eyeing the wall clock. "It's nearly five-thirty already."

"So it is. My, how time passes when you're having fun, huh?" Max tossed her a wink. "Gee, last time I was up this early on a Sunday morning I was a kid and my dad's idea of a great time was sitting in a fishing boat out on the lake before God, or man, or certainly any of the fish, were even awake." Reveling in the memory, Max smiled.

"I'm really sorry, Max."

"About the fishing or about my sexist reading habits—or both?" He fell into easy laughter.

"No, for the way I acted." Raking her fingers through her hair, Angel bellowed a yawn. "I owe you so much for what you've done—and I owe you a giant apology for yanking you out of your house at this hour and...and..." Heaving a growl of disgust, Angel buried her face in her hands. "And treating you like you were some kind of...of..."

"Idiot?" Max offered. Angel peeked up to see his bemused expression. "Moron? Dimwit? Insensitive male chauvinist?"

"Eeeew." She curled her lip into a sneer. "I guess I did kind of imply that, didn't I? I don't know what I can say, other than I was frantic with worry over Henry. My God, you must have thought I was some wild banshee or something the way I came pounding at your door, screeching at you." She shuddered in disgust at her unsuitable behavior. "I am *so* embarrassed and *so* sorry, Max."

"You may find this hard to believe," he said, gently lifting her chin with his fingers, "but it's not often that I'm awakened in the middle of the night by a very beautiful, half-naked, wild banshee, desperately in need of my services." He chuckled as Angel felt herself blush. "Not that I really noticed that all you had on was a flimsy nightgown, of course."

"Of course." The memory of the way Max had eyed her hungrily as she stood before him in her nightgown made her nipples bead, aching for his attention. Raising her eyes again, she peered into the depths of Max Wiley's whiskey-colored eyes and smiled. "You're the closest thing to a knight in shining armor I've ever encountered." She placed her hand against his chest. The feel of his heartbeat sent a shiver jogging up and down her spine, until it finally zeroed in at her pussy. Stifling a moan, her lips parted as desire flowed through her body.

"I will always," she hurried on, licking her lips and trying to ignore the heat pooling between her legs, "be grateful to you for helping me instead of bashing me over the head with that baseball bat you were clutching so fiercely when you opened the door." She laughed. A moment later she cocked her head in surprise when Max didn't follow suit.

Angel let out a little gasp as his eyes flashed dark and hot with unmistakable passion. Yes indeed, Doctor Wiley was staring at her...in a decidedly non-clinical manner.

Chapter Four

The nearness of her was driving Max up the wall. Her sweet, fresh smell. Those liquid pools of sea-blue, dancing with laughter. That flaxen halo surrounding her skin. Those moist lips, just waiting to be kissed. Even that brash, insolent mouth of hers. He watched the whirl of emotions parade through her eyes as he drew closer. Before he even realized what he was doing, Max grabbed Angel by the shoulders. Tugging her hard against his chest, he covered her mouth with his. As his tongue delved into the satiny alcove, her taste satisfied his every expectation. It left him hungry to sample the rest of this delicious creature—whether she was a wild banshee, an avenging angel, or simply a slightly nutty neighbor.

He deepened the kiss. Angel let out a little moan and wrapped her arms around the back of Max's neck, streaking her fingers through his hair.

The sound of a final puff of steam from the coffeemaker rudely intruded, and they parted reluctantly.

Her cheeks rosy with what Max hoped was the bloom of desire, Angel smiled. "Well, I guess the coffee's ready."

If she had any idea how close he was to yanking down her jeans and sliding into her, she wouldn't be smiling at him like that. As he watched her nervously fluff her curls, he stifled a

38

grin. The woman was such an anomaly—a multifaceted jumble of brusque, no-nonsense feminist ideals and soft round, squeezable femininity. Oh, man, what a dame! And he had to go ruin things by shoving his tongue down her throat when what she wanted...*needed*, was for him to be objective, impersonal and professional. Damn.

He plowed his hand through his hair. "Jeez, I shouldn't have done that." His words came out no more than a gravelly whisper. "I don't know what came over me. You must think I'm a real jerk. I'm sorry, Angel."

Taking his hand in hers, Angel smoothed her fingers over his knuckles. She beamed a bright smile up at Max. "On the contrary, my dear Dr. Wiley, I rather enjoyed your, um, bedside manner."

"Just be thankful I didn't smoosh you with a grapefruit."

Angel slanted him a puzzled look. "Huh?"

"You know, Cagney, 1931, *The Public Enemy*..." When Angel looked even more bewildered, Max chuckled. "Long story—never mind."

"Tell you what, Max. Let's make a deal, okay? We'll just chalk up my unforgivable behavior and your unbelievable forwardness to both of us being really overtired. Sound good?"

A wide grin spreading across his face, Max said, "Sounds good to me. How about we start over with a fresh, clean slate and do things right?"

"Like?"

"Like, you bring Henry back here for a follow-up Monday morning, and I ask you out to dinner. You say yes, and we eat and talk and get to know each other a little better. Then maybe we can, uh..."

"Then we can get to the grabbing and kissing part again?" Angel offered.

watched it tighten before trailing a damp path with his tongue to her other breast, repeating the pleasurable process. Her passion and exuberance had his cock more than primed and ready to plunge into her pussy.

"Good God in heaven, Max, you're driving me crazy," Angel nearly growled.

"Then I'd say we're even, dollface."

While her nipples grew stiff as pokers under Max's lavish attention, Angel explored the planes of his chest, his abs and across his back with her raking fingers. Max kissed the tip of her breast, depositing a string of soft kisses up her chest and throat, then his tongue swept into her mouth.

Reckless frenzy mounted within Max as Angel's heady kiss made him constrict with desire. He needed to see her pussy. To feel those concealed curls against his skin. To breathe in her womanly scent. Raising himself slightly, he impatiently fumbled with the fastenings on her jeans, as Angel's fingers tore at his. She nudged his jeans down to his knees and stroked the insides of his thighs, watching the erection in his shorts bobbing in anticipation.

Max tugged Angel's jeans down. His fingers fastened around the lacy scrap of panties, pulling them away from the furry blonde mound that glistened with her juices. The sight of her was so evocative of his erotic dream that his heart skipped a beat.

"I just knew you were a natural blonde," he said, twirling his fingers through her pussy curls as he inhaled deeply. He couldn't wait until his cock snuggled into her silky cunt.

Suddenly Max felt his face fall. Damn. With a monstrous groan, he forced himself off the sofa, leaving a ripe and panting Angel looking bewildered. "Protection," he muttered. "Just a minute." He scraped the remains of his T-shirt from his shoulders and then shrugged fully out of his jeans. He retrieved his wallet from the back pocket, hoping...praying, that it held a condom. "Yes!" he hissed as he drew the foil packet out then tore it open with his teeth.

"Let me see you first, Max. Take off your shorts." Gleefully obedient, Max immediately complied. Angel's warm, inviting smile morphed into a look of surprise when he turned to face her. "Uh-oh..." She looked from his hungry cock to his face and back again—and then she licked her lips. "I don't think we're going to be able to do this."

"What?!" Max's voice sounded strangled and desperate, even to his own ears. "Why not? I've gotta tell you, Angel, I'm teetering on the point of no return here." His forced chuckle came out more like a croak.

"Max, you'll never fit," Angel said, scrutinizing his cock. "I think it's too big."

Max couldn't help but laugh at that. "Oh, don't worry, dollface, we'll make it fit, I'll see to that."

"I want to touch it," Angel whispered. Max's body tightened at her words. "I want to see if your cock feels as remarkable as it looks." She sat up on the couch and kicked off her jeans and panties. She focused her full attention on Max's erection, reaching out to touch it, tentatively at first, then with more vigor and firmness.

The sensation of her cool fingers wrapping around his hot dick nearly pushed Max over the edge. She feathered a touch against his balls and he had to fight with every ounce of reserve not to ejaculate in her soft white hands. He didn't remember his cock ever getting quite this long or hard—and certainly never this impatient. He'd never been on the verge of fucking an avenging angel before, either—at least, outside of his dreams. The thought of ramming himself into Angel's pretty little pussy had him shuddering with unrestrained anticipation.

"You're so stunning, Max," Angel whispered as she stroked the tender underside of his shaft. "So soft and velvety, yet so hard and firm at the same time. It's extraordinary." She shifted her passion-drugged gaze to his face and blinked. "I can't wait to feel you inside of me."

He felt her gently tug on his dick as the fingers of Angel's other hand softly caressed her pussy. Her thighs parted in sweet invitation.

Max's eyes grew wide and his mouth went dry. "Jesus," was all he managed to say as, with lightning speed, he rolled the condom onto his insistent cock.

Chapter Five

Every nerve ending in Angel's body prickled in expectation. She'd never been this famished for a man's body before. God knows she'd never seen a cock like Max's. Sure, she'd read about sizeable appendages, but that was strictly fiction. This was no storybook illusion. Uh-uh. This was the real deal, right in front of her—big and bobbing and so damned striking it made her quiver just to look at him. Her gaze moved to her fingers as they closed around his cock. She smiled...almost drooled, in fact. Her clit throbbed and her pussy clenched as she waited for the powerful sense of fullness when Max pushed inside her.

As it was, her nipples would probably remain permanently puckered after being subjected to the delightful sensations of his copious attention. It was amazing. The tips of her breasts had hardened in response to him long before the notion that they would actually be having sex together. When his teeth tugged and his fingers twisted, she'd been so close, teetering on the verge of a powerful orgasm just from that stimulation alone. Well, that and the way he'd called her *dollface*.

There was just something about the way he said the chauvinistic term that managed to offend her feminist sensibilities, while stoking the flames of desire deep in her belly at the same time. Curious. In any case, this wasn't the time for clinical analysis. Uh-uh. This was the time for getting probed with the doctor's instrument.

Angel almost snickered at the silly analogy, but she was too busy readying herself to get laid. With one hand feathering over her pussy and her other gloving his cock, she pulled Max to her, opening herself to the welcome intrusion.

Relinquishing her hold so Max could sheathe his cock with the condom, her blood slipped through her veins like quicksilver. It was going to happen. She was really going to feel this fabulous hunk of eye candy deep inside of her. Max mounted her. She saw the fathomless pools of molten desire in his eyes. He looked almost predatory now. Serious and focused. Angel swallowed hard. Her pussy juices ran and a hungry cry of anticipation tripped past her lips.

She writhed involuntarily beneath him, impatient for the exquisite pain and punishment to come. Max positioned the tip of his cock at her opening, easing it in just a bit before stopping. The pause was agonizing.

"Are you sure, Angel?" Max managed through raspy breaths.

She gave a throaty chuckle. "Doctor, I appreciate your polite bedside manner, but if I have to wait any longer to feel you inside of me, I swear to God I'll scream." She clasped her hands on his ass, arching her hips as she pulled him into her. Max growled, seating himself with one deep thrust as what appeared to be the last of his control hit the skids.

The sensation of being profoundly pierced by Max's sizeable cock was more intense and sensational than Angel had anticipated. Such fullness...such exquisite completeness... Her cunt tightened around his shaft, relishing the delicious pain along with the pleasure.

Max stilled as she indulged in a passionate moan.

"Are you okay?"

She sucked in a deep breath as her eyelids fluttered closed and she smiled. "Yes. Oh yes." She was better than okay, she was ecstatic.

"I should have eased in slower, but you felt so damn good, Angel. So warm and wet. I couldn't stop myself."

"No, it's perfect, Max. You feel amazing."

He slid his fingers from her belly to her chest, kneading her breasts and pinching the taut nipples. "Your body is so receptive. I could spend days exploring you...every delicious inch of you." He leaned down, swooping his tongue from the beading peaks at her breasts up to her mouth for a lusty kiss. Her clit pulsed with a mighty throb.

"Just in case you hadn't noticed," he added, licking his lips, "we fit together perfectly." Max lifted her hips, thrusting into her again. His strokes were insistent. Fast, hot and wicked. She couldn't help whimpering with needy pleasure.

Then he did something else...a twisty, turning kind of something that made her heart stop and her body stiffen. Deep inside she felt his magical cock abrading a spot she hadn't even known existed. Repeated waves of pleasure gripped her being, intensifying to such a crescendo that it almost frightened her.

"Dear Lord in heaven, what *is* that?" she eked out.

"I think we've just found your G-spot, dollface." Max's voice was low and hoarse.

"Well don't ever leave it," she ordered, panting. As the sensation intensified, she felt a fine sheen of perspiration emerge. "I've never...it's absolutely..." Her words trailed off in a series of sensuous moans. She writhed as Max kept up his mesmerizing rhythm.

It was as if every fiber of her being was alert and in sync, preparing for an extraordinary event. A single swipe from Max's

Chapter Six

Max returned a few moments later and shrugged into his jeans. Amazingly, just one brief glance Angel's way had his depleted cock resuscitating. What a woman. What a doll. What a dame! He was so inspired by their lusty liaison that he was tempted to drag out his laptop and start banging out a new story featuring Jack Clyde's ongoing love interest, Trixie Lang, the sexy, full-figured female character who kept Jack's libido hopping. Yeah, Max was newly inspired. Oh, mama, what he could do with that couple! The pages would be so hot they'd singe readers' fingers. Oh yeah...*oh yeah...*

Trixie was a damn good cop. She was also a strong, opinionated dame who took delight in openly flaunting herself. And, brother, she had plenty to flaunt. I'd always been a tit man and she fit the bill. The first time I laid eyes on those big headlights and curvy chassis of hers, I was a goner. She was a dish and I let loose the expected low whistle. It got me a slap across the face, but I knew I had her when she stuck a cigarette between her lacquered lips and waited for me to light it. The lush fullness of her mouth glistened with a damp warmth of invitation and I knew at that moment that we'd be good together. Yeah, sure, maybe it hasn't been all fire and honey all the time, but it's good.

I almost went bananas when Trixie told me she was going undercover as a whore to catch the jackass who'd been offing all the prostitutes. I'd been a cop once, and I had a healthy respect for the law. I knew the drill, but I didn't trust those wet-behind-the-ears pups who were assigned as her backup, so I tailed her. There was no way I was going to let my doll out on the street alone without me.

I watched from a distance as she connected with the suspect. The guy looked mighty mean under the amber lights and I figured he was probably packing heat. He was an ugly dude with a face like a butthole, but there was nothing cheapshit about those duds he was wearing. I was tempted to eighty-six the guy right there. The thought of another man touching Trixie had been bad enough, but knowing that she couldn't flinch when the creep started running his hand up and down her thigh—

"How about you?"

"Huh?" Max uttered eloquently through a blank stare. Eyeballing that luscious shape of hers, he realized he hadn't heard a word she'd said.

"I said I could sure go for that cup of coffee now." She paused. "You get distracted easily, don't you?"

"Sorry." Max felt the color creep up his neck. "But how can I possibly *not* be distracted when I'm in the same room with you?" He gave her a saucy wink.

"Smooth recovery, doc. Real smooth." She returned the wink. "I'll get the coffees."

Angel began to rise and Max waved her back down. "Uh-uh. You can just sit there and bask in the afterglow while the doctor tends to your needs. How do you like it?"

"Long, thick, fast and hard."

As one of Max's eyebrows shot up, he slanted her a cautionary grin. "Now, now, Ms. Brewster. I was talking about your coffee."

"Oh that." She gave him a casual look. "Plenty of cream and three sugars, please."

"Three...really?" Watching Angel's just-been-happily-fucked features morph into a frown as her posture stiffened had him stifling a smile. He had a hunch he knew what was coming next.

"Yes. I only drink a couple of cups a day, so why shouldn't I enjoy it just the way I like it?"

"Yeah, but three whole packets? Wow..." Shaking his head in mock dismay, Max bit the inside of his cheek to keep from laughing.

"Why not? Are you saying that you think I'm too fat?" Bristling, Angel stood up, arms akimbo. "Granted, I'm not a size twelve, but does that mean I should go along with the rest of the easily led women who blindly ingest those little colored packets of chemicals because they're convinced those will magically make them thin? Sorry, but I prefer not to poison my system with fake non-food products. Why should I drink my coffee black when what I really want is something sweet and creamy? In fact, statistics show that artificial sweeteners do absolutely nothing to—"

Returning to her side, Max swooped Angel into his arms, mashed his mouth over hers and did his damnedest to kiss her senseless—and wordless. Still stiffened with outrage, she tried to push him away at first but soon melted into his embrace as their tongues tangled in an erotic dance. Once he had her soft and pliable again he broke the kiss, unceremoniously let her fall back to the couch and silently went back to preparing the coffee.

He didn't turn around when he heard Angel's audible gasp.
"Max! You did that on purpose. You baited me!"

He turned to face her, leaning one elbow against the small counter. "Dollface, you are *so* easy."

"How could you do that to me after we just made love?"

"Maybe I get a kick out of watching you change from a sweet porcelain-faced doll into a fierce, peppermint pink-faced avenging angel."

Jumping to her feet with hands fisted at her sides, Angel's mouth opened and closed...twice. After a moment of silent fuming she relaxed her body. "Okay, I see what you mean. I do tend to be extremely, um...passionate about things. And maybe just a *teensy* bit too zealous sometimes." Lowering her head a bit, she held her thumb and forefinger about an inch apart as she gave a coy smile.

"It's that passionate nature of yours that I find so irresistible," Max said, emptying the third packet of raw sugar into her mug. "You can be as sweet and innocent as this," he held the packet aloft, "or as bold and powerful as this," he hiked his thumb toward the bag of strong Sumatra coffee. "I find either extreme quite...stimulating. In fact, you remind me of a tigress I've treated."

"You've worked with wild animals?"

"On occasion." Max brought two mugs of coffee to the table in front of the sofa. He sat down, patting the seat next to him. Angel slipped in beside him and sipped from her coffee, murmuring her appreciation. "Some friends own a compound in Africa. I go down there for a visit once or twice a year and make sure their animals are in healthy condition. It's a great experience—quite different than working with cats, dogs and parakeets—and always a challenge. Wild animals are very unpredictable." He sipped from his mug then turned to her with a devilish smile. "Rather like some people I know."

Casting him an amused expression, Angel quirked an eyebrow. "Passion and unpredictability do have their good points. They're part of what make me a good journalist."

"Ah, so that's your calling, huh?" Max studied her. "Yeah, I can definitely see you as a reporter. Stubborn, fiery, and determined. Waving a banner of righteousness wherever you tread."

"Stubborn?"

Lifting her chin with his finger, Max gazed into her eyes. "Come on, Angel. Are you honestly going to try to refute that?"

Angel sniffed. Her expression became haughty as she elevated her chin even higher. "Some people view stubbornness as a sign of strength. If I wasn't stubborn and tenacious I wouldn't be where I am today. It's not easy for a woman to make it in a man's world, you know."

"That's a good point." He skated the fingers of one hand up her thigh, enjoying the flush that immediately tinged her cheeks. "So tell me, my stubborn little angel, just what sort of articles do you write?" His fingers crept higher until they reached her denim-clad pussy. He stroked the material slowly, deeply.

Angel exhaled with a whoosh. "That's not fair. How do you expect me to concentrate when you're doing that?"

His mouth curved into a smirk, Max just shrugged.

"Okay, well then turnabout is fair play." She clapped her hand over his groin, beaming a resolute smile as his cock twitched and he nearly spilled his coffee.

"I specialize in women's issues," she said with a slight quiver in her voice as she massaged the growing bulge in Max's jeans.

Max grinned, perfectly happy to have her hand toying with his cock. "A feminist. Gee, that's a surprise." Angel gave him a playful whap. "I'll bet you're a green-loving, recycling, tree-hugger, too."

"Well of course I am." Angel gave an incredulous huff. "I'm an Oregonian." With an uptilt of her chin, she said it as if it were a proud banner boldly emblazoned across her big, beautiful breasts. "I mean, how can anyone possibly live in our lush, green, clean-air state and not want to preserve our healthy abundance of trees and natural resources? After all, it's the trees that keep our air clean, unlike dirty smog-filled places like California or New York."

"Hey, hey, hey," Max cautioned with an admonishing finger. "Careful, you're talking to a born and bred New Yorker here." He thumped his chest.

Angel hiked an eyebrow. "I thought I detected a distinct Eastern twang."

"New Yorkers don't speak with twangs, dollface. We like to think of it more as *Brooklynese*," he exaggerated the voice inflection that he'd practiced so hard to tone down. "Don't get me wrong, I've been out here for a couple of years now and I love it...well, aside from all the winter rain."

"We like our rain," Angel defended. "It's what keeps Oregon so verdant."

"Yeah, well, it might be greener, and the air might be a lot cleaner and easier to breathe out here, but Portland is sorely lacking in other highly significant areas."

"Such as?"

"Food, honey. It's like the culinary revolution stopped in Chicago and never made it any further west."

"That's ridiculous," Angel said. "Pacific Northwest cuisine is both innovative and widely renowned."

"Sure, if you like salmon and hazelnuts fixed umpteen thousand different ways. Somewhere along the line somebody dropped the ball and forgot to establish a little Italy amidst all the tofu palaces and Asian delis. With the exception of one great little restaurant, there's a painful lack of good Italian food out here. They don't have the vaguest idea how to make and serve a good hot dog, either."

"Tofu palaces," Angel said thoughtfully, and Max could pretty much tell what was coming next. "Do you have something against vegetarians and their philosophy?"

"Certainly not. In fact, I love vegetarians." Angel smiled at that. "Because of them there's just that much more steak, chops, ham, ribs, burgers and bacon left for meat lovers like me to eat." Max snickered and Angel's smile morphed into a frown.

"I'm a lacto-ovo vegetarian," she said, "which means I also eat dairy and eggs, as long as they come from farms where the cows and chickens are treated humanely and given plenty of free space to roam and eat their naturally intended diets. However, I fully respect those who prefer to dine on the carcasses of dead animals if that's their uninformed choice." Chin raised, Angel punctuated her diatribe with a broad I-dare-you-to-challenge-me grin.

"Yeah, I can hear the respect just dripping off your tongue," Max muttered under his breath. Sucking in a deep breath, he eyed Angel silently for a long moment. He could just imagine the two of them out for dinner, with Max salivating over a big, bloody slab of prime rib and dollface munching on radish soufflé with turnip sauce. It was high time he shifted the course of their conversation to safer territory.

"So where do you work?" he asked.

"I'm a columnist for *Women's Wit and Wisdom* magazine. Our offices are just a few blocks from here, actually. We focus primarily on women's rights and equality issues."

Oh brother...

"We're also animal activists and have done several award-winning articles on the abuse and mistreatment of our furry friends by cosmetic companies and the like," Angel added. "As a veterinarian I'm sure you already know about the atrocities being perpetrated on the poor, helpless creatures."

Save me, Lord...save me!

"Right now," Angel continued, "I'm working on a piece detailing the detrimental effects that male-dominated media and marketing has on the way young girls view themselves and their bodies."

"Have I told you that I *love* your body, Ms. Brewster?" Max jumped in with the hopes of derailing little-miss-activist's righteous train of thought before they found themselves tangled in a heated exchange of the non-sexual variety. "So full and round and succulent." His hand trailed a path from Angel's pussy to her breasts, where he caught a tight nipple between his fingers and rolled it. The color rose in her cheeks, cascading down her throat as she swallowed a moan. Max knew he'd found a perfect way to shut her up.

"It's-it's..." Angel sucked in a deep breath. She clutched Max's cock tighter, eliciting a groan from him. "It's an absolute crime that the most requested gift when a girl turns eighteen is breast enhancement surgery. They can't possibly have the stick-figure bodies and huge breasts that they see portrayed in the movies or on the fashion runways. It's just not healthy for females to be emaciated. Women were meant to be—"

"Ripe and plump and juicy." Not willing to lose this round, Max tweaked her nipple more firmly. Maintaining her grip on his fully aroused cock, Angel slithered down in her seat with a protracted moan. "Just like you, dollface." He leaned in close, covering the nipple stabbing through the fabric of her bra and T-shirt with his mouth. *Take that you little rutabaga-munching tree-hugger.*

"Okay. That's it," she growled in a husky whisper as her fingernail dragged along the zipper of his jeans. "I give up. You win, Max. Fuck me. Fuck me now. Hard and fast"

"I'd say we both win," Max said. He shoved the coffee table out of the way, got to his knees and helped Angel shrug off her jeans. "Look how wet you are for me. Your panties are soaked." His cock hammered hard in his jeans as he inhaled her heady scent. It would take enormous strength not to bury himself in her, but he'd only had the one condom in his wallet. Regardless, he was determined to give his mouthy angel a treat that would render her voiceless for at least a little while. He hooked his thumbs through her panties and tugged, dragging them down over her hips and the hot, sweet mound that begged for his attention.

He gazed down at her pussy, fondling it before looking up into her eyes. The expression of unmasked desire he found there hardened his whole body and he shuddered. "You're all woman, Angel. I want to explore every soft, curvaceous inch of you. Open up for me, baby." Her thighs parted to reveal the rosy folds of her cunt. Kneeling over her, Max slipped one hand under her sweet ass before plunging two fingers into her drenched pussy. Her body jerked at the invasion and she clenched around his fingers.

"Max..."

"Shhh," he whispered. "No talking. Take off your shirt so I can see those beautiful tits of yours bounce as I fuck you with my hand. I want to watch you come, Angel. Give me that pleasure." She moaned in response as she removed her shirt and bra, baring her dark, puckered nipples for him. He raised himself just enough to nip at each peak with his teeth, extending them further until they stood out in wet, rosy contrast to her pale flesh.

After a few more strokes, he added another finger, fucking her hard and fast. His gaze became glued to the rise and fall of her breasts as she panted and made ardent little murmurs. Angel's hands smoothed over her belly and rested on her breasts. Max swallowed hard. Watching her writhe was too damned erotic. He struggled, steeling his control so he wouldn't come all over himself like some kid just entering puberty—but he wasn't sure he could make it.

"How close are you to coming, Angel?"

"Pretty damn close." She managed to chuckle a bit.

His fingers still inside of her, Max swiped his thumb over her clit. She stiffened. With the second strike over her engorged flesh, Angel cried out, her body trembling violently. Still cradling her ass, he continued to rub her slick clitoris gently until her orgasm crested. He felt the warm rush of her juices as she came all over his hand.

"That was the sexiest, most beautiful thing I've ever seen," Max breathed. When Angel opened her eyes he brought his hand to his mouth and licked her taste from his fingers.

Chapter Seven

"Just in case you're wondering," Max said, stroking Angel's thighs from her knees to her crotch and back again, "I love the size and shape of your body. You're everything a woman should be, Angel. When I hold a woman in my arms, I don't want bony protrusions poking me everywhere. I want to feel sumptuous curves and padded hips and a soft, sweet ass." He slid his hands up her belly, kneading her flesh. "Women are supposed to be soft here." His hands trailed to her breasts and he squeezed them. "And here." Max scooted his hands back down to rest at her pussy. "And definitely here." He kissed her mound and Angel shuddered.

She'd had men express their appreciation for her behind closed doors before, but never like this. Never with such eloquence and seeming sincerity. Male admiration usually amounted to no more than a string of impassioned grunts, groans and trite phrases as they squeezed her zaftig body parts before jamming themselves into her. In the light of day and out in public, it was a whole different story. The same men who had waxed poetic over her voluptuous curves didn't want anyone else to know they favored double-digit-sized chicks. It just wasn't cool.

She hoped that it would be different with Max.

Max spread Angel's legs open, moving in close. In the next instant she felt his tongue licking her swollen clit.

"*Max!* I can't. Not yet." She tried to clamp her thighs together, but Max held them open. She'd just experienced a second mind-blowing orgasm and she was spent—and sensitive as hell down there now. She knew her body well enough to know that it would be quite a while before she was ready to come again.

Max lifted his head. "Oh yes you can. Trust me"

His mouth was on her again—his tongue piercing and swooping and tickling until Angel thought she'd go insane. A torrent of awareness flooded her senses as Max continued his sweet torture. She wanted him to stop—at least she thought she did—but she found herself threading her fingers through his hair, pressing his head even closer to her throbbing ache. His talented tongue kept on twirling and lapping at her juices. All the while an inferno raged deep in her belly, threatening to ignite her entire being.

"Lord, Max...this is too much. I feel like I'm going to detonate."

And then she did.

As her body bucked and jerked, Max held her close, stroking and kneading her flesh while an unintelligible thread of impassioned cries spilled from her throat. His voice was soft and low as he whispered to her of her beauty and how much he desired her. Never had a man made her feel more cherished.

It was a while before Angel found her voice or could think straight enough to put two words together that made any sense. When she'd recovered a bit she started to chuckle.

"What's so funny, dollface?"

"It's just that I've never been fucked senseless before." She drew Max up on the couch next to her. "Oh, Dr. Wiley, you are a most talented and generous man." She brushed a soft kiss across his lips. "Thank you."

"Believe me when I say that it was entirely my pleasure." He trailed a line of kisses from her mouth to her temple.

"That was the only condom you had, wasn't it?" Angel asked, stroking the light growth of beard along his jaw.

"Yup."

"That's what I thought." She unfastened his jeans and pulled down the zipper. "Your turn, doc." With one tug on the waistband of his shorts, Max's cock sprang from its confines. It seemed even bigger than it had before. "Oh my...look what we have here," Angel teased as she ran a finger along the underside of his shaft. "It appears to be one great big throbbing cock desperately in need of Nurse Angel's rapt attention." She couldn't help but giggle when his cock gave a mighty twitch in response. "Well, let's just see what we can do to make it all better."

She closed her mouth over his cock.

"Oh, Christ..." A groan rumbled from deep within Max's chest. "Angel..."

She took as much of his cock as she could, sucking, nibbling and licking as if it were a gourmet delicacy. Angel kept one hand on the base of his thick shaft while allowing the fingers of her other hand to explore his groin area, his balls, and the firm curve of his ass. Max's enthusiastic response gave her a feeling of power as she brought him close to the edge, doing her best to tease, tantalize and bring him the same sweet satisfaction that he had given her.

She lifted her head, slowly allowing his cock to slip from her lips and bob free before clasping it firmly in her hand again. With a quivering moan, she licked the broad head, savoring the tiny drops of pre-cum. She shifted her position so that she was kneeling on the floor in front of him. She sandwiched Max's cock between her breasts, holding them together as she moved back and forth. The stark contrast of the purple head popping in and out of her pale breasts was quite fascinating and erotic.

"Sexy. Sexy and so goddamned hot." Max's breathing was hard and fast as he watched her fuck him with her tits. "You're killing me, Angel. But what a way to go." He leaned forward enough to grasp her nipples, pinching and tugging on them, causing Angel to halt in her task for moment and moan.

"Oh God...I can't believe this," she said, panting. "I don't know how it's possible, but I'm close to coming again just from playing with your cock." She looked up into his hooded gaze as he groaned. "I love it when you pinch my nipples, Max. Do it harder...please. I want us to come together." She lowered her head and took his long cock back into her mouth, milking him hard. Max increased the pressure on her rigid peaks.

In less time than she could count, Max's primal growl reverberated in her ears as his cum spurted down the back of her throat. Angel felt herself being hurled into another quaking climax.

Oh yes...she was a well-fucked, very happy woman.

She got back on the couch and snuggled next to Max, purring her satisfaction. It was amazing how right it felt...as if they'd known each other a lifetime instead of just several hours. *Hours?* As the realization hit her, a sudden wave of good-girl-guilt washed over her. Dear God, she'd only known this man for a mere blip in time and she'd already fucked him with her mouth! Her behavior was most definitely un-Angel Brewster-ish...but oh what a glorious, soul-shattering fuck. What an extraordinary man.

"Angel, you are so incredible." Max's voice was loose and languid. "That was the most stimulating, powerful experience I've ever had."

"Me too. It's pretty damned funny, though."

"Oh? How so? Max tangled his fingers through her hair, massaging her scalp in wavy strokes.

She looked into his eyes and grinned. "Because I usually don't even kiss on a first date." They looked at each other for a moment and then erupted in joint laughter.

"Believe me when I say that this is not my usual modus operandi either. I like to think that I give all of my clients special attention, but that usually doesn't extend to engaging in screaming orgasms." Max nibbled her earlobe and spiraled a tendril of her hair around his finger. "Ready for another cup of coffee?"

Angel splayed her fingers against his chest, pushing as he started to rise. "Let me get it this time." She got to her feet and stretched, amazed at how fabulous she felt. Renewed, refreshed, and so perfectly pleasured.

"Please don't stretch like that, Angel."

She turned to him in surprise. "Huh?"

Max pointed to his cock. "It needs time to recuperate and watching you arch your back and stretch in all your female glory is definitely not helping. Besides, next time we do it I want to make sure I have a hefty supply of condoms—and someplace a little roomier and more comfortable than this leather couch."

"Next time?" Angel felt herself blush. The sheer sense of relief and happiness she felt at his words startled her. Damn, she was behaving exactly like the needy women she wrote about in her column. She had to be careful. After her disastrous relationship with Robert, she swore she'd never allow herself to feel needy about any man again.

"Baby, I'm not into one-night stands. You stormed into my life for a reason...and I'm not about to let you go. Hell, I even dreamed about you before you came banging on my door."

She eyed him with an incredulous expression. "How could you have a dream about me? You didn't even know me."

"Just before you announced your arrival—with your fist on my door—I was in the middle of an erotic dream. It was unusual because I rarely have such explicit dreams. There you were, an avenging angel with your terrible swift sword. We were just about to make love before I woke up."

"Me, huh?" Angel slanted him a wary look and snickered as she went to fix their coffee.

"I'm telling you, it's true. It was you—all big and bold and beautiful, with your shiny yellow halo of hair and flowing white gown."

"I see...and, um, what was I doing with the sword?" She picked up a sharp knife from the counter and aimed it at him, blowing a kiss down the blade's length.

Max bolted upright in his seat, staring at Angel. He pointed at her, waving his outstretched finger. "That! You were doing just exactly that." He swiped at the sudden perspiration on his brow with the back of his hand. "Whoa...this is too weird..."

"Uh-huh. How do you take your coffee, dream boy?"

"Extra cream and three sugars," he said absently as he stared at her with a dazed expression.

Angel gave him a dubious look. "Seriously."

"I am serious. That's how I've always taken my coffee. That's what I'm trying to tell you, Angel. You, me, the dream, our lovemaking...even the way we take our coffee. It's karma."

"Karma." A throaty chuckle erupted from her throat. "Dr. Wiley, you're a man of science. You're not supposed to believe in such frivolous things."

Max offered a sheepish smile. "Actually, I never did...until now."

"Well," Angel said, setting the mugs down on the coffee table after Max dragged it back towards the couch, "I must admit that I do believe in fate. I think we probably were destined to meet." She gave a throaty giggle. "Especially after you actually fit that unbelievably big cock of yours inside of me and worked your magic to find my G-spot. Now *that*, my dear doctor, was karma!"

Max held his mug aloft. "I'd like to propose a toast."

"Okay. What shall we toast to?"

"To the poisoning of Henry—which," Max added quickly as he saw the shock in Angel's eyes, "while certainly not very pleasant for the poor little pooch, was most definitely the catalyst that brought us together."

Angel nodded. "And to little Henry's rapid and complete recovery."

"And," Max added, "to our upcoming first date."

They clinked mugs and drank.

Chapter Eight

"No, Mom, you don't hear depression in my voice." Angel laughed. "Yes, I'm telling you the truth. In fact, I'm feeling especially good this morning." Propelling herself by pushing off the desk with her foot, she swirled her office chair a few times, engaging in a dreamy, private smile as she thought about the other night with Max.

"Okay, yes, nosy one, it has to do with a man. Satisfied? He's one of my neighbors. I had a bit of a chocolate emergency with Henry and—yes, he's just fine. Anyway, the veterinarian a couple of blocks away came to our aid and fixed Henry right up." *And turned my world upside down at the same time.* Angel stifled an emerging giggle. At her mother's next comment, she stilled her chair and groaned.

"You're not supposed to ask me that, Mother, and I'm certainly not going to answer you." She tsked and her voice went up an octave as she said, "Because it's none of your business, that's why. I don't ask you or Dad about your sex life, do I?" At the mere thought, Angel shuddered. "Please, Mom, whatever you do, don't start telling me about it because, trust me, I do *not* want to know.

"No, he's nothing at all like Robert. I just met the guy, Mom, relax, okay? Give me a chance to get to know him before you put me through the motherly inquisition, okay?" She laughed.

At that moment, Angel's boss stuck her head into Angel's office. "Hey, kid, I just peeked in on Henry and he's still sound asleep." Seeing that Angel was on the phone as Angel swiveled forward in her chair, the woman held up her hand and mouthed a *sorry.*

Angel frantically waved her into her office. "Oh, gee, Mom, my boss just came in and she needs me, so I have to go." Angel gestured to her boss in a pleading manner until the woman nodded in understanding and winked.

"How's the article coming, Angel?" she said loudly. "Don't forget, we're on a deadline here."

Angel grinned and gave her a thumbs-up sign. "Sorry. Gotta run, Mom. Um...no, I don't think I can do lunch today. I'm pretty tied up. Yes, sure, I'll let you know later." After disconnecting the call, she kicked back in her chair and smiled up at B.J. Treedall, the tall, lanky editor-in-chief of *Women's Wit and Wisdom.* "Thanks, B.J. I was getting the third degree about my love life. Again." She looked skyward and sighed.

"Is your mother even half as meddlesome in your brothers' lives?" B.J. asked.

"I wish. They get off pretty easy—probably because they've always got women hanging all over them and Mom figures it's just a matter of time before they get dragged off to the altar. It seems my mother is on a mission to see her feminist daughter— her *only* daughter—happily ensconced in traditional marital bliss and birthing a houseful of children. She's dying to be a grandmother."

B.J. patted her hand in sympathy. "You're not the only one, kid. My mother is eighty and she's still waiting for those grandkids. Seeing as how I just turned sixty, I'd say she's out of luck, wouldn't you?" Angel joined her in a chuckle. "So, how *is* that article on BDD coming, anyway? Almost done?"

"Just about." Angel nodded. "I love this topic. I get so damned fired up about it." She sent the two pages to the printer, snatching them as they slipped out, presenting them to B.J. "What do you think so far?"

Perching her scrawny butt on the edge of Angel's desk, B.J. perused the article silently for a moment and then read aloud. "...they're no more than kids and yet these teens are begging their parents for cosmetic surgery," she read. "Not to correct a birth deformity or a two-inch mole on the face, or even a crooked nose, but to have big, perfectly round, non-moving breasts jutting atop purposely bony rib cages." Uttering a growl of disgust, B.J. threaded her fingers through her long, straight salt-and-pepper hair.

"A girl's driving need to be the fairest in the land," she continued reading, "is one of the oldest fairytale themes. Unfortunately, that need often has deadly consequences if it develops into Body Dysmorphic Disorder. BDD is a preoccupation with an imagined physical defect. The condition tends to be chronic and can lead to depression, social isolation, dropping out of school, unnecessary surgery and even suicide." B.J. looked up from the page, fixing a stony gaze on Angel.

After what seemed like an eternity of silence, Angel swallowed hard and spit out, "So?" She'd worked hard on this story and it was important to her to alert readers to this dire problem that had recently become so widespread.

"It's perfect," B.J. said quietly as she nodded. "This topic pisses me off so much I could scream. Those poor insecure kids end up getting all twisted because of the goddamn motherfucking male-dominated chauvinistic motherfucking media." She pounded her fist on Angel's desk.

"Um...you said *motherfucking* twice," Angel pointed out with a grin.

"Yeah, I guess I did." B.J. smirked. "Shows you how much it pisses me off." She headed out of Angel's office, pausing at the door and peeking back inside. "I need this finished by five o'clock. Great job, kid."

Beaming a smile, Angel glanced at her notes. "Let's see," she mused. "What else do I want to get in here...perfect turned-up noses...plumped up lips...skimpy clothes...summer fat camps for skinny girls..." She sighed. "So much to work into the article."

"Do you always talk to yourself when you're alone, Ms. Brewster?"

With an astonished gasp, Angel clapped a hand against her chest. She looked up, straight into the eyes of Dr. Max Wiley. "Max! What are you doing here?"

"I tried calling you on your cell phone but gave up after leaving the fifth message. I figured you were either trying to avoid me, had the thing turned off, or left it at home, so I decided to stop by in person instead."

After drinking in Max's studly presence, which was just as appealing and sexy midday as it was in the middle of the night, she smiled. This was certainly a first. Angel had definitely never experienced a quivering, dribbling pussy while sitting at the computer in her office before. She squirmed just a bit in her seat and cleared her throat. "Nope, not avoiding you. I leave the phone turned off when I'm at work. Hey," she slanted him a befuddled look, "how did you get in here, anyway? They usually buzz me first when someone wants to see me."

Max waved a hand in the general direction of the receptionist's desk. "When I told them who I was, the girls up front pointed out your office and told me I could just come on back here. Is that a problem?"

One glimpse through the blinds on her window confirmed Angel's suspicions. She wasn't a bit surprised to see the receptionist huddled with three other columnists, craning their necks to see what was going on. After all, it wasn't often that the decidedly feminist offices of *Women's Wit and Wisdom* magazine were graced by the machismo charm and presence of a man like Max Wiley. Angel knew she'd be in for a lengthy third degree later.

"Not at all. I'm glad you stopped by."

"Nice office," Max said, surveying the small, somewhat haphazard room. It's not that Angel was a slob, but she did have a penchant for collecting things. Not classic collectibles like salt and pepper shakers, or limited-edition plates, or cookie jars, but things like old postcards featuring photos and illustrations of Rubenesque women, many of them risqué, lists of favorite quotations, and other assorted oddities that she squirreled away. The postcards were stuffed, pinned, wedged, and otherwise displayed in every spare nook and cranny of her office, including the ones that stood on mini-easels along the windowsills, while the burgeoning sheets filled with quotations were, at least so far, confined to her bulletin board and desktop. Of course, it would be convenient if she also had a penchant for orderliness, but, she reasoned, one can't have everything.

"What are all these?" Max motioned to the glut of postcards then tapped a long sheet of paper tacked to her bulletin board before flipping it up to see several others beneath it.

"Just a few of the old postcards and favorite quotations that I collect," Angel said.

"A few? You mean there's more?"

"Well, aside from what's in the filing cabinet over there, I've got a linen closet full of the stuff at home. I'm...well, just a little compulsive when it comes to certain things. Like postcards and quotations and chocolate. Of course, the chocolate never lasts long enough to be displayed anywhere but on my hips."

"And a mighty fine set of hips they are, too," Max said with a devilish smile.

If she'd been older, Angel would have sworn that she was having a hot flash. There was something about the man... No more than a sexy lift of his eyebrow could send her hormones into overdrive. "I jot the quotations down as I find them," she said, without acknowledging his comment. "One of these days I'll take the time to type them out and frame them along with some of the postcards, or maybe make up some scrapbooks or something."

Max studied a few of the postcards and then looked the top sheet of quotations over and chuckled. "Antique photos of full-bodied nude women combined with women's lib quotes. An interesting and rather curious collection, Ms. Brewster."

"They pair together quite well I think. Pictures of women from an age when full bosoms and hips were prized, and quotes relating to how times have changed since then. What's so curious about that?"

"Quotes relating to the battle between the sexes, you mean," Max said.

"No they're not." Angel muttered a grumble. "Why do you feel the need to slap a label on everything?"

Ignoring her question, Max kept his attention on the list. "Here's one by Nicole Hollander, cartoonist. 'Can you imagine a world without men?'" he read aloud. "'No crime and lots of happy fat women.'" After a brief I-told-you-so glance at Angel, he continued to scan the list silently and then chuckled. "'Remember,'" he read, "'Ginger Rogers did everything Fred Astaire did, but backwards and in high heels.' Faith Whittlesey, former Ambassador to Switzerland."

"It's one of my favorites," Angel said. "Ginger never got the credit she deserved."

"'If the world were a logical place,'" Max read, "'men would ride side saddle.' Rita Mae Brown, author." He thought for a moment then gave Angel a benefit-of-the-doubt shrug as he nodded. "I have to admit, she's got a valid point there."

"Kind of like the whole boy-girl bicycle bar thing," Angel said. "Logically, it should be the other way around."

Max winced. "Yeah...that's one I can vouch for personally." He returned his attention to the list. "Here's a dandy," he said, clearly amused. "'When I first went into the movies, Lionel Barrymore played my grandfather. Later he played my father and finally he played my husband. If he had lived I'm sure I would have played his mother. That's the way it is in Hollywood. The men get younger and the women get older.' Lillian Gish." Max looked up from the page, smirking. "Yeah, I can see how these quotes have nothing whatsoever to do with the battle of the sexes."

"You know," Angel couldn't help but point out, "if you substitute any current aging male actor's name for Barrymore's, that statement could easily be made by any female actor today."

"Actress, you mean."

"No. That's sexist. Today both men and women are referred to as actors."

Max looked unconvinced. "I don't know, makes things sorta difficult to keep straight, if you ask me."

"I don't see why. It just takes some enlightened thinking, that's all. For instance, what about doctors? When's the last time you heard of a woman doctor being referred to as a doctress?"

Max gave a thoughtful nod. "You've got me there." He cleared his throat. "Anyway, I was—"

"You don't hear female butchers referred to as butcheresses, do you? Or bus driveress, lawyeress, teacheress," Angel ticked each example off on her fingers. "Veterinarianess—"

"Whoa! I surrender." Max laughed. "I get the point. I promise never to refer to you as a magazine writeress or columnistess, okay?"

"Thank you." Nodding, Angel chuckled.

"Anyway, what I was about to say before getting an impromptu lesson in gender-neutral language," Max said, "is that I was trying to reach you on your phone to find out how Henry's doing this afternoon. Any problems?"

Rising from her chair, Angel crooked her finger. "Come with me, doctor." She led Max out of the office and around the corner to a small storage room where Henry was lounging on the floor atop a large pillow placed over a thick blanket. His favorite squeak toy and a rawhide bone were nestled between his paws. His food and water dishes stood nearby.

"I just couldn't leave him alone today," Angel said. At the sound of his mistress' voice, Henry sleepily propped one eyelid open, licked his chops and went back to sleep. "I didn't want to leave him with a sitter, either. I called my boss after I left your clinic for Henry's follow-up this morning and she said I could bring him into the office with me."

Max took a few steps over to Henry and squatted, giving Angel a delicious view of his ass through the straining jeans. Her thoughts immediately flew to their lovemaking late Saturday night, or, rather, early Sunday morning, and how good it felt to clasp her hands around those firm butt cheeks of his. It was the same reaction she'd had when she saw Max earlier this morning wearing a white doctor's top over his jeans. When the deluge of tantalizing memories flooded her brain, she felt herself flush and her nipples harden. She did her best to throw a mental bucket of ice water on her libido because this wasn't the time or place.

Angel watched as Max checked her dog, with Henry moving nary a muscle during the examination. "Everything looks good," he said. "He's probably going to be listless like this for another couple of days, then he'll gradually become more energetic until he's back to himself."

"So, do you usually make house calls?" Angel asked as Max rose to his feet. She'd meant the comment to sound witty and urbane, only to cringe when it came out sounding so utterly wispy.

"Occasionally." Max stuffed his hands in his back pockets. "Actually, I stopped by because I was in the area, on my way to a lunch date with a very special lady." His expression grew devilish.

"Oh." Surprised at how disappointed she was to learn that she, er...Henry, wasn't the only reason for Max's visit, Angel's shoulders sagged. Things got even worse as she felt the unwelcome beginnings of jealousy stir at the mere notion of Max having lunch with someone else. Especially since that someone else was a female someone else. Damn. After years of steeping herself in feminist dogma, she was suddenly sliding downhill fast. Well, that's what she got for having mind-numbing sex with a man she'd known for just a few hours.

"I really appreciate it, Max. Thanks." Angel took in a deep breath and glanced at her watch. "Well, I, uh, don't want to keep you from your lunch date." She did her best to project a bright smile.

"How about you," Max said. "Got any plans for lunch?"

"Me? A lunch date?" Max nodded and Angel envisioned the avocado, tomato and sprouts sandwich on five-grain bread waiting for her in the refrigerator. "Well, sure. Of course I do.

Why wouldn't I?" She cleared her throat. "In fact, Jason's expecting me soon, so I should be going, too."

Tsking, Max shook his head. "Gee, that's too bad."

"Um..." Angel studied him wondering what he had on his mind. Maybe he thought he'd coordinate a threesome lunchtime quickie with her and his *very special lady.* Hah! Dream on, buster. "Why?"

"Because I was hoping *you* were going to be my lunch date."

"Oh." Angel nodded. "*Oh!*" she repeated when it finally sank in. "Just you and me, you mean."

Max smiled and nodded. "That was my dastardly plan."

"Well, sure, I can arrange that. Just let me make a quick call to cancel—"

"No, no, that's not necessary," Max said, stepping out of the storeroom. "I wouldn't want you to change your plans on my account." He gave Angel a smile that melted her insides. "Just give me a call or stop by if anything comes up with Henry." He turned, heading back to the front of the office, leaving Angel drop-jawed and flustered.

"Um...Max? Wait. Honestly, it's no trouble," she said, traipsing behind him like a smitten teenager and mentally chastising herself for it. "Just give me a minute, okay?" She waited long enough to make sure Max had stopped walking before she sped back to her office and gathered her purse. She grabbed her cell phone, turned it on and pretended to punch in a phone number as Max stood outside her office door.

"Jason, hi," she said into the phone after a moment. "Listen, I'm sorry, but something's come up and I've got to cancel our lunch date. Yes, I was looking forward to it, too, Jay, but—"

And then Angel's cell phone rang.

Squealing a yelp, she dropped it like a hot potato and erupted into nervous giggles.

Folding his arms across his chest, Max crossed one leg over the other and leaned against the doorjamb, with a big, stupid, knowing grin plastered across his face.

A telltale blush singeing her cheeks, Angel bent to grab the phone, gushing out more giggles as she glanced at Max. Answering the phone, she said, "Hello? Oh, Jason, it's you! Sorry, I guess we must have been cut off. Thanks for calling back so fast." More giggles. "Anyway, we'll do lunch another time again soon, Jay, I promise, okay? Buh-bye." She ended the call, leaving the caller, her nosy, persistent mother of all people, thoroughly baffled. Well, she'd just have to deal with that later.

"Must be some newfangled kind of cell phone you've got there," Max mused, grin still firmly entrenched. "'Cause mine sure doesn't do that."

"Neither does mine," B.J. added as she poked her head into Angel's office, tongue firmly in cheek.

If Angel had access to duct tape she'd have slapped a big strip over her mouth rather than humiliate herself further by spewing forth yet another collection of inane giggles. Regrettably, no tape was at hand and the grating sound of panicky laughter rang through the air.

"Yeah," she said, regaining her composure and stuffing her phone back into her purse, "it's really amazing what they can do with these things nowadays, isn't it? Hard to keep up with the technology." Her gaze shifting from Max to B.J. and back again, she choked back another emerging giggle, thankfully impeding it before it exited her mouth.

"I'm B.J., Angel's boss." B.J. extended her hand. "And you're?"

"Max Wiley." He enclosed the woman's hand with his own and pumped. "Nice to meet you."

"He's the doctor who saved Henry," Angel clarified.

"Of course," B.J. said. "The vet. Angel told us all about how you helped Henry after his chocolate binge. Well," B.J. paused, tossing a bemused glance in Angel's direction, "at least she told us *some* of what happened." She arched an eyebrow at Angel before returning her attention to Max. "Now I'm eager to hear the rest of the story." She winked before scooting off and calling, "Enjoy your lunch," over her shoulder. "Don't forget I need that article by five."

"Not to worry, B.J.," Angel said. "Um, there's a great little Thai place just down the street, Max," she offered quickly, hoping she could sort of slide past her embarrassment without him nailing her on the fake call. "Unless you'd prefer something else."

"Is it vegetarian?" he asked, warily.

Angel gave him a disparaging look. "Don't worry, they serve animal flesh, too—although I'd strongly recommend their panang curry with tofu. It's wonderfully flavorful. Hot and spicy."

"Thai sounds good to me," Max said. "Personally, I like things *hot* and *spicy*." Drawing the words out, Max pushed off the doorjamb and strode into her office, planting both hands on her desk and leaning toward her. He was so close that she could smell him, breathe in that fresh woodsy soap smell mixed with his male essence. With his rugged good looks, wit, and raw sex appeal, Max defined the very essence of masculinity. He was tough and somewhat arrogant, with just the right amount of humor and sensitivity thrown into the mix. He stood there across the desk, staring at her so intently she thought she'd liquefy on the spot.

"So, is that where you and, uh...Jason were going to have lunch?" he said finally.

Angel could tell by the distinct twist of his mouth and jaw that he was trying hard not to burst out laughing. She decided right then and there that she'd been wrong in her assessment of him. Clearly, the man was sadly lacking on the sensitivity front. Ignoring his question, she yanked her keys from her purse. "Come on. I'll drive."

"That's okay, I'll drive," Max countered as she brushed past him.

Angel stopped and turned around. "I *said* that *I* will drive."

Max slapped his hand against his chest. "*I'm* the man, so I'll—"

"*Excuse me?*" Angel practically screeched as her cheeks grew hot with indignation. "What does your gender have to do with anything? Except that perhaps it renders you incapable of being a passenger when a woman is behind the wheel. Does the idea somehow threaten your masculinity, Dr. Wiley?"

"Of course not, don't be ridiculous. It's just that I prefer to—" He stopped when Angel frowned, gazing at him through a narrow-eyed glare. After a pause, during which he seemed to be counting to ten, Max said calmly, "Look, you're my date for lunch, so I'm the one who should do the driving. It's the gentlemanly thing to do." As he swept into a bow, his saccharine-soaked smile didn't fool Angel one bit.

"Uh-huh, well this date is Dutch," she said. "So there's no reason why I can't drive. Case settled."

"Jeezus. Why do you have to make every little insignificant remark into a major issue?" Max said. "From the first moment I laid eyes on you you've been harping at me for one thing or another."

"Me? I'm not the one who started it," Angel said. "If you remember, I said I would drive and then you said—"

"Well, since you've got such a bee in your bonnet about it, Ms. Brewster," Max jabbed an accusatory finger toward Angel, "maybe we should just forget lunch altogether."

"Bee in my...well, of all the nerve!" With a righteous gasp, Angel's chin jutted forward. "Yeah, maybe we should forget about it. That's fine with me." She marched back to her desk, slammed her purse onto it and faced him, arms akimbo.

"Fine!" Max bellowed, turning on his heel to leave.

"Oh for chrissakes, you two!" B.J. yelled from her adjacent office a moment before she marched out, looked at the two of them and then burst out laughing.

Angel sucked in an audible exclamation. Her own boss, her friend, the woman who'd personally coached her in feminist dogma after Robert had drained Angel of her confidence, was laughing at her! She felt downright betrayed. "B.J., how can you stand there laughing like that? There is nothing funny about this whatsoever. If you'd really been listening then you would have heard that Max just insulted my womanhood."

"I did no such thing," Max countered. "If anyone was doing the insulting it was you, not me."

"Children!" B.J. said with authority. Max and Angel's mouths clamped shut. "For heaven's sake, keep your voices down. You're disturbing the entire office with your antics. Honestly, if you could just see yourselves—like a couple of defiant kindergarteners. Max all puffed up with macho indignation and Angel bristling with feminist bravado."

"He's just like Robert," Angel muttered under her breath.

"Who's Robert?" Max said.

"No he most certainly is not," B.J. said.

"Robert *never* let me drive. Remember?"

"Oh brother." B.J. rolled her eyes. "That doesn't mean Max is anything like Robert."

"Who's Robert?" Max said more loudly.

"My niece's husband," B.J. said.

"My ex," Angela said.

"Husband?" Max sounded incredulous.

"Ex control freak," Angel answered.

Max's jaw dropped. "Are you saying I'm a control freak just because I wanted to drive?"

"Robert was her fiancé," B. J. said. "You're nothing like him."

"Well, if the shoe fits—" Angel started.

"Oh, good God in heaven, will you just *stop!*" B.J. bellowed and the entire office came to a standstill. Growling in frustration, she waved her hand at the staff. "Sorry. Everything's okay, just go back to work." She turned back to Angel and Max, her shoulders drooping in a weary sag. "There, now see what you two made me do? You made me lose my cool in front of my staff. That has never happened before."

"She's right, it hasn't," Angel said to Max, disbelief tingeing her voice.

B.J. held out her hand, palm up, and wiggled her fingers. "Both of you. Now. Give me your keys."

"But—" Max and Angel chorused.

"I said *now*. Give. Me. Your. Keys. *Now*," B.J. said quietly through clenched teeth as she fried the pair with a narrow-eyed glare. "Until the two of you stop acting like kindergarteners, your driving privileges have been revoked. So just shut up and walk to the goddamned restaurant already. It's not that far. If you can show me that you can behave like mature, civilized adults when you get back then I'll return these."

Jangling both sets of keys, B.J. turned on her heel and headed back to her office. "You know," she said looking over her shoulder, "if Adam and Eve had been anything like you two, chances are none of us would even be here today."

She closed the door and locked it, leaving Max and Angel with mouths gaping.

Chapter Nine

"And so the night before the wedding B.J. caught her niece, Linda—my best friend and maid of honor—and Robert in bed together," Angel said after swallowing the last of her spring roll.

"Holy shit."

"Yeah," Angel said. "That pretty much sums it up."

"So B.J. called to tell you?"

Angel nodded. "Yup, then I called off the wedding. It was embarrassing, expensive and horrible, but thank God I found out before marrying that rat-bastard and making the biggest mistake of my life." She sucked in a deep breath and exhaled slowly. "So that's pretty much my Robert story in a nutshell, Max. I never should have compared you to him. You're nothing like Robert at all. That was wrong and childish. I acted like a complete jerk and I'm sorry. Truly." Her smile was hesitant, apologetic. "Forgive me?"

Max gazed into Angel's eyes and felt the last vestiges of anger melt away. He gave a dismissive wave of his hand. "Forget about it. I acted like a jerk, too. I just should have let you drive and kept my mouth shut in the first place."

Angel's smile lit up her whole face. "Thanks Max."

"So Robert married B.J.'s niece then?"

Angel nodded. "Pregnant."

"Jeez."

"From what I hear they're very happy together. Linda loves being a doormat and Robert loves walking all over her." Angel reveled in a devilish snicker before sampling her panang curry with tofu, murmuring her delight. "Mmm, this is delicious. Want to try some?" she asked. "Careful, I added extra chili sauce."

"Eh...sure. Want to try my...uh...whatever it is? It's really good, too."

"Pad ga pow," Angel said. "Stir-fried basil with meat. That's one of my favorites, well, not when it's made with meat, of course. I like it with ground portabella mushrooms instead. Mmm, delicious"

"Yeah, thanks for suggesting it. Want a taste?"

Angel gave him a you-should-know-better look. "Max, you ordered yours with ground pork. I don't eat meat, remember?"

"Oh yeah...sorry."

"Here, taste mine."

A discriminating, otherwise known as *picky*, eater, especially when it came to certain vegetables or anything he couldn't pronounce, Max felt like he was ten again. *Aw, gee, Mom, do I have to eat that slimy stuff?* He sucked in a deep breath. "Yeah, sure. What the hell."

She prepared a forkful with a bit of everything on it, including a plump wad of tofu nestled right on top. He tried not to look at it because if he concentrated hard enough the stuff almost seemed to wiggle. Max couldn't help but cringe just a bit as he opened his mouth and she deposited the contents on his tongue. Once he got past the tasteless clump of white stuff it wasn't half bad.

"Your sauce tastes kind of like spicy peanut butter. I like it...I think." Max smiled.

"Good, then maybe you'll order it next time you eat Thai, instead of something with meat." Angel patted his hand.

"Uh...no." Max was proud of himself for not shuddering at the thought of downing an entire plate of the bland, nondescript, poor-ass substitution for meat.

He watched as Angel slipped another forkful of the hot, spicy curry into her mouth. She closed her eyes while savoring the taste. Max liked her like this. Quiet and preoccupied so that being contrary was, hopefully, the furthest thing from her mind. As a writer who spent time observing the habits and personalities of others, he had become particularly adept at reading people. But Angel wasn't easy to peg. She was a true enigma. In the short time he'd known her he'd witnessed her mood change—several times—from practical good sense to wild irrationality in a matter of moments, without a clue as to the cause of the storm. Until now. Her experience with Robert explained a lot.

If Angel was any other woman he would have been gone so fast it would have made her head spin. There was something extraordinary about Angel. Something that drew him to her like iron filings to a magnet. The sex? By far the best he'd ever had.

A curious kind of hostile intimacy had risen between them, like nothing he'd experienced before. No, despite that annoyingly aggressive feminism of hers, not to mention her profusion of opinions on most any topic, Max couldn't bring himself to walk away.

As the thought skipped through his mind, he already knew it was a bad one. If he were smart, if he wanted to avoid trouble, if he had an ounce of good sense, he'd give her the big kiss off. Yeah...that's what Jack Clyde would do. He sure wouldn't let any bold-mouthed babe push him around. No way. He'd—

"See?" Angel said, licking her lips as she intruded on his thoughts. "We can do this."

Slanting a questioning glance, Max said, "What? Have lunch together or sample each other's food?"

"Well, that, too," she said, "but I meant *talk*. As in, have a nice, normal, rational, non-confrontational conversation." She scooped another forkful of tofu into her mouth, practically purring as her eyelids fluttered shut.

Max felt the flicker of a smile curve his lips as he nodded. "Well what do you know. It seems that we can." Goddamn, she was sexy—even when she was eating. Hell, the expression on her face as she relished her meal surpassed those he'd seen on women in the throes of orgasm. Angel Brewster was, indeed, a woman of extreme passion.

"Tell me about your dog, Spill," she said. "What happened to his other leg? Was it an accident or was he born that way?"

Max huffed a humorless laugh. "Some street punks used the little guy for target practice," he said. Angel breathed in an exclamation.

"Oh my God. They shot him. With a gun?"

"Snot-nosed little bastards," Max said. "Apparently it was part of an initiation to join a gang. They got a point for each leg they shot. The cops reached the scene before they could take another shot at Spill, but a couple of other dogs weren't so lucky. One got it in three legs and the other one took a bullet in the belly."

"Did Spill belong to you then?"

"No. Someone else owned him. They brought him to me for surgery. When the owner found out that Spill was going to lose his leg, he said he didn't want him. Told me to put him down or take him to the pound." Max sipped from his tea, returning the cup to the table with more force than he'd intended.

"That's the most awful thing I've ever heard," Angel said, her eyes glistening with tears. "How could he simply abandon his dog when the poor little thing needed him most?"

"Regrettably, not every pet owner shares your values, Angel. It would turn your stomach if I told you the results I've seen from what owners have done to their dogs and cats. Even their birds. Disgusting." Angel was silent and Max studied her for a moment. "Sorry, that wasn't very pleasant or appropriate lunchtime conversation."

"No...no," Angel said. "I'm glad you told me. So you adopted Spill then?"

Max grinned. "Yeah, we became best buddies right from the get-go. He's a spirited little guy. Wasn't about to let the loss of one leg slow him down for long."

"Yeah, he gets around amazingly well. It took me awhile that night I came to your place before I even realized he only had three legs. Did you name him? Spill's such an unusual name for a dog."

"Unlike Henry, you mean." Max snickered. "His full name is Spillane. I named him after Mickey."

Angel frowned. "You named your dog after Mickey Spillane, the author?"

"I'm a big fan, what can I say? Plus I wr—" Max stopped short. Dollface still seemed a little edgy. Something told him this may not be the best time to mention that he wrote hardboiled sexist crime fiction as Frank Coleman.

Angel gave him a peculiar look. "What were you saying?"

"Uh...it was either Spill or Hammer," Max continued quickly, "after Mike Hammer, Spillane's detective character. Another option was Lippy, after Lippy Sullivan, a character that appeared in one of his books, but he got snuffed."

"Got snuffed? You crack me up, Max. You must read a lot of those books because the jargon's definitely carried over into your everyday speech."

"Yeah..." Maybe he should just tell her and get it over with. How bad could it be? She might lose a little respect for him, get pissed because she'd see him as some chauvinistic asshole or something, but that would pass... Wouldn't it? On the other hand, what if she got her feathers all ruffled and stormed out of his life forever? He didn't want to chance that...not when they were just getting to know each other—and had the promise of more stupendous sex just ahead, after their first real date.

"Somehow I didn't think Spill would appreciate being called Lippy," Max said, certain he was making the right decision by not spilling his guts about the writing thing just yet. There'd be plenty of time for that later. "Turns out the name *Spill* fits the little guy just right, seeing as how he's always taking a spill when he zips around corners too fast."

Angel looked up at him with those big baby blues and smiled. "You're really a very nice man, Max. A *good* man."

He swallowed hard. "That's right," he said matter-of-factly, pointing the tines of his fork in her direction. "Don't you forget it. Especially the next time you want to jump down my throat for some harmless comment I've mistakenly made, okay?"

Angel cringed. "I'm...I'm sorry, Max." She dropped her gaze to her plate where she was pushing a trio of green beans around with her fork. "I know I have a way of... Well, I know I can be rather brusque and maybe just a bit stubborn. It's not just because of the things that happened with Robert, it's also because—" She popped her head up when she heard Max chuckle. At first her expression became fierce and then she loosened up.

"It's because I come from a big family," she explained. "There were six of us kids and I was the only girl—the youngest child, and—"

"You've got five brothers?" Max asked incredulously.

"Yup." Angel gave in to a resigned sigh. "The triplets, Bartholomew, Benjamin and Bradley," she ticked the names off on her fingers, "are thirty-eight. They take after my dad with blue eyes and dark brown hair. The twins, Joshua and Joseph, are thirty-five. They take after Mom's side like me, with blond hair and blue eyes."

"Wow. It must have been pandemonium at your house."

"Always." Angel looked at Max's expression and chuckled. "Multiple births run on both sides of my family," she explained. "My parents are both twins. They met at a twins' convention. Practically everyone else on either side of the family are twins, triplets or quadruplets. When singular little old me was born, everyone in the family teased my parents saying I must be the mailman's daughter." Tugging on a curly strand of hair, she gave a lopsided grin.

Being an only child with no aunts or uncles, Max could only imagine what it must have been like in the Brewster household. "So you had to learn to speak up for yourself or get overlooked, I'll bet."

"Damn right. If I didn't elbow my way in and speak up for myself, I'd be pushed aside. I learned early on to hold my ground and not to back down."

"Except when it came to Robert."

"It was so subtle at first I didn't realize what was happening. First Robert told me my naturally curly hair made me look like a floozy. He encouraged me to straighten it—and tone down the color."

Max gazed at her angelic halo of blonde. "What?!"

"Then he told me I should never wear jeans because they're not flattering on overweight women. Plus he wanted me to wear skirts and dresses because he thought I was too much of a tomboy." Max gave her a look of disbelief. "It just escalated from there. Robert's an accountant. He's very conservative and concerned with appearances. Before I knew what had happened, Angel Brewster had disappeared and in her place was a docile woman I didn't even know." She looked thoughtful for a moment. "Anyway, now whenever I feel pushed into a corner, I tend to strike back without thinking first."

"Makes sense," Max said.

Angel stabbed one of the green beans, slid it through the sauce and popped it into her mouth, looking up at him again. "Of course, that's also why I'm not skinny."

"Okay," Max said. "I was following everything right up to the not being skinny part. Then you lost me. You're saying you're not skinny because of Robert?"

"No, because of my family," Angel said matter-of-factly. "I was rail thin as a kid. Partly because I was athletic, but mostly because I never got any cake, or cookies, or candy, or pudding or ice cream. And because I had to have my milk plain, without any chocolate. And because I never got any French fries. And because—"

"Whoa!" Max wiped his mouth with his napkin. He clamped his other hand over Angel's arm. "Slow down a minute so I can sort this out, okay? So, what I'm getting out of this is that your parents were either very strict or very poor. Because of that, you and your brothers didn't have an opportunity to eat many treats when you were kids. Is that right?"

"Hah!" Angel blurted so loudly that the diners at the surrounding tables in the small establishment turned in her direction. "Not by a long shot. On the contrary, with five mischievous boys just three years apart, and one scrappy daughter, my mother was too haggard to bother being strict and my father was always flying off here or there because of business. He made a good living, so we weren't poor. The reason I didn't have any of those things is because my brothers were a bunch of selfish, thoughtless, ravenous pigs who ate up all the treats before I ever got my portion. I got stuck with all the healthy crap they didn't want, like the salads and cooked vegetables."

Enlightened, Max nodded broadly. "Ahh, now I understand. No wonder you're such a pushy, feisty little broad." He watched Angel's relaxed features morph until they bristled with indignation. "Hold it..." he held up his hand, "don't go into one of your tirades, okay? I was just kidding. Damn, you're easy."

Angel sucked in a deep breath, her lips quirking into a restrained smile. "You derive far too much enjoyment from pushing my buttons, doc."

"Sorry. I imagine you already have to put up with enough of that from your brothers."

"I'm used to it. They've learned by now not to give me too much grief because they know damn well that I'll make them suffer for it." Having abandoned her fork for the serving spoon, she ladled a spoonful of spicy peanut sauce into her mouth, humming her appreciation.

"I can well imagine," Max said, smirking until he noted the pink tip of her tongue lazily sweep across her full, sensuous lips. She may have spiced up her sauce with extra chili, but she was still the hottest thing at their table. In the entire restaurant, in fact—he'd bet on it.

"They can still be a pain, especially when they get overprotective. They scared off most of my boyfriends with their threats and inquisitions." Angel laughed. "Actually, the one who gives me the most grief now is my mom. I love her to death, but the woman is a world class buttinski who believes it's a mother's sacred right to interfere with her children's lives— especially her daughter's." Angel rolled her eyes and chuckled. "I know she means well, but I just wish she'd get off my case and trust me enough to let me take my life in the direction I choose."

"Mine sounds similar," Max said. "She's an old-fashioned kind of woman living in a high-tech world and she hasn't quite caught up with it yet. Her latest concern is that her only child might be gay."

Angel bugged her eyes. "Gay? You?"

Max nodded. "There was a time when being thirty-five and unmarried meant a man was a freewheeling bachelor. Nowadays, at least as far as my mother is concerned, it's a sure sign that he's gay. Although Mom's assured me that she'll love me just the same and do her best to accept any partners I may have hidden away—as long as we keep my homosexuality a secret from my father, who'd keel over with a heart attack if he discovered his son was gay."

"Oh, that's just too funny." Angel laughed along with Max. "I've been getting the same thing from my mother, believe it or not."

"Really? Because you're not married?"

"Exactly." Angel nodded.

"You were engaged," Max said. "Doesn't that count?"

"No, because that was several years ago and I haven't been in a serious relationship since. I think she's afraid my bad experience with the rat-bastard turned me against all men and into a lesbian, especially because I've become a feminist since breaking things off with Robert."

"Ah," Max gave a knowing nod. "I see."

"Mom's still in the dark ages when it comes to equality for women," Angel continued. "She still thinks that a woman's place is in the home, catering to a husband's every whim and orchestrating the lives of a hoard of children."

Max shrugged. "Sounds reasonable to me."

"Mmm-hmm. It would." Angel looked cynical. "So apparently Mom thinks I'm a closet lesbian. She's convinced that any straight, thirty-two–year-old woman would be happily ensconced in domestic bliss by now. Never mind that my brothers, all older than me, are still happily single. She never worries about any of *them* being gay. Of course, that might have something to do with the fact that they've constantly got gorgeous, eager women crawling all over them. My *helpful* father has told Mom repeatedly that all feminists are lesbians."

Max reached across the small square table and lifted her chin, brushing his thumb across her skin. "If you think it would help matters, I'd be more than happy to vouch for your heterosexuality." He did his best to look innocent.

Angel covered Max's hand with her own, lowering it to the table and patting it. "Thanks. I appreciate the offer, Sir Galahad. Tell you what...we'll pay my parents a visit right after we finish telling yours that we screwed each other's brains out after knowing each other for just a few hours." She grinned, seemingly unaware of heads turning in her direction again.

What a dame!

"Yeah...maybe we'll just forget that whole idea and find something a bit more, uh...subtle," Max said.

"Maybe we'd get our parents off our backs by telling them we're bisexual." Angel slurped up the last of her peanut sauce, smacking her lips.

Max stalled, fork in midair as enticing scenarios danced across his mind...

It was an area thickly populated with johns and their sluts. The motel room reeked of cigar smoke and drugstore after-shave, but the sweet smell of ripe pussy hit my nostrils, clear as a bell.

I came within an ace of catching them in the act—two busty broads, naked and rummaging around each other with their tongues while their john, a sleazebag peddler of kiddie porn, jerked himself off. Jill, a lean-faced, full-mouthed redhead, had a reputation for giving the best bang for the buck of any hooker on the street. Her old man wasn't earning much, so she got a job at a topless dance club. After he bought the farm, she upped her business, becoming a high-class whore. She was okay in my book. A hardworking dame who didn't fleece her johns. I would have taken her up on her offers to do the horizontal mambo if I hadn't sworn off hookers a long time ago. Sure, I may be a sleazy P.I., but I still have my scruples.

I didn't recognize the other babe. Angel was what Jill called her. I tore my gaze from Angel's bouncy little ass and sighed as I felt my dick get hard. She was stacked. A cute little cupcake with nonstop legs, and the supple body of a dancer. Eyeballing me, Angel fixed a brittle stare across the smoke-hazed room. "You a cop?" she asked, licking the taste of Jill's big tit from her lips. I wanted my tongue there, too, tangling with hers. As if she read my thoughts, Angel's expression of fright mingled with a queer kind of pleasurable expectancy.

"Jack Clyde, private dick," I filled her in. "Relax, dollface. I'm here for the john, not you." As I said the words, I knew I was lying. "Come on, Ernie," I said, pinning the sleazebag with a cold, hard stare. "I'm hauling your ass in." One look at the revolver in my hand and I knew Ernie wouldn't give me any trouble. His eyes were hugely dilated and he was trembling like a wet puppy.

Jill flicked open a lighter and torched a cigarette. "Why don't you stop back when you're finished with business, Jack," she said. "Angel and I could make you feel real good." Then Angel stretched, flaunting herself like a tropical flower as Jill raked Angel's body with her fingers.

"Real good," Angel added, slipping her fingers into Jill's cunt and then savoring the musky tang as she licked them.

"Yeah, I just bet you could," I answered, quirking my lip into a smile. I could think of nothing better than ending the evening with a couple of cold beers and a pair of hot pussies. I had to get out of there fast before I embarrassed myself by having my swelling dick burst out of my pants and shoot a load all over the dolls.

Damn. I shouldn't have thought about that. Because now all I could picture was watching the two dames lick my cum off each other's tits...

Max shook his head, clearing his thoughts. "Are you?" he asked Angel. "Bisexual, I mean?"

Angel took one look at his face and burst out laughing. "You can just wipe that eager, hopeful grin right off your face, Max Wiley. While I'm an advocate of same-sex relationships, I'm totally straight. If there were going to be any threesomes going on it would be with me and two men, not the other way around."

"Nope. Doesn't work for me." Max wrinkled his nose. "I want to keep my woman all to myself...unless, of course, she expresses an interest in a double female, single male ménage, of course." He quirked a brow and smiled.

"Like I said, doc, dream on. It ain't gonna happen. Not with me, at least."

Max scooted back his chair, a solemn look on his face. "Well, if that's the way you feel, then maybe we should just say adios now, Angel. It's been fun."

Angel's jaw dropped with an audible gasp as Max rose. And then it opened and closed like a fish.

"Gotcha," he said pointing at her and erupting with laughter.

Eyes wide with surprise, Angel bolted out of her chair. "Very funny. You're a real riot, Max. Remember that date you mentioned us going on? The one where we would get to know each other before getting back to anything physical?"

"Sure do," Max said, grinning. "I've got a very special evening planned. Saturday good for you, dollface?"

"Um...gee...let me see," Angel said, looking pensive as she tapped her finger against her cheek. "No. I don't think so. How about *never*, you big jerk!" She gathered her purse and clutched it close, withdrawing a tissue from its depths and dabbing her eyes and nose with a loud sob. Angel stormed through the restaurant toward the exit with Max rushing after her, mentally kicking himself for being such a jackass.

"Aw, jeez. Angel, wait," he called out, unmindful of the heads turning and the whispered exchanges that were, no doubt, focused on him and Angel. "Please don't cry. I'm sorry. Honest. I was just trying to be funny."

When Angel reached the door she turned back to Max, pointed a finger, grinned and said, "Gotcha!" before gleefully skipping out the door.

Chapter Ten

"Oh...is that what you're wearing?" Max said, eyeing Angel's holey sweatshirt and worn jeans as she opened the door. "Granted, it's not a fancy restaurant, but," he paused as he gave her another appraisal, "something a little less, uh, casual might be in order."

"Well, good evening to you, too." With an audible exclamation of frustration, Angel folded her arms across her chest. "Up until about thirty minutes ago I looked downright presentable, believe it or not. So, tell me, do you make a habit of being nearly two hours late picking up your dinner dates, just to stop by later and criticize their apparel? Ever hear of the telephone? It's a little thing invented for just these sorts of situations."

"I'm sorry, Angel. I should have called, but I completely forgot about our date because—"

Sputtering a humorless laugh, Angel rolled her eyes. "Oh, well that's real great for a girl's ego. Thanks, Max."

"No, you don't understand, I—"

"On the contrary, I understand perfectly," she said, stiffening and drumming her fingertips against her arm. Just then a car pulled into her driveway. A young man carrying a pizza box ran up to the door. Gathering the money from her jeans pocket, she paid him and walked to the kitchen, setting the pizza on the counter.

"You ordered a pizza?" Max asked with an incredulous expression as Angel returned to the front door.

"Yes I did, and now if you'll excuse me, Dr. Wiley, I'd like to eat it. Alone." Flattening her hand against his chest, Angel shoved him out the door. "Goodnight." Just as she was about to slam it in his face, Max's hand shot out to catch the door.

"It was a pregnant German Shepherd," Max said quickly, his jawbone clenching and unclenching. "Her owners called me just before I was going to leave to pick you up. She was hit by a car, Angel. I had to deliver her pups by cesarean section, then I had to put her down because there was nothing I could do to save her. I needed to spend some time with the family. I couldn't just run out on them when they were so broken up over the loss of their pet."

Angel's hand flew to her lips. "Oh my God, Max. I'm sorry. I am *so* sorry." She was quite certain that she'd never felt more like a selfish, whiny, bitchy jerk in all of her life. She grasped Max's sleeve and pulled him inside across the threshold. "Can you ever forgive me for being such an ass—*again*?"

"No reason to apologize." Max gave a tired smile. "It's not your fault. You didn't know."

"Wanna share a pizza?" Angel asked with a sheepish grin. "It's from my favorite vegetarian restaurant. Everything's organic from the crust to the cheese to the soy-based faux pepperoni and the delicious sausage made from textured wheat protein."

"Oh...uh..." Max sucked in a deep breath and blew it out slowly. "To tell you the truth, I think I could use a pleasant night out at a restaurant with a beautiful woman instead. I need the distraction."

Angel looked under the table, then lifted the pillows from the couch. She peeked behind the door before looking back at Max. "Sorry," she said.

"Angel...what on earth are you doing?"

"Looking for a beautiful woman," she answered matter-of-factly, glad when she saw Max's features relax into a full smile.

"That would be you," he said. He eyed her apparel again. "Well, at least it will be once you get back into your restaurant-going duds."

"Give me five minutes," she said, racing up the stairs.

"I'm positive," Max said ten minutes later. "Trust me."

"But Henry looks so forlorn," Angel insisted. "What if he needs me while I'm gone? He hasn't been left alone since you treated him last weekend."

"Look, it's not like you're abandoning him, you're just leaving him for a few hours, that's all. Besides, he's trying to look forlorn on purpose, to make you feel guilty."

"But..."

"You're like a nervous mother." Chuckling, Max tugged Angel close. "Tell you what, if it makes you feel better we can drop Henry off at my place. He and Spill can spend some time getting to know each other, okay?" Angel gave a tentative nod. "He'll be fine, Angel, I promise."

"You're sure he's strong enough to be left on his own?" Henry cocked his head and whimpered then. "Aw...see? The poor little thing's upset."

"Hardly. He's just clever. He's pushing your buttons just like I do because you're easy." Max sidestepped before Angel could whap him. "Henry's got the stamina of a canine superhero, able to leap tall buildings in a single bound, don't you, boy?" He mussed the dog's fur and got a juicy lick to the hand in return. "See that? He's fine. Now let's go or we'll be late for our dinner reservations. I called the restaurant once I was finished at the clinic and rescheduled." He gave his thigh a pat. "Come on, Henry. We're going for a ride." An eager Henry pranced along as Max took Angel's elbow and guided her to the door.

"I shouldn't be going with you, you know," Angel said, smoothing the skirt of her black after-five dress—the new one with the low neckline that displayed the nice, long cleavage crack, thanks to her push-up bra. It was the first really sexy dress she'd had on in years.

"Angel, I keep telling you—"

"Not because of Henry, Max. Because of you. I've been thinking about us all week. I've come to the conclusion that the only thing we really have in common is physical attraction. Period. That's it."

"True." Max nodded, sidling up close enough so she could breathe in his warm masculine scent. "Sizzling, firecracker-hot, exceedingly stimulating attraction." His voice dropped an octave as their bodies connected. The heated sensation of his body pressed against her was immediate electricity. "Have I told you that you look positively sensational in your restaurant-going duds?" His eyes lingered hungrily at her breasts.

Angel cleared her throat. It took every ounce of her strength to remain composed. Feeling as if her senses were scrambled, she put her hand against his chest in an instinctive effort to preserve what little space she had left. She simply could *not* think straight with the man this close. "Yes, I'll admit that we have a certain chemistry working for us, but—"

Max bellowed a laugh at that. "Yeah, you could say that. I'm so hot for you that I'm walking around in a constant state of arousal. And you want me so bad that your sweet little pussy's creaming right this minute." Angel sucked in a gasp. "Go ahead," Max taunted, "try to deny it."

Angel sputtered, "Of all the nerve. The audacity. The...the..." As outraged as she was at Max's masculine arrogance and presumption, it was really difficult to concentrate with her pussy creaming in obedient response to his confident declaration. Damn the man.

"After dinner I'm going to lap up that cream for dessert."

Angel's face became hot as she squeezed her thighs together, thoroughly cognizant of her dampening panties. Shit. She was in danger of coming, right there, standing in the vestibule of her house for chrissakes. "You're purposely trying to fluster me, Max, and I don't like it."

"Oh yes you do, dollface." His mouth kicked up into a wicked, genuine, all-out smile. His thumb brushed her chin, then her bottom lip and she shivered. "You love it and you know it. You may play the role of the starchy, zealous little feminist during the daytime, Angel, but I know what's really ticking underneath that prickly, righteous exterior. The heat...the passion..." His hands skimmed her curves and a groan of pleasure rumbled up from his chest. "You're all woman. Soft and round and wet and hungry to feel that juicy pussy of yours filled with my cock."

Angel lost track of the objections she'd been about to make when Max's arm snaked around her waist and his mouth came down on hers, stealing a kiss. She loathed him at that moment for being so damned accurate about her. It was as if he could see right through her, into her brain...inside her libido's control tower, wherever the hell that was located. God help her, Max *was* right. She'd barely been able to get through the week at work because all she could focus on was seeing him again and being impaled by his magnificent cock.

Oh, brother...she was certainly one sorry-ass excuse for a feminist.

"The point I was trying to make," she said when the kiss ended, "and it's a valid one," she wagged her finger under his nose, "is that all we have in common is the hots for each other. Yes, I admit that I do find the possibility of us engaging in sex again to be quite pleasing. However, while lust and desire are undeniably enjoyable, we really should have more in common, don't you think? I mean, we can't base any sort of relationship purely on sexual attraction. That's insane."

"Absolutely," Max said, giving a resolute nod. "But you're forgetting all the things we *do* have in common." He couldn't seem to resist dropping a kiss on her jaw.

"Uh-huh...like?"

A light of possibility gleamed in his eyes. "Have you forgotten the shared commonality we have because our parents think we're both gay?" Max pointed out with a chuckle as one finger stroked her cleavage. "And the fact that we're both devoted dog owners?"

"Ah...yes. You have a point there." Head tilted back, her hand resting lightly against his broad chest, Angel tried hard to breathe. "Unfortunately, as far as everything else goes, we have vastly different interests, dissimilar points of view, completely opposing—"

"Opposites attract," Max offered before he bent his head and trailed his hot, wet tongue between her breasts, growling against her skin.

"Oh lordy..." After catching her breath, Angel stepped back. She looked Max up and down. He was so damned handsome, dashing and debonair in his dark suit and tie, she wanted to rip everything off him with her teeth right then and there and feast on him. "Well, *we* certainly do," she acknowledged with a nod.

"How about if I promise to be on my best behavior all evening," Max said.

His low, seductive voice sent shivers down her spine, tightened her nipples. As sexual hunger scratched through her mind and body, Angel licked her lips. "Oh...well, maybe not *all* evening," she cooed, surprised when her voice came out as seductive as any siren.

With a husky chuckle, Max presented his elbow and Angel slipped her arm through it as he led her and Henry out the door.

🐈 🐈 🐈

"This is wonderful, Max," Angel said after they were seated on bentwood chairs at a small, intimate table draped with a red and white checked tablecloth and she had a chance to look around. The lighting was low. There were tiny twinkling clear lights artfully strung above picturesque murals of Mediterranean villages and the seaside. Each table was adorned with a straw-wrapped Chianti bottle, thick with wax-drippings and brandishing a candle. Sounds of Dean Martin crooning "That's Amore" wafted over the sound system. The tiny restaurant had the look and feel of a set from one of those wonderful old romantic movies Angel loved to watch on cable. And here she was sitting across the table from Mr. Tall-Dark-and-Handsome, right in the middle of it all. She sighed. "What wonderful atmosphere. Perfectly charming."

"Spinelli's Trattoria." Max nodded. "It's my own little slice of New York heaven, right here in Portland. I heard about it a couple of months ago from one of my medical suppliers who moved here from New Jersey a few years back. We were lamenting the lack of good food out here and he told me this was the only place in Portland with true, authentic Italian cuisine. I've been here at least twice a week for dinner ever since."

"Well, now I'm *really* eager to try the food," Angel said, perusing the substantial menu. "I see several meatless dishes. They sound scrumptious."

"I haven't had a disappointing or poorly prepared dish here yet," Max said, "and I've been through nearly half of the menu already. See that couple in the corner?" He motioned to a man and woman who looked to be seventy-ish, both plump and wrapped in long, white butcher-style aprons. "They're the owners. Moved here from back East about a year ago to be closer to their two daughters and their families. Real salt-of-the-earth types. They go out of their way to make everybody feel like family. I think you'll really like them."

"Ah, Maximilian!" the man cried with arms outstretched as he crossed the room. "You come back to visit again, eh?" He clapped Max on the back. Angel noted the man had dark, graying hair, a noteworthy mustache and twinkling eyes.

"You bet, Mr. Spinelli." Max grasped the older man's hand and shook it. "Most of all I came to fill my belly with more of your delicious food."

"Each time you come I have to tell you the same thing," the man said in his rich Italian accent, wagging his finger at Max. "It's Dominick. Mr. Spinelli is my father." He chuckled and pointed to the thin, elderly man sipping red wine at a small table near the bar, who raised his hand and waved.

"Dominick," Max said. "This time I brought Angel with me. She's a native Oregonian, and she's never had *real* Italian food before." Max shook his head mournfully.

Dominick's eyebrows shot up. "Oh...I'm so sorry," he said, as if he'd been told that she'd just been orphaned.

"There's just, uh, one more thing you should know..." Max said, and Dominick leaned close, cocking his head with concern. "Angel is a vegetarian," Max added apologetically and Angel rolled her eyes, huffing a humorless laugh.

Jaw dropped, Dominick stiffened, sucked a deep breath and then let it out with a protracted whoosh. "No problem," he said to Angel, recovering quickly. "I fix you a meat-free Italian meal so good it will make you want to sing." He nodded with a broad, confident smile. "Is cheese okay? Ours is all organic from local farmers we trust."

"Perfect! Yes, I love it." Angel nodded. "That's so very kind of you," she said. "Max has already assured me I'll have the very best this evening."

"The *best* of the best!" Grinning, Dominick's gaze rested on Angel. "Ahhh..." He tucked his chin in close and gave an approving nod. "*Bellissima.*" He curled his fingers and brought them to his lips, smacking them with a kiss before splaying them in the air. "Beautiful," he repeated in English. Angel felt her cheeks color. "Tonight, Angelina, Mama and I make a special dinner, just for you and Maximilian." He picked up the menus from the table. "With Maximilian's permission, of course." He gave Max an inquisitive nod.

"Absolutely," Max said. "I leave it in your capable hands."

Angel was thoroughly charmed. "Thank you, Mr—"

"No...please," Dominick said with one finger outstretched in protest. "It would honor me to have you call me by my given name, Angelina." He took her hand, bent over it and kissed it.

Angel's hand flew to her chest in delighted surprise. "Why...thank you. Dominick." While Angel was her full name, she loved the way *Angelina* sounded rolling off his tongue and wasn't about to embarrass the sweet man by correcting him.

"Papa, you're always flirting with the beautiful young women." His wife strolled to the table, wiping her hands in the flour-sack towel that hung from her waist. She had apple cheeks, salt-and-pepper hair pulled back into a bun and a warm, welcoming smile.

"You know I only have eyes for you, Mama," Dominick said, cupping his wife's face and smacking a kiss on her lips. "Angelina, may I present to you the sunshine of my life and the mother of my children...my beautiful Francesca."

Francesca's eyes crinkled as she gazed lovingly at her husband and smiled. Then she turned her attention to Angel. "If Papa gives you trouble, you just let me know. I keep a nice heavy rolling pin in the kitchen." She winked before heading to Max's side of the table and pinching his cheeks.

"Oooh, look at him. He's such a handsome boy. You're so beautiful, Maximilian, that I just want to eat you up." She smooched his forehead and gave his cheeks another pinch.

Angel found it amusing when Max actually blushed.

"Ah, so now who's flirting, huh, Mama?"

Waving a hand in dismissal, Francesca sped over to the bar and was back in a moment with a bottle of Chianti and two wine glasses. "Our best. On the house."

"Thank you," Max and Angel chorused while Dominick opened the bottle and poured.

Dominick looped his arm through Francesca's and led her from the table. "Come on, we have to fix a very special dinner. Angelina was born here in Oregon. She's never had real Italian food." Then he added in a not too quiet whisper, "And she doesn't eat meat."

Angel watched them retreat, chuckling when Francesca halted in her tracks and sucked in a gasp. "Papa, no. Oh, the poor girl." The last thing she heard Francesca say as the pair rounded the corner on their way to the kitchen was, "No wonder the poor little thing is so skinny."

Dominick followed up with, "Don't worry, Mama. We'll fatten her up."

Their unexpected remarks had Angel collapsing in fits of laughter. That was, without a doubt, the first and only time in her life she'd ever heard anyone even remotely imply that she was deficient in the weight department.

"Oh, Max, I love them. They're positively adorable. I feel as if I've known them for years and we only just met a little while ago." The Spinellis seemed to have the same kind of warm, loving relationship her parents had, the kind of permanent relationship that Angel longed to have with a good man someday. A man like Max. The unexpected thought shocked her and Angel sucked in a little gasp.

"That's just how I felt on my first visit," Max said. "Besides the great food, that's one of the reasons I keep coming back. With my parents living so far away back in New York, it's almost like having family here."

"Are your parents happy together, Max?"

"Very much so." He looked a bit confused.

"That's nice." Angel smiled.

"Why do you ask?"

"No special reason. I was just curious because the Spinellis still seem to be very much in love at their age. They remind me a little bit of my parents and it made me wonder about yours."

Max reached for Angel's hand. He grasped it, smoothing his thumb over the surface. The gesture created a sharp frisson of pleasurable sensation that began at the tips of her fingers and traipsed clear through to her core. "I'm glad you like it here. Just wait till you taste the food."

"While we're on the subject of food, my dear Dr. Wiley," Angel poked his forearm, "that reminds me. Shame on you for teasing me on the way over here. Bubba's Beef and Oink Barbecue House, indeed." She screwed her features and made a derisive sound.

"I couldn't resist. I told you before, you're just too damned easy, *Angelina*."

Angel's eyes widened. Hearing the name tumble from Max's lips had an entirely different effect on her than when Dominick spoke the word. Max had done it deliberately, of course—spoken the name with such rich, honeyed, sexy inflection that it couldn't help but make her pussy cream. Lord, she was pathetic. Even Max's voice set her libido spiraling. After settling her lusty hormones with a few calming breaths, Angel leaned close and whispered, "So, are you really a Maximilian?"

"Nope." Max grinned. "As much as I hate to admit it, I'm a Maxwell." He wrinkled his nose. "I just don't have the heart to correct them. Besides, I think Maximilian has a certain air of distinction, don't you?" Max sat up straight. With a tug to his lapels, a straightening of the tie knot at his neck, and a shot of his cuffs, he transmitted a self-assured smile.

Angel watched the shift of hard muscle and tendon beneath his suit as he posed. God, he was such a deliciously attractive man—confident and comfortable in his own skin. Boldly masculine and blessed with the gift of easy laughter. He also possessed the elusive knowledge of how to pleasure a woman perfectly...generously. The icing on the cake was that Max Wiley was a good man. Okay, so he was a little sexist and chauvinistic...and more than a bit bullheaded, but at least he was open and honest. Angel respected that, especially after being with someone sneaky like Robert.

"Definitely," Angel answered, bringing the glass of Chianti to her lips and regarding the chiseled perfection of Max's face over the rim. "The name suits you well."

"I think it makes Dominick feel good to christen his favorite patrons with his own names," Max said. "What about you...are you an Angelina, an Angeline, or maybe an Angela?"

"None of the above. It's just plain Angel. I like the way Angelina sounds though. It makes my name sound beautiful and romantic."

"It is...and you are," Max said, his crystal brown eyes sliding over her.

Before Angel had a chance to respond, a young server appeared at the table, spreading an assortment of delectable edibles from his large round tray before them. Lifting the corner of the red cloth napkin from the basket of rolls, Angel sniffed the air with an *aaaaahhhh* of appreciation.

"Hey, Tony," Max greeted the server. "How's it going?"

"Great, Max," he answered with a bright smile. "Grandma and Grandpa are cooking up some terrific stuff for you and the lady tonight." He sprinted back to the kitchen.

"A good old-fashioned family-operated business," Angel said. "That's nice." She helped herself to a fragrant bread roll, topped with chopped fresh garlic, olive oil and oregano, splitting it in half. On one side she slathered some of the soft, sweet butter from one of the ramekins. On the other half she spooned some green olive pesto, dotted with pine nuts and pimento.

After the first bite of her butter-slathered roll, Angel murmured her satisfaction. "I think I just died and went to heaven," she said before sinking her teeth into the other half of the warm bread. "Oh...mmm, Max, this is so good. The flavors are sensational."

A moment later Tony brought a variety of antipasto platters to the table, crammed with what he described as white bean bruschetta on crostini, grilled portabellas with tapenade, and fried zucchini flowers with ricotta and roasted tomato oil. And not a speck of meat to be found anywhere.

For the next few minutes, Max and Angel were caught up in gustatory appreciation as they savored the flavorful bites, waxing poetic over the exceptional flavor and texture of each intricately seasoned offering.

"I'll bet even a meat lover can appreciate these dishes," Angel said. "Everything's so hearty and substantial."

Wolfing down one of the huge mushrooms, Max nodded. "I knew whatever Dominick came up with would be delicious. And I knew there wouldn't be any tofu." He shuddered a bit. "I honestly don't miss the meat at all."

"So tell me about your past relationships, Max." He gave her a startled deer-caught-in-the-headlights look in response. "You've had to listen to all of my whining about Robert, so I thought it was only fair to return the favor," she explained. "Unless all of your relationships were whine-free, of course."

"There's really not all that much to tell," Max said. "Never been married or engaged, although I've come close a few times."

"What stopped you from doing the aisle-walk?"

"Cold feet mostly." Max grinned. "Kathy had happily-ever-after on the brain right from the start. She was always yapping about how much she wanted the whole white-picket-fence and houseful-of-babies thing. Everywhere we went she'd point out ideal houses, adorable babies or perfect furniture. That scared the bejeezus out of me." Max screwed his features. "And Marla was one of those women who looked at men as lumps of clay she could mold into something more to her liking. Kind of how Robert was with you. Marla was always picking away at me with stuff like, 'Gee, Max, don't you think you'd be happier being an attorney?' or 'Your place would look so much better in shades of mauve, why not let me decorate it for you' or 'Dogs are so messy, why don't you trade Spill in for a cat instead?'"

"That one was the corker," Angel said, "right?"

"You got it. Marla was history after that remark." Max got a far-away look in his eye. "I guess the woman who came closest to getting me to pop the question was Laura. Catching her and my buddy Lenny screwing in the backseat of his car kind of put a damper on that relationship."

"Ouch."

"Yeah. But she's got a ring through Lenny's nose and is making him miserable now, just like Robert and your maid of honor, which goes to prove there is justice after all." He laughed. "So you said there wasn't anybody important after Robert?"

"Not really. Well, except for Nate, the one right after Robert. I met him at one of those eight-minute dating functions." She groaned and took a sip of wine.

"I did one of those once. Hated it," Max said. "So what happened with this Nate?"

"He was nuts. Seems like I attract all the weirdos."

"Gee, thanks." Max lifted an eyebrow and smirked.

Angel's hand flew to her mouth and she gasped. "Oh my gosh, I'm sorry. I didn't mean you, Max." She swallowed hard and plunged ahead. "Anyway, Nate was a world-class liar. Not only was he dating me and two other women while none of us knew about each other, but he lied about his age, too, saying he was twelve years younger than he really was."

"No way. I thought just women did that."

"Apparently not. Oh, but that's not all," Angel added, sitting forward in her seat. "He also just happened to have a wife and three children he neglected to mention."

"Ouch." Max cringed. "You've had some mighty bad luck with relationships, dollface."

"Yup. Seems like we both have." Sipping from her wine, she silently prayed that this time things would be different.

They returned their attention to the food. Just when Angel thought she'd experienced the optimum in Italian cuisine, Tony returned to serve a perfect mushroom-asparagus risotto and a platter of spinach and goat cheese gnocchi.

"By the rapturous expression on your face, Ms. Brewster," Max said, chuckling, "I take it you're also very happy with the food."

"Happy?" she said after swallowing her first forkful of the creamy rice dish. "Max, I'm ecstatic. Positively euphoric." She sat back in her chair and took in a deep breath. "Everything was superb. I'm stuffed. The Spinellis did a fabulous job and I can't wait to tell them."

"Stuffed? That was just the beginning, dollface—only the appetizer and the pasta course. We haven't even had the main dish yet."

Angel felt her eyes bug. "You have *got* to be kidding. There's more?" Her appetite and capacity could keep right up with her six-foot-something brothers, but even they would be hard pressed to pack in any more food.

Nodding, Max gave a knowing smile. "It would break Mama and Papa Spinelli's hearts if you didn't eat up, *Angelina*."

"Ooh...I guess I shouldn't have gobbled down all those rolls." She patted her distended belly.

"So it appears that now we have something else in common," Max said, a teasing twinkle gleaming in his eye. He stabbed a few of the tiny potato dumplings with his fork and brought them to his mouth, closing his eyes and murmuring his approval as he chewed.

"What's that?" Angel said, licking a smidgen of the green olive pesto from one of her fingers after she'd scraped the last speck from the ramekin.

"The appreciation of fine food." Max grinned. "See, we're not such opposites after all." He held his wineglass aloft and they clinked, toasting their precious few commonalities.

"While I'm glad to toast to your observation," Angel said, "I'm afraid our differences far outweigh our similarities, Max. The two things we have most in common are being stubborn and being horny." She sipped back more Chianti. "I mean, one, I don't eat meat and you do. Two," she kept tally on her fingers, "I bristle in the face of chauvinism and you embrace it. Three, I read and write feminist tomes and you read sexist genre fiction. Four—"

"Wait...let's go back to number three for a minute," Max said. "The, uh, so called sexist fiction. I need to tell you something about that." Angel gave an inquisitive nod and Max continued. "A man reading—or," he cleared his throat, "even writing, for that matter—hardboiled crime is really no worse than a woman reading romances when you think about it. It's all wishful thinking and make believe, right?"

"Funny you should make that particular comparison. Actually, Max, I'm not a fan of romance novels either. They perpetuate false stereotypes and do little to empower women."

Max slumped down a bit in his seat. "Oh." He reached for his water and took a sip.

With a wave of dismissal, Angel said, "Look, I honestly don't mean to pick on you because of your preference for blatantly sexist, clichéd reading material. I mean, yes, in my eyes those books diminish women just as surely as any media that treats women like sex objects but, jeez, Max, it's not like you *write* the stuff." She burst out laughing. "If you did, we certainly wouldn't be sitting here having this conversation right now."

Just as she began chuckling again, Max made an awful choking sound. Soon he was coughing, spewing and dribbling water from his mouth and nose.

Angel's eyes went wide as she leapt up from her chair, circled behind Max and gave him a few hearty claps on the back. "Hey...are you okay? You look kind of...green."

Nodding with a limp semi-smile as he dabbed at his face, shirt and tie, Max sputtered through another cough. "Yeah...water just went down the wrong way. Sorry."

Just then both Dominick and Francesca arrived tableside, burdened with an assortment of steaming plates. As full as she was, Angel couldn't help but lick her lips at the sight and aroma of the various dishes. The rundown the Spinellis gave included stuffed baby artichokes, vegetable *fritto misto*, and, finally, eggplant-stuffed peppers topped with marinara sauce and shaved *Parmagiano Reggiano* cheese.

"What do you think so far, eh, little Angelina?" Dominick asked.

"Oh, Dominick... Honestly...I don't even have the words to describe how absolutely delicious everything is. Not to mention filling. *Really* filling."

"Good, good. That's what I like to hear," he said proudly, pouring them each another glass of wine. "I see you need more rolls. I'll have Tony bring another basket." As Angel was about to protest, he added, "After you finish your dinner, you won't believe the dessert Francesca made for you."

Francesca leaned close with a conspirator's gleam in her eye. "Chocolate tiramisu," she said in a low protracted whisper. One look at you, Angelina, and I could tell you're a chocolate lover just like me, eh?"

Angel was done for. "It's my favorite food in all the world," she said, shoulders slumping and cognizant that she was salivating at the thought of sampling the rich dessert even though it might mean she'd never be able to rise from the chair to leave the restaurant. She wondered how she'd get through the rest of the evening without exploding—which would make her a terribly undesirable dinner date.

Closing his eyes with a blissful expression, Dominick curled his fingers and kissed them. "Mmm, *delizia!*"

"*Mangia, mangia!*" the Spinellis urged in unison before walking away, arm in arm.

"That means *eat, eat,*" Max clarified as he plopped servings from each platter onto his plate. "The Italians don't feel they've done their job of feeding you properly until you're ready to be rolled out the door."

"Well then, I have a feeling I won't be disappointing them," Angel said, measuring small portions of each dish onto her plate and taking a deep breath before tackling the dollops of food. As she nibbled on the divine fare, she wished that she'd gone braless instead of wearing the push-up bra with the underwires because it didn't allow her much leeway for comfortable breathing on a full stomach.

"I love watching you eat," Max said, and Angel looked up, surprised.

"You mean because I make such a pig out of myself?" She popped a forkful of saucy eggplant into her mouth, moaning in epicurean rapture.

"No. Because you do it with such passion...such enthusiasm." Max moved closer, his tone dipping to a seductive murmur. "Dollface, watching you enjoy the hell out of your food gives me such a raging hard-on you wouldn't believe it. It's the same blissful expression you have when I'm pleasuring your pussy."

Fork paused in mid-air, Angel's jaw dropped. "Oh," was all she managed to say. The fact that Max had the power to melt her with just a few words from his sensuous mouth made her uneasy. Never had she reacted so strongly to a man, or felt so entirely feminine in one's presence. She heard a moan escape her lips when a curious mix of sensations spiked through her system. First there were the enticing new flavors baptizing her taste buds, and then there was the distinct feel of cream drenching her already moist pussy, making her fully aware of its aching need.

This presented a major problem because, as hungry for Max as she was, it would be damned difficult attempting to make love with her belly protruding like a super-inflated blimp.

"Relax and enjoy your food," Max said as if he had read her mind. "We're in no rush, Angel...we've got all night."

Chapter Eleven

While Max and Angel relaxed in front of the fire, Henry and Spill sprawled out near the hearth. They looked like a couple of old pals who'd just come in from a long night of boozing and playing poker—just like the dogs in those paintings Max couldn't help but like.

Max sat back against the sofa, keeping thigh contact with Angel. He couldn't have asked for a better, more perfect evening, from the delicious dinner, to Angel's appreciation of Spinelli's and its owners, to the pleasant, mostly non-confrontational conversation they'd shared, right down to the fact that Henry was not only alive, but hale and hearty upon their return to Max's house.

Max couldn't see any reason why the night wouldn't just keep getting better...especially once they got hot, sweaty and naked together.

"See? Didn't I tell you Henry would be just fine?"

Angel looked satisfied. "It seems they've become best buddies. I'm amazed at how well they get along."

"All it took was a round of grrr-ing, teeth-baring, a few butt sniffs and a little male posturing before they accepted each other." He poured them each a second glass of champagne. "There's nothing like a couple of bottles of bubbly to settle a belly full of food. I'd originally planned to serve this with some cookies I bought, but I think that might be overkill about now, don't you?"

"I'll say. It's a damned good thing that we didn't take my little economy car tonight because I honestly don't think either of us would have fit behind the wheel." She cradled her full stomach and groaned.

"Well, in that case," Max said, "I'm thankful that you acquiesced earlier when I said I was driving my new red convertible tonight."

Angel's lips quirked into a smile. "Taking turns is fair. I drove once, now you have, and that means it's my turn again next time."

Max gave a protracted groan. "This women's lib stuff will be the death of me yet."

"Yeah...if you don't die from withered-brain disease reading those cheesy crime novels of yours, first." She snickered, pointing to the crammed bookcases on either side of the room. "Just look at all that mind-deadening claptrap." She turned to Max, fixing him with a determined stare as she crossed her arms over her breasts. "I have a new mission," she declared.

"Oh boy." Groaning again, Max gave her a skeptical look. "I'm not sure I want to hear this."

"It's time you broadened your horizons, my good Dr. Wiley. And I'm just the woman to help." Angel blazed a bright smile. "The next time I come over I'll bring you something really good to read."

"Yeah, I can just imagine," Max said, smirking, "Like, *How to Turn Your Macho Lover into a Pansy in Five Easy Steps*, or maybe, *Learn to Pussy Whip Your Man until he Whimpers*, or perhaps *Squeezing the Last Ounce of Masculinity from Your Man*, or what about—"

"Okay, wise guy," Angel said in mock anger. "Very funny." With an agonized *ooph*, she rose from the sofa and headed for one of the bookcases. "At least those titles are better than..." she cocked her head to read the spines, "*Dead Redhead with Ruby Red Lips*, or *Busty Blonde Assassin in the Cellar*, or *Ditzy Dame with a Motive*, or any of these other books by Frank Coleman—of which you seem to have an awful lot of, by the way. Honestly, Max, these *Jack Clyde, Private Detective and his Crime-Busting Dog, Billy* books are the absolute worst, and yet the most hysterically funny examples of raw, idiotic sexism I've ever seen. They're so bad it's as if they were written as parodies." She examined one of the book's spines. "Were they?"

"They most certainly were not. Hardboiled crime fiction is a time-honored genre, Angel. It spawned all those great old movies like *The Maltese Falcon, The Big Sleep, To Have and Have Not, The Thin Man* series, and dozens more. Plenty of readers would disagree with your negative assessment of Frank Coleman's books," Max defended, puffing out his chest a bit. "For your information, Coleman is making quite a name for himself."

Angel huffed a laugh tinged with incredulity. "Yeah, by propagating negative stereotypes that belittle, offend and diminish women. I can't figure you out, Max. Here you are a clearly intelligent professional man—a nice, honest, hardworking type of guy—and how do you spend your valuable and limited leisure time? By reading hackneyed drivel written by some pea-brained second-class purveyor of chauvinistic fiction."

She was talking about him and the work he took such pride in, damn it!

Feeling the pulse throbbing at his temple, Max paused to take a few deep breaths before he spoke, otherwise he'd forget he was a gentleman. And he'd forget that Angel was his dinner date. Then he'd find himself jumping down her throat and ripping out her vocal cords to shut her the hell up—after which she most likely wouldn't want to get hot, sweaty and naked with him.

"Look, Angel," he started cautiously, "I know you get your feathers ruffled real easy, but don't you think you're being just a little bit unfair? I mean, being a writer yourself, how can you just rip apart an author and his books without ever having read them?" Under the circumstances, Max was proud of the slow, measured evenness of his voice.

Surrounded by blessed quiet for a long moment, save for the rattling snores of the dogs, Max breathed a sigh of relief. His well-stated, logical assertion seemed to take the wind right out of Angel's sails, thank God. The absolute last thing he wanted to do was to get into a tussle when what they should be doing was engaging in a bout of lusty foreplay.

"You're absolutely right, of course," Angel finally said, smiling sweetly as her shoulders slumped a bit. "As a journalist it was completely unjust and out of line for me to make assumptions about material I've never read. Since Robert was such a controlling chauvinist, anything I perceive as demeaning to women automatically makes me bristle. It brings back all those bad memories. My apologies, Max."

Yeah, that was more like it. That's how Max liked her, all soft-spoken, smiling and agreeable. "Good. It takes a strong woman to admit her mistakes," Max said. "Now let's finish our champagne." He patted the cushion next to him, beaming an expectant smile and doing his best to look charming.

"I'll reserve my opinion until after I've read one of these books," Angel said. "Then we can discuss it further. You don't mind if I borrow one, do you, Max?" she said as she tugged on one of the books Max had written.

"Holy shit! Stop!" Max leaped from the sofa, hurdling the coffee table and clutching his chest as if he were having a heart attack. Instinct told him that once Angel got a load of his author photo on the back of that book she'd be all righteous and bristly and livid and stomping out of there so fast he wouldn't know what hit him. Max and his eager cock had entirely different plans in mind for the evening.

Angel jumped nearly a foot from fright. "Good grief, Max. What in the world is wrong with you? You almost gave me a heart attack."

"Yeah, well that makes two of us," he muttered under his breath.

"What?" Angel said, her fingers still clutching the book's spine.

"Nothing." Max clasped his hand over Angel's and eased the book back into place.

"Look, Max, if you don't want me to borrow your precious book, just say so. There's no need to have a conniption fit, okay?"

"No...no, you can borrow any of my books anytime you like." Holding the book firmly in place as Angel tugged on it again, Max broadcast a too-wide grin. No fucking way was he going to let her get her hands on one of his Frank Coleman books. "Actually, I just hopped over here to say *touché*, that's all."

"Before or after you scared the hell out of me by bounding over that table and practically knocking yourself on your ass?"

"Sorry about that. Guess I'm...uh, jumpy. Yeah, that's it. I'm jittery from those four cups of espresso I had with dessert. See?" Holding out a hand, he made it vibrate as he erupted in nervous laughter.

"You only had two," Angel reminded him.

"Tell you what, Angel, let's say we just call it even, okay? I'm not a fan of feminist-themed books and you don't like sexist ones. Different strokes for different folks. Fair enough?" He clutched her fingers, sliding them from the cover of *The Sinister Brunette in Boots.* "Now let's relax and finish up our champagne so we can enjoy the rest of our evening together. I thought we might start things off with a nice warm shower. How does that sound, dollface?" He brushed a kiss at her temple and led her back to the sofa, relieved when she offered no resistance and, in fact, uttered a soft little moan.

He'd tell her all about it another time. How he had somehow omitted the fact that he spent most of his nights working as his alter ego, Frank Coleman, penning clichéd genre fiction so blatantly sexist and politically incorrect it would frizzle the ends of that silky blonde halo of hair on her head. They'd have a good laugh over it. She'd see the humor in it and would forgive him for not being straightforward with her from the get-go.

Until that time—especially until he had her all dreamy-eyed and quivery after a couple of powerhouse orgasms—he had to keep her away from those damned books.

Trixie's gaze scoured me from head to toe as I parked myself all neat, clean, shaved and sober at her front door. Then she gave me the kind of smile a guy can feel all the way down to his dick. I wondered how she was going to react when I spilled the beans and she found out I'd been lying to her from the get-go. Damn, I didn't want to risk never seeing those kissable cherry-red lips curling into a fuck-me smile again. But I felt compelled to confess. I had to lay it on the line. I owed the doll that much.

I was only human, though, so first things first. I bent over her, taking her mouth hard, loving the way Trixie trembled under my hands wherever I touched her. I dug my fingers into the cheeks of that squeezable hot-to-trot ass of hers and felt my dick saluting in my pants.

As I enjoyed the hell out of crushing her soft pussy against my fly, I looked past Trixie into the living room of her apartment. I was hit with the aroma of bubbling beef stew, lit candles and the sounds of Dean Martin singing some mellow tune. Yeah, tonight dollface had the place staged for serious fucking.

"There's something I've got to tell you, baby," I said, already missing the feel of her hot flesh as I held her at arm's length. "Something important. It's about your brother, Frankie, and what really happened the night he got shot." She looked up at me with those big baby blues and I felt my gut twisting. "There's no easy way for me to tell you, Trixie, so I'm just going to get to the point." I sucked in hard and then blurted it out. "It was me, Jack Clyde. I was the one who killed Frankie." With that single remark I watched her passion cool with the suddenness of nightfall and then I watched as a multitude of whys came clamoring alive in her brain.

"What? My baby brother? No...Jack, you can't mean that."

"It was about six months before I left the force," I told her. "Just after you and I met. Eddie, one of the other detectives, and I were on our way for a couple of shots of bourbon after work when we spotted some action going down in the alley behind that little Italian place on Jersey Street. The two guys there made a run for it but we nabbed them. One of them had the swivel-headed jumpiness of a heroin addict badly in need of a fix...and the other one was the dealer. It was Frankie, dollface."

Trixie slapped her hands over her ears and shook her head. "No! I don't want to hear this. Frankie was a good cop. He'd been working citywide Narcotics for thirteen years He'd never deal dope. He died in the line of duty. He was shot by a dope addict."

"Look, baby." I grabbed her trembling arms and made her listen. "Frankie may have started out as a good cop but

somewhere along the way he went crooked. The lure of all that easy dope cash must have got to him. Frankie became a bad cop who came from generations of good, clean cops like you and your dad and your grandfather."

"No!" She tried to pull away but I held tight.

"When Frankie recognized us he pulled out his piece and fired. Eddie reeled back with lead in his thigh and collapsed. 'Drop it, Frankie,' I yelled at him as Eddie just lay there moaning. 'You don't want to do this,' I told him. Frankie beetled his eyes in puzzlement for an instant, but then he took aim at my skull and I plugged him before he could get off another shot."

Dollface was crying now. She was just as ballsy as any male cop on the force, but I'd just delivered a real punch to her gut.

"You motherfucker, you shot my brother right through the heart." Her features constricted in hostility until her expression was somewhere short of homicidal. "You could have just wounded him, you bastard."

"I'm sorry, Trixie. I had no choice. It was Frankie or me. All the blood in me turned cool and slow when I pulled that trigger. After the incident I went through an Internal Affairs review and got cleared of any wrongdoing. The department kept it under wraps because your old man was about to retire after coppering for thirty years. It would have broken his heart to know Frankie was crooked, dollface."

Her eyes narrowed against the hot acrid odor of burning beef stew. She looked like she wanted to cut me up into one-inch squares. "I'm sorry my father died without knowing you murdered his only son, Jack. I'm even sorrier that Frankie didn't shoot you first."

I felt my face twitch at the thought of my relationship with Trixie dying such a painful, ugly death. After the throat-freezing shock of realization, I finally found my tongue. "We can work *through this, Trixie. I don't want to lose you, baby. You're the sunshine of my life," I said, wincing at the pleading tone in my voice. Jack Clyde never begged or pleaded with anyone. But this was dollface. And I was losing her forever.*

"Please, dollface." I reached out and stroked her cheek only to have her crack me hard across the face and shrug off my hand like I was a leper. I didn't mind. I deserved it.

"You shouldn't have lied to me, Jack. You should have told me the truth right away. Maybe I could have forgiven you then, but not now. You're nothing but a lowdown, cowardly liar. Get out of my sight. I never want to see your ugly mug again for as long as I live."

She slammed the door in my face and left me standing there feeling as if I'd been coldcocked with a brick and left for dead.

Chapter Twelve

After they'd polished off the second bottle of champagne, Max had a light, pleasant buzz. Angel was getting all girly and giggly and so horny he could smell the sweet musk of her arousal. Bubbly seemed to have that sort of effect on women. It upped the passion-factor and decreased inhibitions. When Angel cuddled at his side, pressing her big beautiful tits against his arm and chest, Max knew she was perfectly ripe for fucking.

He nuzzled against her hair, breathing in her flowery scent, loving the feel of her fluffy corn silk curls as they cascaded over his face. All the rough, sharp edges of Angel's pigheaded women's lib traits were soft and fuzzy now. That's just the way Max wanted it. Spirit and feistiness between the sheets was one thing, but that motor-mouth of Angel's outside the bedroom didn't do much in the way of keeping his dick stiff. There were so many times since first encountering her, frantic and irrational at his door, that he longed to put her over his knee... The thought of her rump positioned high in the air while she was draped over his lap brought to mind some of the things he'd like to do with that delicious ass of hers. At this moment, as he felt her warm, perfumed body plastered against him, Max wanted his hands on her so bad they almost burned with savage desire.

He lowered his head and trailed a path of kisses from Angel's collarbone to her ear, circling it with a swoop of his tongue, loving the way it made her shiver. "Get ready to have me eat that pretty little pussy of yours once we're in the shower," he whispered, smoothing a finger over her delectable mouth. He wedged a hand between their bodies, fondling her lush breast in his palm. In a low, husky rumble, he added, "I plan to bring you to a screaming orgasm with my teeth, Ms. Brewster."

After hearing the little catch in Angel's throat, Max rose from the sofa, extending his hand.

Her mouth fell open and she sputtered before clearing her throat. "Is that so, Dr. Wiley?" she said with bravado as she took his hand and stood up, teetering just a bit.

By now he knew that bold, brash exterior of Angel's, annoying as it could be, was just a front because when she looked up at him, he could see her eyes glaze over and her pale complexion turn several shades of pink. That made him smile. He loved how quickly she reacted to him, how easily he could push her buttons. Yup, there was nothing quite as satisfying as rattling a mouthy, strong-minded feminist—except for when he was screwing her brains out, of course. That was next on the agenda.

Holding hands, Max led Angel from the living room to his bedroom. He was already so damned hard his dick was hammering against his zipper, eager to bust out and get on with the show. As they scrambled up the stairs he suddenly felt like a kid again, ready to get laid for the first time. That's what she did to him. Angel Brewster, with her full, succulent tits, round, curvy hips and mass of wild flaxen hair was every fantasy he'd ever had rolled into one perfect package—the only flaw being her insistent feminist views. Since Max had every intention of sticking around for a while, he'd either have to keep her liberally plied with champagne or figure out some other way to tame that nasty obstinate streak.

Once in the bedroom, Max walked into the connecting bath and turned on the shower. When he returned it was just in time to lock his gaze on Angel's sweet ass as she bent over to roll off her pantyhose. She thought she was fat. He shook his head and chuckled softly. Just like a dame. What Max saw was a sensuous, voluptuous woman with a body made for hot, lusty, vigorous sex. He'd sure as hell never be satisfied with one of those bony, anemic chicks again after savoring Angel's soft, inviting flesh.

After she had divested herself of clothing, the gloriously naked Angel turned her attention to Max. "Your turn," she said, yanking him by the belt and pulling him close. She opened his fly, snaked her hand inside and clutched his cock.

"Trust me, dollface, you don't have to tell me twice," Max said, his voice nearly croaking. Primal desire punching through his system, he yanked at the tie that was suddenly too tight, then clawed off his jacket and shirt, flinging them in different directions. He left his slacks and shorts in Angel's capable hands. With the impatience of a woman who wants everything at once, she stripped him of his remaining garb and took a few steps back.

Taking a good long gander at his goods, Angel nodded her approval. "I may be a vegetarian, Max, but, mmmm, I can certainly appreciate a big, thick hunk of prime beef when I see one."

"One hundred percent red-blooded male. Just what the lady ordered," Max said, grasping his erect cock and presenting it to her in the palms of his hands. "I'd just love being responsible for turning an avowed vegetarian to the dark side, dollface."

As if Max had died and gone to heaven, Angel's hand scooted down to the silky blonde curls covering her pussy. Her fingers dipped inside. "Eat me," she said matter-of-factly, offering her glistening fingers to Max.

Max's eyebrows shot up in surprise. Momentarily taken aback by her blasé request, he chuckled as his dick bobbed in response until it saluted the ceiling. Imparting a lusty growl, he wasted no time closing the distance and licking the proffered cream from her fingers. The woman was an enigma. A luscious combination of innocence and sin, peppered with a more than adequate portion of tenacity. No, he didn't think he'd ever find Angel Brewster boring, that's for sure.

Like an adoring puppy dog, Max followed her into the shower, where they proceeded to soap each other up. After lathering her superb tits for the third time, Max's hand stilled in the valley between her breasts. He looked at her thoughtfully.

"Something wrong, doc?"

"No...I was just wondering if you have any idea just how positively gorgeous you are, dollface."

"Oh, Max," Angel beamed a come-hither smile. "Thank you." She reached up to plant a kiss on his jaw.

Not yet finished with his appraisal, Max slicked his hands over her soapy curves, adding, "From the crowning glory of gold on your head, to big baby blues and cherry-red lips on your pretty face, to the bounce of your breasts and sway of your hips as you walk, to the lush, dewy pussy between your thighs... Beautiful, dollface. Every goddamned inch of you."

Angel's eyelids fluttered closed. She took in a deep breath, expelling it with an impassioned moan. "I don't mind telling you that you made big points with that one, Max." She grabbed his family jewels and squeezed. "I'll bet you have no idea how I've fantasized about doing all sorts of wicked things with that great...big...king-sized cock of yours. Mmm-mmm." Curling both hands around his shaft, she gingerly gave it a twist and bubbled with throaty giggles from the effects of the champagne that still lingered.

"Oooh, damn, woman. You're wicked." Max lifted the showerhead from its holder, watching the water as it sluiced over her generous, soapy curves. "And wicked girls need to be reprimanded...with a good tongue lashing." He replaced the showerhead and went down on his knees in front of her. "Ready for your punishment?"

"Oh, yes." Her voice was no more than a whisper.

Max loved hearing her sharp intake of breath as he spread her legs and glossy pink inner folds and plunged his tongue inside her honeyed depths. He pulled back just long enough to say, "Sweet, juicy and delicious," before exacting the rest of her punishment. Baring her clitoris, he licked it with a light touch at first, aware of her thighs clenching around his head. He sucked and licked at her sweetness harder, enjoying the cries of passion his stubborn little feminist tried to muffle.

"More, Max," she said, her voice quavering. "Don't stop...please"

"Oh don't worry," Max said, pausing long enough to heed her pleas. "I have no intention of stopping. You've been a very, very wicked girl, harboring fantasies about your neighbor's cock. You need to be punished to the maximum." Angel pushed his head back to her cunt and Max chuckled.

Exposing her clit once again, he breathed in her warm musk scent. "I love the way you smell. Better than anything on Spinelli's menu. In fact, the one thing I neglected to see on their menu was fresh berries." He took Angel's ripe berry between his teeth, alternately nibbling, sucking and licking.

"Oh!" Angel's legs trembled and her breathing became rapid. He knew she was close to shattering. The lusty, rapturous expressions she voiced became increasingly loud as he continued his pleasurable assault. When she fisted his hair and her body stiffened, Max increased the pace and pressure, determined to send Angel where she'd never been before—and screaming as she went.

"Oh God...*Maximilian!*" Angel screamed as her entire being convulsed and shuddered.

He clamped his hands around her waist, holding Angel steady until the quaking finally subsided. He was pleased as hell that he'd apparently succeeded in his mission. He rose to his feet and drew Angel to his chest, smoothing her wet tresses and dropping a series of kisses from her forehead to her throat.

"That was...oh, God, that was awesome, Max." Angel reached up to give his chin a kiss. "I definitely have to be wicked more often." She erupted in throaty laughter and glanced down at his cock, clasping it before raising her eyes to his again. "You know, you were so right about how champagne helps the food to settle. In fact, I think I'm ready for a second dessert." She offered a come-hither look.

Sucking in a deep breath as his gaze settled on Angel's pale hand wrapped around his straining cock, he smiled. "Then may I suggest you select this fine sweet specimen of cock from the dessert tray? It's guilt free," Max said. "No calories."

"Oh that should satisfy my craving perfectly." Angel lowered herself to her knees. "You know what, Max?" She gazed up at him with a teasing expression.

"What?" He smoothed damp strands of hair from her face.

"I hear tell you've been giving your poor neighbor a very hard time about her feminist beliefs. Is that true? Because, if it is, I think you deserve to be punished, too."

The anticipation was almost too much. Angel's pretty mouth was poised to accept his cock and it was fucking killing him. It was all he could do not to ram it into her luscious mouth, fucking it until he shot his load. "Yes. It's all true," Max managed to answer through ragged breaths. "I'm nothing but a disgusting, male chauvinist bastard. Down with feminists."

"Tsk, tsk...wrong answer." Angel's hot tongue swiped at the head of his cock, swirling tiny, hypnotic circles down the length of his shaft.

"Jesus!" Max held her head close to his groin. "And...and I demand to drive every damn time we go out, do you hear me, woman?"

"Ooh, you not only need punishment, Dr. Wiley...you clearly need some rehabilitation, too." Angel took his cock into the warm, wet recesses of her mouth and sucked, twirling her tongue around him as she did. Moaning, she raked his cock with her teeth.

Max pulled her head back, grunting. "Stop, Angel. I'm not going to be able to hold back."

She licked her lips and dragged her bottom lip through her teeth. "Oh, but I don't want you to hold back. In the immortal, albeit slightly altered, words of my sexist neighbor, *I plan to bring you to a screaming orgasm with my teeth.*" She actually had the nerve to giggle as he stood there before her, lust coiling in his gut more tightly than ever before in his life.

She wickedly flicked her tongue at the tip of his cock. Back and forth, faster and faster. "Admit to me that reading those trashy, hardboiled crime fiction books is wrong because they portray women as brainless sex objects." She did that mind-blowing thing with her tongue again, glancing up at him with lusty determination in her eyes. "It's your choice, Max," she said, polishing his cock between her great big gorgeous tits. "You can finish this off using your hand, or you can admit that you were wrong and give me the pleasure of swallowing your cum."

"Sonuvabitch," Max barked. "Anything. Anything you want. I was wrong. Hardboiled crime fiction sucks and men shouldn't read it because—"

"Good boy." Angel's sumptuous mouth closed over him again, milking his steel-hard cock with unbridled enthusiasm. Every muscle in his body clenched and his hot cum spurted down the back of her throat.

A primal yell rumbled deep inside his chest, rising up until he actually heard himself scream, "Holy fucking shit, Angel!"

He looked down at Angel to find her sitting back on her heels, licking his cream from her lips with a gratifying, lip-smacking sound. The woman was incredible.

She grinned up at him. Although still a bit wobbly himself, he helped her to her feet. "That was pretty cool," she said. "You know, I never really thought I could make a man scream when he climaxed."

"And I would have sworn that no woman would *ever* hear me scream, so that makes two us." He captured Angel's mouth in a tender kiss. "Come on, let's get out of here and dry off. Besides, I'm starving. How about you?"

"Ravenous. Still have those cookies?"

"Yup, and a pint of mocha-almond fudge ice cream, a jar of chocolate sauce and a can of whipped cream."

"Oooh, Maximilian...talk about wicked." Angel shook her hand through the air as if to cool it. "Can you just imagine the scintillatingly sinful things we can do with that mini-menu?"

"Oh yeah...lickable, luscious things." Max gave a husky chuckle.

"Of course, we'd have to get right back in the shower," Angel said.

"Or we could just clean each other off with our tongues." Max's gaze swept over her curves. "I can assure you that I'd do a very thorough job."

"I'd be happy to return the favor," Angel promised.

Max bent to nibble on her breasts. "For the first course I'd like to ring these beautiful pink nipples with a few spurts of whipped cream. Not too much, just enough to top off the deliciousness of your sweet flesh." He kissed each pebbled tip.

"Mmm, I like that idea." Angel squirmed in delight. "After that you can scatter little dollops of chocolate sauce all over your body so I can play hide and seek with my tongue." She licked her lips.

"Creativity is definitely one of your strong points, Ms. Brewster."

As they toweled off in Max's bedroom, he paused to pull her close. "You're very special, *Angelina*. There's something whimsical and magical and intoxicating about you. One minute you're driving me crazy with your feminist babble and the next you're making me insane with that incredible passion of yours."

Angel murmured a soft little moan as she traced her fingers over his chest. "I guess I pretty much feel the same way about you, *Maximilian*. You drive me batty in more ways than one." She trailed little kisses down his abdomen, stopping just short of the dark thatch of hair at his groin.

Max sucked in a sharp breath as a jolt of electricity galvanized his nerves. Grasping her upper arms, he dragged Angel flush against his length. "I want you to stay overnight, dollface, so I can fuck your beautiful little pussy all night long," he said, smoothing the damp tendrils of hair from her ear. "I want to keep you gasping and quaking until the sun rises."

The words he heard tumbling from his mouth surprised him. In the past he'd purposefully gone out of his way to avoid spending the entire night with a woman. Dames had a way of reading more into a situation than there really was, and then ingratiating themselves into a man's life before he knew what hit him. Caught up in a daze, the big clueless sap would soon find himself doing the aisle-walk. Uh-uh. Max didn't want any part of that scene. The last thing he wanted was for some woman to start pressing for a commitment, to get all clingy and possessive—to snap a ring through his nose and drag him away from his independence.

So what the hell prompted him to suddenly spill over at the mouth and invite Angel to spend the night?

Mistake. Big mistake.

Angel let out a delighted squeal. "Mmm, I can think of nothing better than waking up in your arms, Max."

Warning bells clanged in his brain.

Squirming in his embrace, Angel crushed her lush curves against his chest and groin. "God, I just love the way you feel," she said, her fingers raking over the muscles in his back as she leaned in, inhaling his scent. "And the way you smell. All hot, hard male flesh."

Still overcoming the shock of issuing her the uncharacteristic invitation, and Angel's all-too-eager acceptance, Max took a step back, tripping over his shoes and losing his balance. With Angel still wrapped around him, he fell back against the bed, half on, half off. Sprawled on top of him, Angel started to roll off, but he held her tightly in place.

God damn the woman felt good. Too good.

"Uh-uh. Don't even think about moving," Max said, adrenaline slamming through him with primal force as Angel's skin glided over his. "I want you right where you are, dollface— your slick cunt perched right over my cock, ready for action." As if wielding a broom, his brain whisked away any concerns, and then flooded his senses with a hot new torrent of desire. Settling his mouth over Angel's in a deep, passion-packed kiss, he lost himself in the warmth of her sweet, intoxicating wetness.

In her position atop him, Max knew Angel could feel his burgeoning arousal adamantly throbbing against her. Cupping one of her breasts, he relished in the considerable weight of it in his hand. He pinched and twisted the rigid nipple as he further deepened their kiss. No matter how many times his tongue danced with hers, Max couldn't imagine himself being any less ravenous for her sweet taste.

His cock continued to mushroom as he heard the soft feminine whimper and distinct catch in Angel's throat. She got to him the way no other dame ever had before. He was beginning to feel like some helpless, vulnerable addict, which meant he was going to have to tread mighty carefully to keep from getting sucked in too deep. Unfortunately, it wasn't going to be easy to convince his dick to see the logic behind that train of thought.

As their lips finally parted, Max and Angel panted in hard, ragged breaths.

"You should let me up, Max," she said, trying to slide off while he held her firmly in place. "I'm too heavy. I'm going to crush you."

Max had to laugh at that. "Oh, baby, what a way to go."

"I'm serious." She wiggled against him.

Max uttered a growl of exasperation. "Shit. It's that damned Robert again, isn't it?"

"Huh?"

"He must have made you feel like you're fat and unattractive in bed, right?"

Angel nodded, lowering her head as if she were ashamed. "He said it was really hard for him to get turned on because of my weight. He hated it when I sat in his lap or anything. Said I was crushing him."

"Trust me on this, Angel, Robert was not only a rat-bastard, he was an idiot. He had Botticelli's Venus all to himself and was too stupid to appreciate it."

"Oh, Max," Angel stroked his cheek, "what a beautiful, thoughtful thing to say. Thank you, but you don't have to worry about pumping up my ego. I know I'm too fat to be really attractive."

"That's ridiculous. Your ex really did a number on you, dollface. I'll have you know that throughout history men have fought bloody wars just for the sake of being crushed by gorgeous, zaftig women boasting soft, womanly curves like yours." Dragging Angel up a bit, he flexed his hips, wedging his cock into the cleft of her pussy lips.

Angel stilled before sinking against him with a sigh. "Are you sure you're a veterinarian and not a writer?"

Max felt the blood drain from his face. "What?" Lifting Angel and setting her to the side, he bolted to his feet.

"Boy you can really move fast when you want to." She positioned herself on the edge of the bed, gazing up at him. "It's just that you have a truly wonderful way with words. More so than any other man I know."

"Oh." Max felt a wave of relief ripple through his body.

"Thank you for making me feel truly beautiful." Angel kissed him. "So are we going to go downstairs and get the chocolate sauce and whipped cream now?" Bouncing in place, she looked particularly appealing.

Max's pulse went haywire as he gazed from her teasing lips to the puckered nipples at the tips of her jiggling breasts, and finally, to the cluster of blonde curls at the balmy notch between her legs. She'd just taken him from lust to panic and back to lust again in the matter of less than a minute.

"We'll do the chocolate later," he said, feeling a rush of urgent desire, unwilling to wait long enough to gather the edibles before thrusting into her. She was *his* Botticelli's Venus now, dammit, and he was eager to show her just how much he appreciated her lushness. He stepped to his nightstand and grabbed a strip of condoms from the drawer, wasting no time in ripping open one of the foil packets with his teeth and rolling it on his throbbing cock. He stood in front of Angel, glowering down at her.

"Max...what's the matter? All of a sudden you look like you're angry or something."

"Get on your knees, Angel."

"What?"

Hopping on the bed, Max grabbed Angel at the waist. He swiveled her around, positioning her so that she was kneeling. Promptly taking his place behind her, he gripped her hips firmly enough to pin her in place, zeroing his cock in on the opening of her silky pussy.

"Max!" She tried to look over her shoulder. "Do you mind telling me just what in the hell you think it is that you're doing?"

"Getting ready to send you to paradise, dollface," he said, prepared to plunge his hard-enough-to-hammer-nails cock into her juicy depths and show her who was boss.

"Excuse me?" With the speed of light and the agility of a cat, Angel whipped her body around so that she was facing Max. "Since when did we start playing caveman and cavewoman?" She sat up on her knees, planting a fist on each hip. "What's gotten into you? You can't just toss me around as if I were a mindless rag doll, Max."

"I was just—"

"Besides," Angel continued, and Max knew he was in for it, "what if I wanted to be on top this time? You should have—"

Max took her mouth, smothering her screech of outrage. It seemed like the only alternative, seeing as how he was totally clueless as to what to say or how else to shut her up before she completely annihilated his vigorous erection with her incessant jaw-flapping.

"You should have asked me," she blazed on as soon as the kiss ended. "We didn't even discuss it."

"What's there to discuss?" Max countered with a shrug. "We're having sex. We've *been* having sex for more than an hour. So far you haven't had any complaints. So why are you getting your panties all in a ruffle all of a sudden?"

Sucking in an irate gasp, Angel crawled off the bed to retrieve her panties and yank them on. She followed up by shimmying into her bra. Max groaned. This definitely wasn't turning out the way he'd planned.

"There. Is that better?" she said, standing before him, arms akimbo, as he sat back on his heels in the middle of the bed. "Now you can see more clearly if my panties start to get into a ruffle." The look she shot him was lethal at best.

"Come on, don't be like that, Angel. Why do you always have to start a fight?"

"Me? Oh, puhleeze! The question should be, why do you always have to push my buttons?"

Max held out his hand like a stop sign before she could open her mouth again. He looked down at his dwindling hard-on, growling in frustration. "I'm sorry because I took it upon myself to initiate a sexual action before asking you, okay, Angel? It wasn't me, it was the lust." Angel rolled her eyes and huffed at that. "That's what you do to me," Max continued. "I can't help it. I look at you and those big baby blues, and those sinful curves of yours and my primitive instincts just sort of take over and I just want to fuck that beautiful little pussy of yours right on the spot."

"Oh."

Seeing evidence of the icebergs in Angel's eyes melting ever so slightly, he smiled. Complimenting her was obviously a smart move on his part. He had to remember that a little Flattery 101 could work wonders with women on the rampage.

"I'm sorry, Max. It's just that—"

"Please don't tell me this has something to do with Robert again," Max said, cutting her off. "Because I'm really getting tired of having your ex-fiancé come between us, you know?"

"What can I say?" Angel looked dejected. "You're absolutely right. I still have all these...*issues* about men because of Robert. He always took full control in bed and totally disregarded what I might want. I felt like a piece of meat." She gave an almost imperceptible chuckle, then added, "A piece of fatty, lumpy meat."

"I'm not Robert, dollface," Max said softly. "Or Nate, or any other jerk who treated you wrong in the past. You need to come to terms with that."

"True. You're nothing like either of them. Unless you've got a wife and three kids tucked away someplace that I don't know about." She chuckled.

"Trust me on this, Angel, that's one worry you can eliminate."

She smiled. "You're a good man, Max. An honest man. I know that. Nate was a cheat and a liar. You're certainly neither of those."

Max swallowed hard. Well at least he wasn't a cheat. He really needed to come clean with her about his alter ego, but the time just never seemed right. Now definitely didn't seem like a good time to cough up the information. "I'm certainly not perfect," Max said. "I'm just a man—and a flawed one at that— but a man who happens to find you deliciously attractive and desirable." Angel nodded and smiled. "Listen," Max continued, "I promise you can be on top next time." Knee-walking to the edge of the bed, he reached out to stroke her arm. "But right now I really want to take you dog—"

Angel gasped. "If you value that three-piece package between your legs, Max, you will not refer to me and the term *doggy-style* in the same sentence." Angel shot him a glare icy enough to wither the most powerful erection.

And it did.

"Aw, jeez, Angel," Max said, flipping his half-erect dick. "Now look what you did. You killed it."

"No, I'm not the one who's responsible for your deflated erection, Max, you are. If you would have taken the time to be considerate enough of my feelings to consult me as to whether of not I wanted you to take me from the back or if I preferred another position, then you'd still be sporting that big old flagpole you had a minute ago and I'd be sitting on top of it after licking chocolate sauce off of your body and we'd both be well on our way to a rip-roaring orgasm."

Shoulders slumping, Max just sat there drop-jawed and silent for a long moment. "Damn, woman, you sure know how to put a crimp in a guy's style, not to mention his ego."

She opened her mouth to reply and Max readied himself for another onslaught of righteous indignation. The dame was making him crazy, but this time he was ready. Oh yeah. Once Angel stopped spouting off at him, he'd grab her and her clothes, bodily haul her down the stairs by her hair and deposit her and her dog outside his door, never to cross his threshold again.

The idea made him smile. He was relatively certain it was an evil, maniacal smile. As he steeled himself for her spewing outrage, Angel did the absolute last thing he expected. She covered her face with her hands and started to cry. Hard. Her shoulders shook and all Max could do was stare, dumbfounded. Damn. He'd rather put up with the righteous indignation.

"Oh God, Max, I'm hopeless," she sobbed. "I don't know why I can't keep my big mouth shut. I'm so sorry."

His gaze followed her as she grabbed a tissue and wiped her eyes and nose. Then she started to hunt and peck around the room.

"What are you looking for?" Max asked, his voice tentative.

"My dress," she said, sniveling and getting on her knees to look under the bed. "And these." She held the pantyhose she'd retrieved aloft before scurrying to the other side of the room where she found her dress in a heap with Max's shirt and tie. "And these." She sniveled again as she bent to scoop up her high heels.

Max felt totally out of his element as he looked at Angel's tear-stained face and red nose once she stood up. A knack for comforting weepy women was not high on his list of natural abilities. He was tempted to draw her into his arms and hug her, telling her not to cry, but he wasn't sure that's what she wanted. What if it just made her cry even harder?

"You don't want to put all that stuff back on," Max said finally. "That can't be comfortable for lounging around." He hopped off the bed and went to his dresser, drawing out a sweatshirt and sweatpants, holding them out to Angel. "Here, put these on instead. You might have to roll the sleeves and legs up a few times, but at least they're warm and comfortable."

"No thank you," Angel said, slipping into her dress and balling the pantyhose into one of her fists. She headed for the bedroom door.

Max shouted. "Hey! Where are you going?"

"Home, of course. As soon as I get Henry."

Tossing the sweats on the bed, Max was at her side in a flash, catching her arms at the elbows and drawing her close. "You said you'd sleep over." He rolled his eyes. Nothing like sounding like a goddamned whiny ten-year old.

Angel was silent for a moment. "Well, I don't really think that's a very good idea now...considering," she said with a tiny shrug. "It's pretty clear that this just isn't working, Max. We're just too different. I mean, here we were having this beautiful evening together and I went and spoiled it all."

"You didn't spoil it," Max lied. Angel twisted her face into a disbelieving smirk. "Well, yeah, you did kind of let the air out of my pecker," he admitted, looking down at his limp cock. "The good news is that it's not terminally damaged. It's got amazing recuperative powers."

"Thanks for being so sweet, so gallant, Max, but you don't have to be...really." He saw her chin quiver then. "Thanks for dinner and...um...everything else. I had a wonderful time with you tonight and I'm just sorry it didn't end on a better note."

Max turned back to glance at the digital clock on his nightstand. "Angel, it's nearly two in the morning. You can't leave now...I don't want you to go. Besides...we haven't even had our dessert yet." Angel stiffened, but before she could say anything, Max added, "I'm talking strictly platonic dessert here, dollface. We can sit at the kitchen table and have ice cream sundaes and cookies with a nice pot of coffee. I promise I won't even touch you for the rest of the night if you don't want me to." Doing his best not to think about the *really* stupid vow he'd just uttered, Max held up his fingers in salute. "Scout's honor."

He could tell Angel was softening. He could feel it as her posture relaxed. "Stay. Please, Angel."

To tell the truth, Max didn't know why he was going to so much damned trouble when having Angel stay over clearly went against his bachelor principles. After all, wasn't he intent on preserving his male independence? Angel had just given him the perfect out when she'd said she wanted to leave. They'd had a wonderful dinner followed by some great sex...so, what else did he need her for tonight?

He sure as hell wasn't a wuss like some of his friends who started out as regular guys but then got tangled up with pushy women. Now they let their wives and girlfriends walk all over them, dictating every little aspect of their lives. Not him. Uh-uh. No way. Never. It wasn't as if he appreciated being emasculated by little Miss I-Am-Woman-Hear-Me-Roar. Hell no. The dame was a ball buster, sure as shit. That single trait alone should have him running from Angel like a zebra from a tigress.

So why was he was standing here asking her to stay? He hadn't a clue, other than there was just something really special about her. Something soft, sweet and vulnerable beneath that bristly exterior that made him feel like protecting her...keeping her safe. As the thoughts galloped across his mind, Max did his utmost to give her a smile he hoped would melt a little corner of Angel's heart.

"Please stay," he said again, drawing Angel into a soft embrace and smoothing his hand over her back until her muscles relaxed. As she grew pliable, he heard a telltale little purr vibrate in the back of her throat. Yeah...he had her now.

"Really? Are you sure?"

Max smiled and nodded in response.

"Okay," she said softly. "I'll stay." She stepped back and smiled. "We always seem to be butting heads, Max. Why is that?"

As Angel looked up at him with those great big baby blues, he got lost in them for a minute before his brain had time to register several valid answers. *Because you're an aggressive feminist? Because you're a mouthy, ball-busting broad? Because you're the sort of pigheaded dame who drives a man to drink? Because you're intent on comparing me to the rat-bastard who did you dirty?* Wisely, Max decided that none of those responses would be very well received. Instead, he said, "Gee, I don't know Angel. But I sure hope we can get past it."

She walked over to the bed and picked up the sweats. "I'll put these on then we'll go down together and fix those sundaes and a pot of coffee." She graced him with a warm, genuine smile.

"If you'll allow me," Max said, "I'll go down and prepare things while you change your clothes and get comfortable. Just take your time." He figured that being gallant and seeing to the preparation himself was a good move because it gave dollface even more time to calm down, relax, and perhaps reflect on how damned unreasonable she'd been.

As he padded down the stairs, Max thought about safe, non-confrontational topics of conversation to broach as they enjoyed their ice cream. Religion was out. Politics was a definite no. World affairs? Probably not. Movies? That's it. A nice harmless subject. They could talk about her favorite old movies, all those sappy chick-flicks that made dames cry. She said she liked Cary Grant...maybe he'd even slip in his *Judy, Judy, Judy* impersonation and they'd have a laugh over it.

He peered into the living room once he got downstairs, noting that Spill and Henry were still sawing logs. His thoughts returned to Angel. Yeah, he could still salvage the evening if he played his cards right. He'd set the mood with some music. She seemed to like the Dean Martin songs playing over the sound system at the restaurant. He'd put on one of Dino's CDs. Nice and mellow. They'd do a little schmoozing, he'd offer an ample amount of flattery. He'd make sure he appeared to be listening, even when he wasn't...

Yup, within ninety minutes he could have Angel all hot and sweaty and girly and naked again and they could pick up right where they left off. Hell, he'd even let her choose the position if she wanted to—on top, doggy-style, vertical—whatever the hell she wanted, it was all the same to him. All he cared about was gloving his cock in that soft, creamy pussy of hers again and sucking on those amazing tits. The only sounds he wanted to hear coming out of that mouth of hers were cute little purrs and deep rapturous moans.

He took the jar of premium chocolate fudge sauce out of the cabinet, smiling as he hefted it in his hand. Knowing how much Angel loved chocolate, he'd picked up three jars of the stuff, just in case. Later there'd be plenty leftover to follow her suggestion of plopping it all over himself and letting her lick it off. Naturally, he'd slather his cock with an extra thick layer so he could watch her little pink tongue linger there. He'd watch as she wrapped her sensuous lips around his chocolate-covered dick, sucking until she drank down a savory combination of sweet chocolate and salty cum. Just the mere thought had him hardening in anticipation.

And then Angel's bloodcurdling scream jolted him to full awareness.

Henry and Spill jumped up from their sound sleeps, barking their fool heads off and racing up the stairs.

"Angel?" Max called as he followed the dogs, taking the stairs two at a time. "Angel, what's wrong?"

"Frank Coleman!" he heard her screech.

Max froze in his tracks.

And that's when he remembered the book resting on his nightstand.

Chapter Thirteen

Angel loved wearing Max's sweatshirt and sweatpants, especially relishing the fact that she was swimming in them, which made her feel damned near petite. Wrapping her arms around herself, she breathed in Max's scent and hummed a wistful sigh.

The man was as different from Robert or Nate as she was from a chocolate-hating anorexic. Comparing Max to either of those jerks was ridiculous. It was stupid, highly unfair and he didn't deserve it. Dammit, she knew better. Here was a man who appreciated her and made sure that she knew it, which catapulted Max closer to The-Ideal-Man status than anyone else she'd ever known. And how did she react? By deflating his big, beautiful cock. If she didn't get her shit together and knock it off she'd be in danger of losing this truly good, decent man forever.

The trouble was that whole damned sexist thing he had going—right down to the way he called her dollface, which, for some weird reason, set her heart all aflutter whenever he said it. The man could be positively incorrigible, a walking illustration of conventional, backwards male thinking, and yet...he had so many good qualities, not to mention killer looks and phenomenal skills in bed. But their conflicting personalities kept getting in the way, and he kept pushing her buttons.

The last thing Angel had expected from Max was an invitation to spend the night. It pleased her probably a lot more than it should have, considering she was determined not to get too involved with the hunky, chauvinistic veterinarian. She also hadn't expected Max to be so nice or understanding after their disagreement. Now he was downstairs fixing them make-up ice cream sundaes, which, if things progressed smoothly would segue into a scintillating round of chocolate-covered make-up sex. The guy could really be very sweet. She could tell Max was trying hard...and Angel realized she was falling for him...*hard*.

Having struggled to regain her confidence and sense of self after Robert all but obliterated it, the very idea of kowtowing to a man and being satisfied to walk in his *manly* shadow curdled her liver. Clearly, sometimes the heart has a way of overruling the brain...and the liver. Besides, with all his redeeming qualities, it wasn't as if Max was a hopeless case. If she could just learn to keep her big mouth shut and give the guy a break when he screwed up, she'd be just the woman to smooth out Max's rough, sexist edges. After all, he already had the essentials. Aside from the obvious lip-licking factor, he was intelligent, caring, hard working, had a great sense of humor...and he was a good man. Decent. Genuine. Honest.

Sitting on the edge of Max's bed as she cuddled against the soft fleece lining of his sweatshirt, she listened to the sexy crooning of Dean Martin coming from downstairs, and anticipated a warm, lusty night in Max's arms. What could possibly be better? She noticed a book titled *Ain't That Just Like a Dame?* on his nightstand and picked it up, shaking her head and chuckling at Max's appalling choice of reading material. That was definitely the first thing she'd work on in her mission to reform the man.

A moment later, Angel's contented smile morphed into a silent mouth-gaping scream that gripped her entire being as she gazed down at the photo of Max Wiley and his dog Spill on the back of the Frank Coleman book. The front cover boasted an impossibly busty, cheesy-looking blonde in stiletto heels with a smoking gun at her side, just under the equally cheesy title. It was only after opening the book to a random page and reading a few paragraphs that Angel's voice finally gurgled up and out in an audible shriek.

Her mind flooding with a violent flow of emotion, Angel stormed out of Max's bedroom. With her blood boiling hot as molten lava and her pulse stomping out a raging flamenco, she could barely see straight. Logic told her that she should probably be taking a deep breath and counting to ten, but she was *way* past the point of being calm and rational. And Max was the one who'd pushed her to that point. Once again, like so many naïve, trusting women before her, Angel had been played for a fool by a fatheaded male chauvinist pig, plain and simple.

She'd made the idiotic mistake of convincing herself that Max was different. That he wasn't a stereotypical sexist. That he was genuine. And honest. Hah!

She had to get out of there, get as far away from Max Wiley as possible. Goddammit, there'd better be plenty of chocolate at home because she sure as hell needed it now. Before Angel had a chance to make her escape, Henry and Spill were barreling up the staircase, barking up a storm.

Max was right behind them, looking all caring and concerned, the big fake.

She wasn't normally a woman of violence, but thank God she didn't have Max's baseball bat in her clutches at the moment because she was afraid she'd make damned good use of it by imagining his head as a ball in serious need of whacking. Come to think of it, she was still holding the hardcover book she'd found on his nightstand. If she aimed just right, she could do a fair amount of damage to his thick skull.

"Oooooh!" she growled out as she marched down the stairs. "What an idiot I am! I believed you, Max. I trusted you. I honest to God thought you were different. How could I be that gullible?"

"Angel, I can explain," Max said.

"Come on, Henry." Angel ignored Max, bashing her shoulder into his arm as he clasped her. "We're going home." Agitated by all the commotion, the dogs barked in chorus as they jumped up on her legs. She could tell genuine dog concern when she saw it—it was a hell of a lot more consideration than Max had given her.

"It's not what you think," Max said, racing ahead of her and bracing himself against the front door, blocking her passage.

"It's exactly what I think. Now get out of the way and let me pass, Max." Fuming so hard she was sure steam was about to blow out of her ears, Angel crossed her arms under her breasts and did her best to laser a hole right through Max Wiley's miniscule male brain with her gaze.

"Just give me ten minutes," he said.

"Ten minutes my ass, *Mr. Coleman.* You couldn't explain this," she waved the book in the air, "away in ten *years.* You lied to me, Max. Flat-out lied."

"Well, not technically," Max said, wincing as Angel's seething glare grew even more blistering. "I'd call it more of an omission. I mean, you never actually came right out and asked me if I wrote those books, did you? If you had, I would have told you the truth. In fact, I was going to do just that over our ice cream sundaes and coffee." He gave a hopeful smile.

Angel focused on the deep percussion beat thumping inside her head for a moment before responding. "And then you and I could sort of talk about it and have a good hearty laugh over it. Is that what you had in mind?"

Nodding, Max beamed a bright smile. "Exactly. It's really quite a funny situation when you think about it."

"Oh yeah, it's funny all right," Angel said, bobbing her head up and down so fast she was afraid she'd cause permanent neck injury. "Especially the part about how you wheedled your way into my pants by pretending to be someone you're not." Angel growled in frustration. "That was a regular riot, Max. Gee, I could just laugh my fool head off thinking about it."

"Angel, it wasn't like that." He reached a hand out to her and Angel slapped it away. "You're not being fair."

"No, you're right, I guess I'm not. I forgot to mention the rip-roaring hilarious part about how, even though you started out on the wrong foot by lying, you could have come clean and told me your secret over dinner when we were discussing trashy books like these." She waved the book again. "To make the episode even more side-splittingly comical, you made damned sure to get your cock serviced by me tonight, *before* you had this big epiphany about making a clean breast of it and being honest with me. Oh, Max, that's the most laughable part of all."

"Jesus, is that what you really think?" Max asked, and Angel responded by jutting her chin. "It just so happens that I tried to tell you about it over dinner tonight, but then you just went off on one of your righteous rampages again, spouting about how writers of hardboiled crime are one rung up the ladder from Satan. I sure as hell wasn't going to spill my guts to you after that. Has anyone ever told you that you have an annoying way of twisting everything to suit your agenda?"

"Twisting things to..." Angel sucked in an audible gasp and slapped her hand against her chest. "Please tell me that remark did *not* just come out of your mouth, Max. Because if it did, I think you ought to hang your big fat head in shame."

She noticed that Max had the decency to flush with embarrassment.

"Angel, you have to believe me when I tell you that I absolutely did not use you for sex."

She shifted her weight to her other hip. "Uh-huh."

"I'm serious. Yes, I was wrong for lying—I mean *omitting* the fact that I write as Frank Coleman, but you were so adamant about hating the books and saying how much you detested liars that I was afraid to fess up. Honestly, dollface—"

Angel wagged a warning finger in his direction. "Do *not* call me that."

Max sighed in frustration. "Angel, I care about you. I would never do anything to hurt your feelings or make a fool out of you. I'm not that kind of man, regardless of how hard you try to paint me as one."

"Right," Angel said, sucking in a deep breath, "because a good man would never purposely try to manipulate a woman. He wouldn't lie to her for the express reason of having her suck his dick. Or flatter her solely because he wants to fuck her, right?"

"Right." Max's posture relaxed. "I knew you'd understand if you just let me explain my side of it."

Feeling a maniacal grin take hold, Angel answered, "Oh, I've already got your side right here, Max." She thumped the book then flipped it open to a page conveniently bookmarked by her pantyhose. She scrolled down for a moment and then read aloud. "I was a private dick, a gumshoe looking for a way to fight the tedium. That's when Trixie came into my life. A bottle-bleach blonde with cherry-red lips, pearly-white teeth, mile-long legs, and a great set of tits, the dame was half good and half hussy—"

"Uh-oh." Cringing, Max scoured his face with his hand. He backed up a few steps, plopping his ass onto the stairs. Spill ambled to his side, licking Max's face, while Henry cowered under a table.

Shaking, Angel continued, "She was a mouthy, self-assured broad and being around her I felt dirty and outclassed. I knew Trixie would hightail it unless I came across as a regular, upstanding Boy Scout type, oozing with awshucksness and all that other crap dolls like to hear. So that's what I gave her—and plenty of it. Soon I got caught up in a diabolical game of deceit, but I didn't care," Angel paused long enough to nail Max with a knife-edged glare, "because a man's gotta do what a man's gotta do. And I was one horny lug in need of a blowjob." Angel could almost feel the floor rumble with the intensity of Max's humongous groan.

"You made your point, Angel. There's no need to continue." Elbows propped on his knees, Max buried his face in his hands. "Besides...that's fiction," he said through his fingers. "It's not about me and you."

Angel bellowed forth with a laugh at Max's ludicrous remark and then went on reading. "I gave my spiel to Trixie in dribbles and half-truths, twisting it around to suit my agenda. And then, just for good measure, I threw in a bunch of malarkey about how pretty and classy she was. Told her she had a great ass, nice tits, and a pretty little pussy." Her eye twitching with fury by this time, Angel looked up from the book again to find Max mumbling and shaking his head.

"Oh, Jesus. Just shoot me now," he muttered into his hands.

Boasting a triumphant smile, Angel finished the passage by reading, "I would have told Trixie anything just to get her to wrap those soft lips of hers around my stiff dick and suck me all the way to China. I gave out with some real humdingers about how special she was and how nobody ever made me feel so good. After I oiled her up real slick with compliments, she spread her legs open for me, all needy and quivery, practically begging me to shoot my pecker home. Ain't that just like a dame?"

Angel slammed the book shut with a resounding thud. Then she opened it and clapped it closed even harder. Aside from Henry's whimper and the jingle of Spill's dog tags as he sped around the corner to hide, the room was so quiet it seemed like a mausoleum.

After a seeming eternity, Max looked up, a dejected half-smile on his face. "I don't suppose I could talk you into planting your righteous rage on the back burner long enough to sit and have a nice little chat over a cup of coffee and couple of melting ice cream sundaes." He cocked his head toward the kitchen. Angel just stood there scowling, still too livid to engage in casual repartee. "Yeah," Max said, noting her rigid stance and probably catching sight of the steam venting from her ears. "I didn't think so."

"Henry." Angel snapped her fingers. "Come on, we're leaving now."

"At least let me drive you home, dollface. Don't let your stubbornness stand in the way of your safety."

"The name is *Angel.*" She huffed noisily. "And no thank you, I can easily walk the two blocks myself. I have a guard dog to protect me, remember?" She snapped her fingers again at Henry, who was still cowering. Then she clapped her hands...and patted her thighs. Henry didn't budge.

Crossing his arms over his chest as he observed the shivering cocker spaniel skulking in the corner under the small occasional table, Max nodded. "Oh, definitely. I mean, he'd sure scare the bejeezus out of me if I was an attacker."

After transmitting another seething glare Max's way, Angel walked over to the table, bending to hook her fingers through Henry's collar and giving a tug. "Come on boy. Time to go." She grumbled in frustration as she dragged the reluctant Henry from his safe haven. "Traitor," she mumbled under her breath as the dog gave her a woebegone look.

"I'd mention that it's nearly three in the morning," Max said, "but you probably already know that. Seems to be your chosen hour for taking neighborhood strolls." He scrubbed his chin with his hand as he appraised her. The jerk actually seemed to be amused by all of this. "While you look mighty damned cute in those sweats," he continued, "I must admit that I'm partial to that flowing white nightgown you wore the last time you wandered around the streets at this hour." He had the audacity to wink.

Angel looked down at her clothes, her shoulders slumping. She'd forgotten that she still had on Max's sweats. There was no way she wanted to stay there long enough to change now. "I'll launder these and have them returned to you promptly," she said.

"Don't worry about it," Max said. "Just hang on to them until you have some time to cool off and come to your senses. You can drop them off and we'll have a nice levelheaded conversation and that cup of coffee."

"Come to my senses?" Angel gasped. "You have *got* to be joking. Why you arrogant, egotistical...uh...uh..." She sputtered and stammered, looking for the right words.

"Pigheaded male chauvinist?" Max offered helpfully.

"Yes!" Angel jabbed a finger toward him. "Thank you."

"No problem." Max shrugged.

"Let me make this perfectly clear, Dr. Wiley, so even you and that infinitesimal male brain of yours can understand. I do not *ever* want to see or hear from you again. Period. Got that?"

Brandishing a mighty scowl, Max rose from the stairs and stood quietly for a moment, just staring at Angel. His gaze was so solemn, intent and menacing she could practically feel the tiny hairs at the back of her neck stand at attention. The sonuvabitch had the unmitigated nerve to stand there looking more handsome and sexy than she'd ever seen him before.

"Loud and clear, Ms. Brewster. You won't ever have to worry about me bothering you again, I can guarantee that."

"Good." Angel nodded, returning his nasty glower and doing her best to ignore the warm trickle emanating from her traitorous pussy as well as the fact that her nipples were tightening. "As long as we understand each other."

Max chuckled through a sneer.

Fisting her hands at her hips, Angel said, "Just what in the hell is so damned funny?"

"It's just that for a moment there I actually made the mistake of forgetting that you were a belligerent, unbending shrew, instead of a warm, rational, understanding woman with a heart." He chuckled again. "*Dollface*," he added purposefully, clearly just to get her goat. And he succeeded.

Huffing an incredulous grumble, Angel tugged Henry to the door.

"Allow me," Max said, slipping past her and opening the door.

"Thank you, Dr. Wiley, and goodbye. I wish I could say it had been a pleasure."

The instant she and Henry were over the threshold, Max barked, "So long, Ms. Brewster, and likewise."

Like the uncouth cretin he was, Max Wiley slammed the door on her butt.

🐈 🐈 🐈

"He called me a b-b-belligerent, unbending shrew," a sobbing, hiccupping Angel wailed into a wad of tissues. "I'm not a shrew...am I B.J.?"

"Of course you're not, dear," Angel's boss said as she patted her softly on the back. "Although you do tend to be a bit on the dogmatic side where certain issues are concerned."

Angel's jaw dropped and she looked up, feeling as though she'd been stomach punched. "Are you saying you think I was wrong? That I'm at fault? Because I really don't think so, B.J." She paused to dab her eyes and blow her nose, and when she continued, it was with an indignant spark. "I mean, I'm not the one who pretended to be something I'm not. I'm not the one who was busy making a fool out of him. I'm not the one who—"

"No, sweetie," B.J. interrupted, "but you're the one who is crying her little heart over a man she claims means absolutely nothing to her."

Angel's quivering chin elevated. "Well, it's true. I never want to see Max Wiley again, and I *don't* care about him." Dragging the tissue box closer, she grabbed a handful and sobbed harder.

"Yes," B.J. said, pulling Angel into a buddy-hug. "I can see that."

"He's a sexist, B.J. A diehard male chauvinist. Exactly the kind of man we warn women about in our articles." Angel slapped her hand against the stack of *Women's Wit and Wisdom* magazines atop her desk. "He-he-he calls me...*dollface.*" The dam broke again and the fresh flood of Angel's tears soaked through the tissues.

"Well, we should string him up by his thumbs for that alone," B.J. said, nursing a smirk. "Maybe the two of you should sit down and talk this out, Angel. Perhaps if you gave Max a chance to explain—"

"Explain what?" Angel cut her off. "How he flattered me and told me whatever he thought I wanted to hear just so I'd sleep with him?"

"Well...I'm kind of thinking that you might—just might, you understand—be blowing this out of proportion." B.J. winced when Angel shot her an accusatory look. "Don't misunderstand. I'm certainly not saying that Max is blameless in this. He really should have told you about his writing, but can't you understand why he may have been reluctant to share that fact with you? After all, from what you've told me, you let Max know in no uncertain terms that you abhorred hardboiled crime fiction, thought it was clichéd and sexist and good for nothing but the trash. Plus you repeatedly compared him to Robert and Nate." She rubbed the tense muscles in Angel's neck until her stiff posture relaxed a little. "Is it any wonder why Max didn't enthusiastically blurt out the fact that he writes as Frank Coleman?"

"He had ample opportunity to tell me." Angel opened a desk drawer and snatched an elastic hair-tie from its depths. "I honestly don't understand why you, of all people, are defending him, B.J." Angel smoothed back the tear-soaked strands from her face and gathered her tangled mop of hair into a ponytail at her nape. "You were my mentor. I learned most of what I know about feminist principles and the empowerment of women from you." Taking a small mirror from the drawer, she glanced at her swollen-eyed reflection, wrinkling her red nose in distaste. She scrubbed the mascara smudges from under her eyes with a tissue. "You were the one who told me that any man who didn't fully respect my beliefs and embrace them completely was unworthy of my time or affection. Remember?"

"Hmmm..." B.J. tapped her jaw thoughtfully. "I suppose I did say that."

"You also said that chauvinistic men hate liberated women because they're innately weak and intimidated by our strength," Angel continued. "That a man who truly cares for a woman will readily renounce his sexist ways and openly support feminist dogma. And you said—"

"Yes, yes, I know, but you should know better than to take everything someone says literally. Especially me. I mean, what do I know?" B.J. waved her hand in a dismissive fashion. "Angel, I'm an aging, twice divorced, bisexual woman who can't seem to get a relationship right whether it's with a man *or* a woman. Hell, I'm probably the last person who should be spouting advice on the subject of amour."

"You know, I actually took notes when you told me all that stuff, B.J." Drawing two chocolate bars out of her desk drawer, Angel offered one to B.J. and tore the wrapper from the other, sinking her teeth into it. She narrowed her eyes, studying her boss for a long moment. "I looked up to you. Admired you. Patterned myself after you...well, all except for the bisexual part." Her lips hiked into a half-smile. "I believed everything you told me, B.J." She slammed her desk drawer shut. "Now you're telling me that it was all just a crock?"

"No, of course not. I'm just saying that, while it's difficult to admit, I'm not right a hundred percent of the time, Angel. No one is. A lot of what I told you came from all the angst I was going through because of my breakup with my second husband. The guy was a snake, a first-class bastard."

"Like Robert...and like Nate," Angel said softly as she nodded in understanding.

"Not really, Jeffrey was a strictly unique sort of jerk." B.J. chuckled. "Speaking of your ex-fiancé, don't forget that you were pretty much a basket case after that whole calling-off-the-wedding thing. Somehow Robert succeeded in robbing you of your spunk and confidence and left you a subservient shadow of your former self."

"You can say that again. I was a mess."

"I guess I took it upon myself," B.J. continued, "to try to turn all that around. To make you stronger so no man would ever walk all over you again. Since my idiot niece was involved in the breakup and I'm the one who told you about it, I felt partially responsible."

"Oh, B.J. how can you say something like that? If it hadn't been for you helping to bolster my ego after everything happened, I'd still be struggling to come back from doormat status. I'll never forget how much you helped me."

"Well, both my negative experiences and yours may have tainted my way of thinking at the time. I probably slipped into man-hating mode a bit stronger than I should have. I'm sorry if that's the case because I don't think Max is the creature from hell you're making him out to be."

"You have nothing to be sorry for." Angel raked her fingers through her hair and groaned. "Oh, B.J., I'm so damned confused. It's like I have the feminist part of me warring with the hopeless romantic side, and neither side is winning. I can't make up my mind what in the hell I really feel about Max."

B.J. walked around to the front of Angel's desk and perched her bony butt on the edge. She covered Angel's hand with hers and smiled warmly. "When it comes to matters of the heart, you need to look within. From everything you've told me about Max, and from my brief meeting with him that day the two of you were scrapping about who was going to drive," B.J. rolled her eyes and snickered, "he seems like a good man. Not perfect, but then, who is? I know I'm not and—newsflash—you're not either." Chuckling, she patted Angel's hand as she slipped off the desk.

"What do you think I should do, B.J." Angel asked as her boss headed for the door.

B.J. paused before turning the knob. "Why don't you take some time off? I think it would do you some good."

"Oh, no, I couldn't do that, I have too much work. I have—"

"Oh, puhleeze. Spare me, Angel." B.J. tsked loudly. "You have a gazillion hours of vacation time backlogged because you have the fool notion that you're indispensable." Angel gasped at that. "Well, listen, kid, I have news for you. This magazine will survive just fine without you for a couple of weeks...or even a couple of months. And your job will be waiting for you when you get back. Go for a cruise or for a retreat somewhere...or what about staying at your parents' cabin out on the coast? You need to get away from work and from home. Go someplace where you can relax and do some serious thinking."

"It's not fair to burden you and the other women with my workload, B.J. What if I agree to take an afternoon off, instead? That's a fair compromise."

"No it most certainly is not!" B.J. whipped her arm forward, jabbing the air with an admonishing finger. "Stop playing the martyr, Angel. Get your ass out of here for at least two weeks, or else you'll leave me no choice but to call someone to come pry your fingers from your keyboard and bodily haul you away." She left the office.

As soon as B.J. closed the door, Angel ripped into the last two bars of chocolate in her desk drawer, devouring them as if she were a starving hyena. "She can't just force me to take a vacation if I don't want to," she mumbled to herself as she chewed and swallowed the creamy candy. "She's just bluffing. I'll refuse to go," her voice rose. "What is she going to do about it? Fire me?" She turned her attention to her keyboard.

"These walls are paper thin and I can hear you, Angel." B.J.'s voice interrupted Angel's thoughts. "And you're damned right. I *will* fire your sorry ass. Now get the hell out!"

Angel sank back in her chair, shoulders slumped and arms dangling over the side. "But, B.J." she called out, "if I don't keep myself busy with work then I'll be forced to think about Max."

"Well," B.J. offered, "I suppose you're right, kid. Maybe it's better if you just stick around and risk running into your hunky, trash-writing neighbor seeing as how you only live two blocks away from each other. Yeah...I hadn't thought of that. Maybe you just want to hang around the office moping and hoping that he charges up on his tarnished white stallion to take you to lunch. With you at the reins, of course."

At the thought of running into Max, Angel's emotions coiled and knotted until her thoughts were nothing more than a bundle of scrambled sensations. No. She definitely wasn't ready to see him.

"Okay, I'm going," Angel called to B.J. "Satisfied?"

"Remember. Two weeks. Minimum."

"B.J.?"

"Yeah?"

"You're such a bitch."

"Flattery won't get you out of this one, kid."

The effervescent echo of B.J.'s laughter crackled between their offices.

Angel picked up the phone and punched a speed dial number. "Hi Mom. I just wanted to let you know that I'm taking a little vacation and I—" She dropped her head into her hand and groaned. "Yes, Mom, I'm okay. Yes, Mom, I know you've been trying to get me to take a vacation for the past two years. No, Mom, I didn't get fired. No, Mom, I'm not depressed or unhappy. No, I'm not lying." With a glance toward heaven, she sent up a silent prayer.

Then, to Angel's horror, she began crying again, setting her mother's radar off. "Okay," she sniffed, "maybe I was lying just a little." She tried to laugh, but it came out sounding more like a needy snivel. "Anyway, Mom," she said after gathering her wits, "I need some time to think, so I thought I'd spend some time out at the cabin, maybe a week or two, unless you have somebody else staying there now." She dabbed her eyes and nose as she listened to her mother. "That's great. Yes, don't worry, I'll...I'll...I'll be...fine," she sobbed into the phone before disconnecting.

Chapter Fourteen

"It's not supposed to work this way," Max grumbled as he sat staring at the computer monitor in his small office next to the kitchen. "It was supposed to be a clean break. She says adios, I say adios, and that's it. Done. Finished. Finito."

Spill cocked his head, looking up at his master, uttering a guy-type moan of camaraderie.

Max leapt out of his chair and rounded the corner to get himself a beer. "But no, it's *not* over because I can't get the ditzy dame out of my head. Damn it!" He slammed the refrigerator and twisted the top off the bottle, taking a swig. "And here I've got an overdue manuscript and I can't put two fucking words together to save my life." He stood looking at the blank computer screen, grumbled, and then stomped into the living room where he plopped onto the sofa and turned on the TV.

"Maybe I could understand it if Angel was some sweet, soft-spoken little cookie-baking, sweater-knitting type of gal," he said, flipping mindlessly through the channels, "but she's not. She's a know-it-all, mouthy, stubborn, ball-busting women's libber, Spill." At the sound of his name, the little three-legged beagle jumped up to the sofa and onto Max's lap, where he sniffed the contents of the beer bottle, licking his chops. Max poured a bit into his hand and held it out to Spill, chuckling as the dog lapped up every last drop.

Max wiped his hand on his jeans and mussed Spill's short fur. "On top of that she keeps comparing me to a couple of fiends from her past. I just can't win. Angel's poison for me, buddy. She's like some mind-altering street drug that grips you in its claws," he squeezed his fingers into a fist, studying it, "and never lets go until it wrings you dry, strangling every last ounce of independence." He relaxed his hand and let his head drop back against the sofa.

"Shit. What am I gonna do, Spill? That woman's got me hooked like a fish on a line. And that's no good." He pounded the sofa cushion and groaned as an image of Angel, naked and needy, flitted across his mind. "Goddamn sonuvabitch. Look at me. For chrissakes, dollface has got me acting all cow-eyed and sulky." With a solemn expression, he patted his dog on the rump. "I'm a man, Spill. We don't sulk." He flipped through more channels until he came to an old movie.

"Aw, damn." Waving the remote toward the TV screen, he sputtered, "There, see? What did I tell you? She's everywhere. Everything I see or do reminds me of Angel." Max recognized the old Cary Grant movie, *Arsenic and Old Lace*, from the first night he met Angel. The night she came banging at his door with her wild, nonsensical story about having poisoned Henry. "Remember how she looked that night, Spill? I mean, aside from being nuts, of course. She was the spitting image of that big, bold, beautiful avenging angel from my dream." He closed his eyes and smiled. "Sexy as hell with that halo of golden hair, the filmy white gown, those amazing big tits..."

Groaning as he felt his dick stiffen, Max nudged Spill from his lap. It was getting mighty damned inconvenient walking around sporting a boner all day at the veterinary clinic, or anywhere else he went for that matter, just because he couldn't keep his mind off Angel's bouncy breasts, or her slick, warm pussy, or the way she looked when she wrapped those cherry-red lips around his dick and sucked.

"I'm turning into a regular sap, Spill. Just like my buddies—the ones who lost every last semblance of manhood when their pushy dames snapped those rings through their noses. The ones I laughed at and made fun of. If I'm not careful I'll be no damned different from them." He shuddered at the thought. "Max Wiley is in danger of joining the sorry ranks of hopeless, hapless, female-addicted mopes. Ain't that a kick in the pants?" He gave a humorless laugh and slugged back a hefty swallow of beer.

"She won't even answer my calls. Five days in a row I've called her house, her cell phone, and her office. Nothing. All I get is voicemail. I need to talk to her. It's driving me nuts, Spill. If I could just have one sane, normal conversation about what happened, I know I could get her out of my system once and for all and get my life back on track." Max sat forward, resting his elbows on his knees, with the beer bottle at his side. Spill took immediate advantage of its location by licking it and sticking his tongue into the neck of the bottle.

"Now you see," Max said, lifting the bottle to his lips and drinking, "if I weren't a veterinarian, if I were just a random know-nothing pet owner like, say, the aforementioned Ms. Brewster, I might be grossed out by dog germs. However, I'm aware of the fact that, generally, dog germs are harmless to humans. Unless, of course, you've been licking your butt hole recently, Spill. You haven't been doing that lately, have you buddy?" Max glugged down the rest of the brew and shrugged. "It doesn't really matter. The beauty of it is, since beer kills off bacteria, I guess we've got all bases covered."

He sat back, and rested his feet on the coffee table, crossing one ankle over the other. "That's the difference between men and women in a nutshell. Men talk in concise statements. Simple, uncomplicated guy-logic. Not like that convoluted, muddled stuff that constantly stirs around inside women's brains and blurts out of their mouths sounding like a bunch of complex, garbled nonsense."

He spoke to Spill as if the dog clearly grasped the gist of the conversation, and Spill, performing his dogly duty, gifted his master with rapt attention.

"As a man," Max continued, "I would simply say, *beer neutralizes dog germs*. Period. Now if I were a woman, I'd feel compelled to start off with the history of the brewing process, going all the way back to ancient Egypt, explaining the hows and whys, before ever getting to the thing about the dog germs. By that time, the man would be asleep—then she'd get all over his case because he wasn't listening. And she'd withhold sex from the poor shmoe for the next week to punish him." Max sneered as he went back to flipping through channels. "Women. Who the fuck needs 'em?"

🐕 🐕 🐕

Max watched with wonder as Dominick Spinelli gave his wife a saucy wink and an impromptu butt squeeze as he passed her on the way to Max's table.

"So, tell me, Dominick," Max said, aware of the slight slur in his words as he gazed into his fourth glass of Chianti, "how do you and Francesca stay happy after all these years together? What's your secret? I mean, does she ever drive you crazy?"

Dominick Spinelli erupted with laughter. "All the time," he said, giving Max a hearty pat on the back then placing a shushing finger to his lips. "Don't ever tell her I said so. She'd pound me flat with that big rolling pin of hers." He sat across from Max, studying him for a moment before speaking again.

"Troubles with the beautiful young lady, eh, Maximilian? With Angelina?"

"We had a fight." Max nodded. "She won't talk to me."

"Tell Papa all about it," Dominick said, patting Max's arm.

Max did. He didn't really know why, because spilling his guts certainly wasn't something he normally did, especially to a relative stranger, but there was just something about Spinelli and his wife and their restaurant, and the happy memories with Angel there, that had Max regurgitating the entire story inside fifteen minutes.

"So, basically," Max said, finishing his tale of woe with a weighty sigh, "I knew she was wounded and vulnerable because Robert and Nate had already hurt her by lying to her, and so what did I do? I acted like a real jerk and lied to her too." Pushing aside the lunch plate of Veal Marsala he'd barely touched, Max picked up the wine bottle and tipped it into his glass, turning it over completely. He waited as two final drips plopped into his glass. "How about another bottle of wine, Dominick? You can share it with me. I'm buying."

"Eh...I think maybe it's time for some espresso," the older man said with a knowing smile. He called one of the servers over, giving him instructions to bring Max a quadruple espresso and some biscotti. "Women are unique creatures, Maximilian. Strange and wonderful. Sometimes...you know, especially at those certain times of the month," Dominick paused to look skyward and cross himself, "they can get a little scary and a *lot* crazy. *Mama mia!*"

"You can say that again," Max agreed. "So what's a guy to do? Other than swear off dames entirely, I mean."

"A wise man learns how to treat a woman right if he wants to keep her happy. And keep his sanity." Dominick chuckled. "You're in love with Angelina." It was a statement rather than a question.

"Hell no I'm not!" Max protested. "I never said anything like that."

Dominick studied Max and smiled. "Ahhh...my mistake," he said, nodding slowly. "What you need to do is to come up with a very special plan to win Angelina back. She's worth the trouble, Maximilian. I can tell. Preferably," he said, poking Max in the arm and winking, "it should be something that will make her cry. That always works the best."

After a couple cups of strong coffee, a bellyful of Italian cookies, and some healthy man-to-man sharing of ideas, Max was armed with a plan guaranteed to make Angel cry as he headed for Angel's office to talk to her boss.

🐈 🐈 🐈

"Just tell me if she's okay."

"Max, I've already told you that she's okay—all two dozen times that you called." B.J.'s frustration was evident. "Like I keep telling you, Angel's just taking some time off, that's all."

"I've been calling her cell phone and leaving messages for more than a week now and she hasn't returned my calls. I figured she would have cooled off by now and be willing to talk about what happened." Max plopped down in the chair opposite B.J.'s desk, bracing his elbows on his knees and dropping his head into his hands.

"Sit down, why don't you?" B.J. said, smirking.

"I suppose she told you I acted like a jerk."

"She may have mentioned something to that effect. Look, kid, from what I've been able to piece together you *did* act like a jerk." Max's head popped up at that. "But then," B.J. held up a finger, "Angel didn't exactly react with discretion, either."

"She drives me crazy," Max admitted, memories of his clashing encounters with Angel storming through his mind.

"She's different from other women I've known. She's just so damned hard to figure out, you know?" B.J. simply raised an eyebrow in response. "Every time I think I've got Angel pegged, she surprises me and, before you know it, I'm back in the doghouse for something I said. Usually something that reminds her of her former spawn-of-the-devil boyfriends, or something *politically incorrect.*" Max hung invisible quotation marks around the phrase with his fingers.

"She knows she has a bad habit of making unwarranted comparisons. I've told her that she really needs to move on and let go of those old hurts." B.J. got up from her chair and stood at the window, gazing out at the rain-slicked street. "Angel is a very passionate woman," she said after a long moment.

"Aw, jeez...you mean she went and told you about the sex?" Max groaned. "What is it with all you dames always blabbing to each other all about what goes on in the bedroom, huh?"

B.J. glanced over her shoulder at Max with a withering glare. "I was talking about her personality in general, Max. I meant that Angel is extremely passionate about her beliefs and sometimes her zealousness tends to cloud her thinking."

He slunk down in his chair. "Oh."

"Your knee-jerk response to what I said is a perfect example of why Angel becomes upset with you so easily."

"I don't get it," Max said. "What do you mean?"

"I couldn't help but notice that you tend to speak not only in clichés, but in bigoted absolutes," B.J. explained, turning fully toward Max. "Of course, it comes across as a superior attitude, which only helps to promulgate the negative stereotype of the sexist male."

"Huh?" Max slanted B.J. a befuddled look. "Maybe you could repeat that, but this time in English."

B.J. laughed. "You said 'all you dames always blabbing to each other.' In that snippet of dialogue, you managed to get *dame*, which is an undesirable clichéd sexist term, in there right next to an all-or-nothing sexist absolute, wherein you imply that *every* woman engages in identical, objectionable behavior. You clearly have a habit of zeroing in on fixed black-and-white concepts without allowing for any of the variable grays to emerge. If this is typical of your speech habits, and I imagine it is, Angel would clearly find that objectionable. Understand?"

Max just stared at B.J. for a moment, doing his damnedest to make heads or tails out of what she'd just said. "You got all of that out of one little sentence I spoke?" he said finally.

"Yup."

"You see, that's exactly the kind of complicated womanly gobbledygook Angel would come out with. She feels the need to dissect everything I say, pushing me to the point where I'm afraid to even open my mouth."

After returning to her desk, B.J. rested her hip against the edge and folded her arms. "Which is why you put off telling her that your pseudonym is Frank Coleman."

"Exactly. I figured she'd react just about the way that she did when she found out."

"Why is it so important for you to find her?" B.J. asked, leaning in closer and making Max feel sort of twitchy and nervous because of that no-nonsense eagle-eyed gaze of hers.

"No special reason." He gave a cavalier shrug. "I felt bad about the way things ended and I just wanted to make sure she was okay."

"Mmm-hmm." B.J. rapped her fingertips against her desktop. "Is that all?"

Max wasn't too crazy about the way B.J. made him feel all squirmy—as if he had something to feel guilty about. "Yeah. That's all."

"I see," B.J. said. "Well, in that case, I think we can say goodbye then." She held out her hand, never taking her gaze from him.

Ignoring B.J.'s gesture, Max said, "Oh, I get it." He sat up straight, crossing one leg over the other and shaking his foot like a nervous tick. "You're looking for me to profess my undying love for Angel or something sappy like that, right? Well you can just forget about it, B.J., because that's not going to happen. The last thing I need in my life is some screwy dame who drives me up the wall whenever we spend more than ten minutes together." He shoved back his chair and leapt out of it, pacing across the room.

"Life as I know it would be over if I got hooked up with Angel," he barked. "My independence would be kaput. She'd squash my masculinity every chance she got. She'd be after me to change the way I think and talk and, Jesus, maybe even the way I write. I've already been involved with one woman on a mission to change everything about me and I certainly don't intend to get mixed up with another. Uh-uh. No way. I don't need that kind of trouble."

"Hmm, it seems to me that Angel isn't the only one guilty of making comparisons." B.J. chuckled.

Ignoring that, because, dammit, he knew she was right, Max plowed his fingers through his hair and groaned. "Just forget any fancy notions about me falling in love with Angel, okay? Like I said, it's *not* going to happen, got that?"

"Oh you poor kid," B.J. said, wincing. "You've really got it bad, don't you?" She shook her head in commiseration.

Max opened his mouth to respond but nothing came out, so he closed it. After he repeated that a couple of times, B.J. said, "Come on, kid, spit it out. Like it or not, you're in love with Angel. Go ahead. Tell me I'm wrong."

"You're the second person today who's told me that and, yeah, you're *both* wrong!" Max growled without hesitation, waving a finger at B.J. and stiffening in his stance. "Goddammit, you're wrong. You couldn't be more wrong if you tried." With a few giant strides he reached her office door, grasping the handle. "I don't know why I bothered to come here to talk to you, B.J."

"Maybe because you're looking for someone with a level head to set you straight," she answered.

Max let go of the door handle. "And you think that's you, huh? You think you've got all the answers, right? Well let me be the first one to tell you that you don't. You're way off base with that crack about me being in love with Angel. I don't know her well enough to be in love with her. If I *did* know her better, you can damn well better believe that I'd be absolutely certain that I didn't love her."

"I've heard about couples who have known each other for less than a day before realizing they were in love," B.J. said. "Some of those unions last a lifetime."

Max crossed his arms over his chest and pinned B.J. with a glare meant to fry her. He was chagrined at its ineffectiveness when she just smiled back at him, perching her skinny butt on the corner of her desk. "When I fall in love it's going to be with some nice, quiet little doll whose deepest desire is to cater to my every whim," he said with conviction. "Some cute-as-a-button dame without strong opinions who'll bring me a beer whenever I want one and whip up a big pot of beef stew and a batch of popcorn just because it makes her happy as hell to please me."

B.J. feigned a yawn, fluttering her hand over her mouth. "Boring," she said in a singsong voice. "You couldn't take it, Max. You're a strong, spirited man. The kind who needs plenty of stimulation. Feistiness. Mischief. You need a gutsy woman who can give as good as she takes." Max shook his head in denial as she spoke and B.J. just sighed. "You can refute it all you want, Max, but you know it as well as I do. Love is funny. It's a strange and unpredictable thing that can't be regulated or planned."

Love? No. No way. It just wasn't possible. Max had his life planned out nice and neat, and love and marriage and baby carriages and the whole shebang that went along with that stuff, were definitely not on his agenda. Not until he was at least sixty...maybe even seventy. It was about time he set B.J. straight.

"It's not love," Max said. "If you absolutely have to slap a label on it, and I know how you women feel compelled to do that," he rolled his eyes and B.J. just smirked, "then I suppose you could call it fascination," he finished. "I mean, yeah, sure, Angel's attractive, and she's interesting...in an odd sort of way. Sometimes she's even nice for more than five minutes at a time, and yes, she's very sexy, too. Sorry to disappoint you, but all that doesn't add up to love, B.J. I'm just temporarily fascinated by Angel because she's different from other women I've known."

"If you say so, Max." B.J. engaged in a knowing smile.

Shaking his head in wonder, Max tsked and chuckled. "You women are always searching for something more when there's nothing else there. I told you when I came in here that I just wanted to make sure Angel was okay. That's all. Look what you did with that little snippet of information. You ran with it, B.J. Hell, in your mind you've already got me hogtied and shackled to Angel."

"My mistake," B.J. said with the kind of I-know-something-you-don't smile Dominick had plastered across his puss when he'd used those same words earlier. B.J. slid her butt from the desk and walked toward Max with her hand outstretched again. "Thanks for stopping by, Max." After shaking his hand she reached for the door handle and pulled the door open, clapping her hand against Max's back to push him out.

Standing firm after crossing the threshold, Max turned to stare at B.J. a moment and then chuckled. "Giving me the bum's rush, I see."

Broadcasting an expression of pure innocence, B.J. said, "I don't know what you mean. I just assumed you'd be leaving now that your question about Angel's well-being has been answered. After all, as you already reminded me, that's the only reason you came here...right, Max?" She rapped her fingernails against the doorjamb.

"Right. And, uh, well, I thought you might tell me where Angel is, too."

"Sorry. No can do."

"Why not?"

"Because she doesn't want to see you, Max."

"Aha! So she's *not* okay. She's upset. I knew it. Come on, B.J., just let me know where I can find her so I can talk to her. I just want to apologize, that's all."

B.J. put her finger to her lips, shushing him. "How about reining in all that male testosterone and keeping your voice down to a roar."

"Sorry," Max whispered. "If you just tell me where I can find Angel I'll be on my way. I won't bother you again, okay?"

"I can't do that, Max. Angel's asked me not to tell you where she is. Besides, what's the big deal? By the time she gets back I'm sure your," she paused to clear her throat loudly, "*fascination* with her will have run its course and you'll be on to some other...*dame*." She started drumming her fingers on the doorjamb again.

Max really hated the way women did their snaring. Like spiders in a web, they just kept shooting out their silk threads, spinning them around their unsuspecting victims until they were good and caught. Dames had a tricky way of being low down and dirty while coming across as the perfect picture of innocence, charm and good manners. It just wasn't fair.

"Okay," he said, "so I care about Angel. Are you satisfied now?"

"That's a start." With an ear-to-ear grin, B.J. fisted a chunk of Max's shirt, dragging him back into the bowels of her office so fast he was tripping over his own feet.

Suddenly Max had that sick kind of *come-in-to-my-parlor-said-the-spider-to-the-fly* feeling roiling in his gut. Angel had already made it crystal clear that she didn't want to see him or talk to him. She hadn't answered any of his calls and she'd even left instructions with her boss not to let Max know where she'd gone. He didn't need someone to hit him over the head with a bat for chrissakes. The reasonable, logical thing to do was to just turn around and leave. Get out of the building, away from Angel's clever and too brainy feminist boss, and get back to his computer and finish writing his damned book.

The smart thing to do was to forget all about Angel, purge all thoughts of her from his mind. Eradicate recollections of their conversations together and the way everything she said captivated him beyond reason. Flush the bright, joyful sound of her laughter from his system. Obliterate the image of those great big baby blues staring up at him. Forget about her soft, full, luscious curves and the way she purred when he took her nipple into his mouth. Disregard all memories of the way she moaned when he sank into her...

"No. No, no, no, no, no," Max said, barely above a whisper as he rocked his head from side to side. Dazed like a little lost puppy, he allowed B.J. to guide him deeper into her office and just stood there stupidly as she crossed the room to close the door.

"The more macho they are, the harder they fall," B.J. muttered as she led him to a chair and gave him a shove, seating him.

"Jesus Christ, B.J., you're right. I *am* in love with her." Feeling like a deer caught in headlights, Max looked up at B.J. as she stood over him, arms akimbo, and smiled her *well-of-course-you-are-you-big-dope* smile at him. In a sad, sorry gesture of resignation, he dropped his head into his hands, heaving a gargantuan sigh that was just about two steps removed from a girly sob. "That's it. I'm done for. My life is over."

"Well, when you're through with the drama, poor baby," B.J. patted him on the shoulder, "we can put our heads together to come up with a plan to get you back in Angel's good graces."

"Plan?" That snapped Max back to attention as he recalled the idea he and Dominick had come up with—the one guaranteed to make Angel bawl like a baby. He figured it probably wasn't a good idea to share that little tidbit of male wisdom with B.J. "I don't need a plan," he said. "All I need is to sit Angel down and make her listen to reason. Make her understand that she needs to be more compliant and levelheaded."

"Hah!" B.J. erupted with a staccato burst of laughter. "Yeah, that'll work." She snatched a tissue from the box on her desk and dabbed at the tears coursing down her cheeks.

Giving some real thought to what he'd just said, Max joined in the laughter. "I see what you mean." Suddenly feeling hemmed in by the realization that he'd become a full-fledged lovelorn sap, he rose from his chair. "I don't think this is a good idea, B.J. Just because a guy is dopey enough to fall for a doll doesn't mean he can't get over it in time."

B.J. gave Max's shoulder a shove hard enough to plant him back in the chair. "Oh, sit down and stop being such a baby."

"Damn," Max said, rubbing his shoulder and chuckling. "For a skinny little thing, you sure do pack a lot of power."

"You definitely need to come up with a strategy if you want Angel to give you the time of day when she sees you next," B. J. said. "You might only get one shot, so you have to make it good. I'm here to help coach you. I figure it's the least I can do because part of the reason she's such a pigheaded feminist is because of my mentoring."

"Well you sure did a damn good job," Max said, blinking in frustration. He sat quietly for a moment, reminding himself not to mention anything about making Angel cry when he told B.J. about his plan. "Actually, now that you mention it, I already did have a plan of sorts in mind," he said. "I think it's a good one. I'd be making big points with Angel. I'd need your help carrying it off, B.J." He began fidgeting and squirming in his seat. "The whole problem is that I'm just not used to playing games and getting involved in lovey-dovey schemes. Men don't work that way, it's not in our genes. So, I don't know if I can do this. I don't even know if I *want* to do this."

"Oh brother." B.J. groaned. "You're quitting before you've even gotten started. Well, if that's any indication of how men work things out, it's no wonder our world is in the sorry shape it is. Look, if you want Angel back, then I'd suggest you quit your pissing, moaning and whining, Dr. Wiley. Suck it up and be a man." She punctuated her command with a good solid pound of her fist on her desk.

"All right already," Max said. "You know, B.J., you're worse than my agent."

B.J. got nose to nose with Max, locking gazes with him as she poked a finger against his chest. "Yeah, well I'll be your worst nightmare if I help you win Angel back and I ever find out that you hurt her. Remember that."

"Sheesh, and here I was worried about those five burly brothers of hers," Max said, rubbing the sore spot on his chest. "Don't worry, B.J. I'm not going to break Angel's heart. I promise. Of course, that doesn't mean I won't give her a good spanking now and then if she needs it." He waggled his eyebrows.

B.J. glanced toward the ceiling. "Oh puhleeze, spare me the carnal details. Just tell me all about this plan of yours. I can't take any more of your pleading, whiny telephone calls, and I really don't want to see you moping around my office and depressing my staff, so, for the sake of my sanity, I figure I'll either have to help you or kill you."

Something about the conviction in B.J.'s voice and the beady look in her eyes made Max believe her.

They spent the next thirty minutes discussing the idea Max and Dominick had devised, leaving out the tears part. B.J. told him she actually liked his scheme—thought it was brilliant— and she'd be happy to do what he asked.

Max figured getting everything ready would involve at least two or three days of work, which meant that his already tardy manuscript would be on hold for a while longer, which would put him in the doghouse with both his agent and editor, but, damn it, Angel was worth it.

"So now you just need to tell me where I can find her," Max said as he got ready to leave.

"I can't." B.J. shook her head as she rose from the chair next to Max's and walked behind her desk, sitting in the chair. "I promised Angel I wouldn't say anything." She tapped her finger on a pad of paper atop the desk and gave Max a weird, intense sort of look. "So I won't *say* anything," B.J. said, now tapping two fingers on the paper, looking at her fingers and then back up at Max.

"I don't get it. What do you mean, you can't, B.J.? Why go to all of the trouble helping me out when you're not even going to tell me where I can find Angel?" Max cocked his head, watching as B.J. tapped and widened her eyes at him. Granted, the woman was a little unusual, but he hadn't seen her act like this before. "Is something wrong?" Max finally asked. "You look sick or nervous or something."

"No...and I'm not trying to *tell* you anything, either," B.J. said slapping her hand against the pad of paper. "Of course, if you just *happen* to find anything out on your own, Max, without me *telling* you anything...without me *saying* anything," she did some eyebrow jiggling and slapping then, "it wouldn't be my fault and I wouldn't have broken my promise to Angel." She gave him that real wide-eyed look again, picked up the small pad of paper and dropped it back on the desk before drumming her fingers against it. The poor woman was full of some quirky nervous ticks.

"How am I supposed to find out on my own?" Max said. "Why are you looking at me like that? You look like you're mad. I already told you I wasn't going to hurt Angel."

"Ugh!" B.J. let out a lengthy growl. "How is it that men can all be so impossibly thick-skulled and dense?" She practically barked. Then she grabbed the pad of paper and threw it to the floor at Max's feet.

Max picked up the pad and held it out to her. "Why, B.J., that wasn't a sexist sort of *absolute-no-gray-area* type of statement now, was it? Because, if it was, then as a man I think I should be offended."

"It appears that certain stereotypical observations do, indeed have merit, Max." B.J. raked her fingers through her long gray mane and snarled. "Now, for crying out loud, will you please get a clue and look at the goddamned piece of paper I've been trying to get you to notice for the past ten minutes!?" She gestured to the pad of paper in Max's hand.

Max looked down, read the address and grinned. "Oh! Cannon Beach. So that's where Angel's been for the past week. Why didn't you just say so?" B.J. glared at him as if he were a moron. "I remember her saying something about her parents having a cabin out there on the coast," Max said, folding the sheet of paper and pocketing it.

"Oh no you don't." B.J. flexed her fingers in a give-it-to-me gesture. "If Angel sees that piece of paper with her handwriting on it in your possession she will eviscerate me." She tossed the pad of paper at him. "Here, make a copy and I'll give you directions. Just remember," B.J. warned, "you didn't hear it from me."

"Right." Winking, Max aimed a finger at B.J. "Gotcha."

He had a few late afternoon appointments at the veterinary clinic, a sneezing parrot, a poodle with parasites, a hamster with conjunctivitis and a diabetic cat, and then he had some shopping to do—and a hell of a lot of work to complete before he made his drive out to the coast. By the time he was finished and Angel got a load of all the trouble he'd gone to just to make things up to her, he'd have her all soft and sweet and docile. And naked. Just the way he liked her.

He'd have her eating out of his hand.

And then he'd have her eating him.

Chapter Fifteen

Snuggled in a corner of the large, overstuffed loveseat, Angel watched the flames in the fireplace flicker as she breathed in the delicious scent of hot-out-of-the-oven cookies wafting from the kitchen. She smiled, thinking that she and her mother couldn't possibly be more different. Jeanne Brewster loved nothing better than to cater to her family's wants and needs. The woman clipped and collected recipes with the same enthusiasm that Angel had for amassing her antique Rubenesque postcards. Jeanne happily filled her days with cooking and baking, sewing, knitting, quilting, and doing all of those other traditional housewife-type things that Angel typically shunned.

She'd been annoyed when her mother showed up at the cabin unannounced two days ago, especially after Angel told her explicitly that she needed some time alone. Even though her mom could be a royal pain in the butt, always sticking her nose where it didn't belong and forever prodding Angel to find a good man, get married and have kids, Angel loved her dearly. Not only because Jeanne made the best damn chocolate chip macadamia nut cookies in the world, either. However, even her mom's prize-winning cookies, as good as they smelled, couldn't tempt Angel to indulge. Ever since that awful episode with Max,

Angel's appetite had been miniscule, which certainly wasn't the norm for her.

"Drink your hot cocoa before it gets cold, dear," Jeanne said, rounding the corner with a piled-high plate of the freshly baked cookies in hand. "You haven't been eating right and I don't want you getting too thin."

A shot of laughter burst forth from Angel's lungs, the first sound of joviality that had escaped her lips in days. "Mom, you're hysterical, you know that? Of all the problems I'm having right now, trust me, fear of becoming emaciated is definitely way at the bottom of the list."

"Well, just the same, drink it up," Jeanne Brewster said, nudging the large mug on the coffee table toward her daughter and setting the plate of cookies next to it. "The cookies cool off quickly. You should eat them while they're still soft, warm and gooey, just the way you like them."

"I really appreciate all the work you did, Mom, but I'm just not hungry right now." As soon as she caught sight of her dog's longing expression, Angel scrambled to the edge of the loveseat. "Don't even think about it, Henry," she said, tugging on the cocker spaniel's collar as he padded closer, sniffing the air and licking his chops. "You've had quite enough chocolate, mister, and have caused more than enough trouble, thank you very much." She picked up the well-chewed rawhide bone from the floor and held it out to Henry, who refused it with what looked like a pout.

Angel watched her fussbudget mother arranging and rearranging the cocoa and cookies on the hand-quilted placemat and smiled. "Why don't you sit down and relax for a while, Mom? Better yet, why don't you head back home. I'll be fine. Honest. You don't have to stay here and fuss over me. It makes me feel guilty."

Jeanne stepped over to the large natural stone hearth and stoked the fire. "Are you warm enough? Should I put on a couple more logs?"

"I'm fine, Mother. Really."

Nestling herself on the loveseat next to Angel, Jeanne tucked the crocheted granny-square afghan tight around Angel's legs and then drew her daughter close, pulling her into a hug. "I get worried when I see you ignoring chocolate," she said. "The only time you do that is when you're really upset."

Angel chuckled. "I'm not that upset. Max isn't worth it. I just needed a few days away to sort things out, that's all."

"You never take vacations unless you're distressed, Angel." Jeanne positioned her daughter's head on her shoulder and stroked her hair. "The last time I remember you taking any time off is when Aunt Jayne broke both arms and legs after she was struck by that drunk driver."

"Believe me when I say that my problems with Max Wiley are inconsequential compared to Aunt Jayne's horrible accident, Mom. I just needed some time off, that's all. I've been putting in a lot of hours at work lately and B.J.'s been after me to use up some of my vacation time so I don't get burned out." Angel tried to raise her head, but Jeanne held it in place. "Mom," she chuckled, "you're treating me like I was five. I'm a big girl now, and, believe it or not, I can handle this."

Jeanne ignored Angel's protests and continued to stroke her hair. "Don't you think you're being a bit too hard on the boy? After all, he's been calling your cell phone and leaving messages several times a day for more than a week now. You said he's left messages on your answering machine at home, and even with your boss at work. He obviously must care very much about you."

Uttering a loud grumble, Angel struggled to sit up. She turned to her mother, shaking her head in frustration. "Mom, haven't you been listening to anything I've said? You know how much I value honesty, especially after the last couple of relationship fiascos I've had. Robert not only made mashed potatoes out of my ego, he was also cheating on me with my best friend practically the whole time we were supposed to be engaged. Then there was Nate who—"

"Yes, yes," Jeanne cut in, "I know the story by heart. Don't you think it's about time you put all of that in the past and move on, dear?"

Angel trilled a sigh. "You've been talking to B.J., haven't you?"

"Well, she's right, you know. It's wrong to compare them to Max. B.J. said he's nothing at all like either of them."

"The thing is, he wasn't honest with me. Do you see a pattern here, Mom?"

Jeanne looked thoughtful. "Well, it's not as if Max was cheating on you like Robert or Nate, dear."

"If he lied about his writing, who knows what else he's been lying about," Angel said, absently poking her fingers through the afghan's crocheted design. "A man like Max Wiley has no place in my life. He's sexist, bullheaded and totally uncompromising."

"Hmm, sounds rather like your father," Jeanne said, chuckling. "Dad would have been here, too, if he didn't have to fly to Chicago for that business meeting two days ago. I tried to get him to change his plans, but he—"

"I prefer my men brainy, intellectual, civilized and quiet and unassuming," Angel continued, oblivious to what her mother was saying.

"Oh, you mean like Robert the accountant and Nate the professor?" Jeanne said, holding up her hands in surrender when she saw the molten glare on her daughter's face. "No man is perfect, dear. You need to lighten up a bit. Be more forgiving and tolerant. Besides," Jeanne added as she sipped from her own mug of cocoa, "you're not getting any younger, Angel. Neither am I for that matter."

Angel let her head fall against the back of the loveseat and groaned. "Please don't start with the grandchild guilt again, Mom. I'm only thirty-two. There's still plenty of time left on my biological clock—*if* I decide to get married and *if* I decide to have kids." She turned to look at her mother. "You've got five single sons, all older than me. Why don't you nag them about finding wives and providing you with dozens of mini-Brewsters, hmm?"

"Because they're men," Jeanne answered matter-of-factly. Angel groaned at her mother's painfully unenlightened attitude. "It's different. They're still sowing their wild oats."

"No, it's *not* different, Mom. Maybe I've got a few wild oats of my own to sow. Have you ever thought of that? As soon as I find myself a good oaty kind of a guy I'll commence to sowing. Of course, with my luck, that's easier said than done."

Jeanne nodded thoughtfully. "Granted, you've had lots of negative experiences with men, but you shouldn't let that sour you on *all* men." She took Angel's hand, clasping it tight. "Remember, sweetheart, you can always talk to me about anything." She kissed Angel's forehead. "*Anything.* I promise not to sit in judgment."

"That's it, Mom. This conversation is over. O-V-E-R." In a flash, Angel had the afghan off of her, she'd retrieved her hand from her mother's clutches and she sprang to her feet.

"But, honey, I just—"

"Yes, I know exactly what you wanted to do." Angel jabbed an accusatory finger toward her mother. "You wanted to ask me for the nine thousandth time if I'm a lesbian. I have told you repeatedly that I am not gay. I am not a lesbian. I am not interested in women in a sexual way."

Jeanne broadcast a helpless look. "You're always participating in all those man-hating lesbian rallies and protest marches. I naturally assumed—"

"Mother, listen to me. Please. I'm an activist for women's rights. I believe in equality for women and do everything I can to promote it. That doesn't make me a man-hater or a lesbian."

"But you have all those lesbian friends..." Jeanne was absently fingering the colorful afghan and worrying her bottom lip. "It's not that I have anything against lesbians, of course, but..." She trailed off and offered a shrug.

Angel tried to rein in her patience. "Yes, Mom, I do have lesbian friends and sometimes the rallies have lesbian participants. Just because I associate with people who are gay doesn't mean I'm gay, just as associating with meat eaters doesn't mean I'm a carnivore." Giving in to a growl, Angel plowed her hand through her hair. "I honestly don't know what else to say, how to get through to you, Mom. I am no more a homosexual than any of my five brothers—who are all older than me and still unmarried."

"I just want you to be happy, Angel. That's all I care about. You're my baby and—"

"I know you mean well, Mom." Angel kneeled on the loveseat next to her fretting mother and bent down to give her a hug. "And I know how much you love me, but I'm not a baby anymore. I'm a grown woman and I need for you to have enough faith in me to let me make my own choices and, yes, even to make my own mistakes." Patting each other's back, she and her mother exchanged loud lip smacks on their cheeks.

Angel started when she heard a car horn blaring and Henry raced to the window and started barking. She and her mother hopped to their feet.

"Who could that be?" Angel said, crossing the room to peek out the window. As soon as she spied the big van, she groaned. "Oh no."

Jeanne joined her daughter, giving a joyous little yelp when she spotted her five sons pouring out of the van. "Oh, good, they made it." She raced for the cabin's door and threw it open, running to meet her boys.

"You invited them?" Shoulders slumped, Angel grumbled. "Peace and quiet. That's all I wanted. Just to be left alone with my misery for a few days. But no, the entire Brewster clan has to stick their noses in my personal business." Shoulders sagging further, she gave in to a sigh of resignation and got ready for the onslaught.

In less than a minute, the big, brawny Brewster boys had barreled into the cabin, with Bartholomew, the oldest of the fraternal triplets, carrying Jeanne in his arms. One by one they hugged Angel, picking her up off her feet and swinging her around as if she weighed no more than a basket of laundry.

"What are you clowns doing here?" Angel said in mock annoyance. "I told Mom I wanted to be up here alone for a few days."

"We can't have our baby sister all alone up here crying in her beer," Joseph, the youngest twin by five minutes said as he smoothed an errant lock of blond hair from his forehead.

"If you notice," Angel pointed out, "I'm neither drinking beer nor crying."

"No problem," Joshua, Joseph's identical twin said, thumbing over his shoulder at the van. "We brought plenty." He ran out to the vehicle and was back in a moment carting four six-packs of beers, ales and stouts from a variety of Portland's craft brewers. "These are just for starters."

"Hey, Mom's chocolate chip cookies," Benjamin, the middle triplet said, hopping over the cases of beer and heading for Angel's plate of cookies.

"Oh no you don't!" She dove for the loveseat, grabbing the plate and scooping it from the table before Ben could swipe any.

"Tickle time!" Bradley, the youngest triplet said as he bent over Angel and dug his fingers into her ribs. Eager to join in all the fun, Henry leapt up to the loveseat and planted himself half on Angel's stomach and half on the cushion, barking his fool head off. Helpless with screaming fits of laughter and admonishments to stop, Angel quickly lost control of the plate, only to have Ben and Brad catch it and down the cookies in nothing flat.

"Not fair!" Angel griped. "You guys are bigger than me and I don't have a chance. Look, you hogs ate all my cookies! Ugh! Some things never change." She plopped into a corner of the loveseat and folded her arms across her chest, pouting. Cocking his head, Henry scooted over to Angel and licked her face.

"You bums didn't leave any for me," Bart bellowed as he leapt over the coffee table and gave Ben a knuckle noogie on the head.

"Yeah, and what about us," the twins protested in unison as they jumped on their brothers, wrestling them to the floor. Henry, of course, made sure to position himself in the center of the fray.

"Don't worry, I made six dozen cookies," Jeanne said. "A dozen for each of you." She stepped over to Angel and patted her daughter's head. "Don't worry, dear, I have yours stored away separately. Oh and...I'm glad your appetite for chocolate has suddenly returned, sweetie."

The last thing Angel had wanted when she made the trip to the quiet cabin tucked away in the woods on a hilltop overlooking the ocean was to be smothered by her meddling mother and bombarded by her rowdy brothers. On the other hand, she liked nothing better than to be caught up in the midst of her noisy, boisterous, loving family. It always made her feel safe and secure. Maybe with all of them here with her she'd miss Max less.

For more than a week now she'd been cloistered alone—well, except for Henry—mulling over all that had happened. Try as she might, Angel simply could not get that man out of her thoughts. It was crazy. Max made her want to pull her hair out by the roots sometimes, but then, at other times...

Sitting in the middle of the bustling Brewster commotion around her, Angel's thoughts slipped back to the last time she and Max made love, just before she found out about his alter ego. Oh, dear Lord, the way he made every cell in her body shiver with excitement...with ecstasy. Max had a way of making her feel cherished, as if she were the only woman in the world and he was focused on nothing but pleasing her. The feel of his hands on her breasts, and his mouth exploring her pussy...it was enough to drive a poor girl insane!

It wasn't just the sex that was great. No, it was Max's scrappy attitude and razor-sharp wit that made him extra appealing. Well, that and the fact that he had the most mesmerizing whiskey-colored eyes and the cutest—

Being bodily picked up and plopped on her oldest brother's lap scuttled any further musings of Max Wiley from Angel's mind.

"So tell me about this creep who broke your heart," the dark-haired Bartholomew said, handing his sister a beer and then dribbling some of his own into his hand for Henry to lap up. "Want us to break his legs for you?" He snickered.

"Bart!" Angel shrieked. "Are you crazy? You can't give beer to a dog. And, no, of course I don't want you to break his legs...Max's legs, I mean, not Henry's."

"A little bit of brewski's not going to hurt him," Bart said, mussing Henry's fur. "It'll put some hair on his chest, that's all."

"Yeah," Bradley chimed in as he sat on the floor, "lighten up, sis. We've been giving beer to Henry ever since you first got him." He just laughed when Angel blustered in horrified astonishment. "Along with nice, big, juicy pieces of blood-rare steak."

"And *sausage pizza*," Joe added, drawing the words out as he looked at Henry, who gave an obliging shiver and licked his muzzle.

"Brad, Joe! How could you do that?" Angel said, sucking in another audible gasp. "Henry's a devout vegetarian. I keep him on a very strict, healthy diet. Even his faux-rawhide bone is vegetarian. It's made from soy."

All of the brothers cracked up with laughter.

"Trust me, Angel," Josh said, "Henry's not a vegetarian by choice."

"He just pretends to be," Joe said.

"That's not true," Angel said, folding her arms across her chest. "Henry finds the thought of eating other four-legged creatures thoroughly appalling."

That comment had her brothers dissolving into laughter again.

"So what's up?" Brad asked, wiping tears of laughter from his eyes. "Mom said you've been a basket case for a week now."

"I have not!" Angel gasped. "Mom!" she called to no avail, because her mother was in the kitchen, happily ensconced in getting dinner ready for her brood. Angel took a swig from her beer, a creamy dark porter. She shooed Henry away when the beer-guzzling, flesh-eating dog came around begging. Damn, even her own dog was nothing but a stereotypical male animal!

Soon, all of her brothers, each brandishing an open beer bottle and munching on the cheese twizzles, potato chips and cookies that Jeanne had set in the center of the coffee table, were sitting around her in rapt attention. That made Angel nervous because the Brewster boys *never* gave her their full attention. She could only imagine what her mother must have told them about her and Max to get them all up to the cabin together on a Saturday. Jeanne must have made it seem as though Angel was practically suicidal.

"Who is this guy," Joseph said. "How'd you meet him?"

"Well, I—" Angel began.

"Mom said Angel went to his house at three in the morning," Joshua added helpfully. "In her nightgown. That's how she met him."

"What?" Ben said, looking horrified. "Were you drunk or something?"

"No, of course not. I—" Angel started again.

"She poisoned her dog," Ben said.

"You poisoned Henry?" Brad said, a look of disbelief plastered across his features. At the sound of his name, Henry moaned and offered his most forlorn look. "So what happened? You catch the poor meat-deprived dog snacking on a leg of lamb and decided to do him in?"

Angel tsked. "That's not funny, Brad. Actually, I—"

"Mom said she poisoned Henry with chocolate so she could meet the veterinarian down the street," Ben explained.

"I never said that," Jeanne hollered from the kitchen.

"You're in big trouble, Mother," Angel called out. "Now, if you guys will just keep quiet long enough for me to get a word in edgewise and tell you what really happened, I will."

"So who's stopping you?" Bart said and Angel just groaned.

"Hey...hold on a minute," Joe said. "What's that?"

"Gravel crunching," Josh said. "Sounds like somebody's coming up the drive." He got to his feet and went to the window. "Yup."

Henry, the fierce guard dog, scampered over to the window and growled.

"Dad?" Ben asked.

"No, he's out of town," Josh said. "It's somebody in a red convertible."

"A red—" Angel stiffened and blanched. The only person she knew who owned a car like that was Max, but it couldn't possibly be him. How could he know where—

"B.J.!" Angel screeched, hopping off her brother's lap and racing to the window for a peek. Sure enough, it was Max.

"Your boss?" Josh said. "Gee, I know you said she was a lesbian, but, hell, I never expected her to look that much like a guy."

"No, you big ninny," Angel said, already scurrying to the other side of the room. "It's Max. The guy I came up here to get away from. B.J. must have told him where I am, unless...Mom?" Angel bellowed.

"It wasn't me," Jeanne called out, running into the living room and wiping her hands on her apron. "I'm innocent. So the boy is here? Oh good, I can't wait to meet him."

"Mother! I absolutely do *not* want you welcoming Max as if he were the future father of your grandchildren, do you hear me? I would die of embarrassment."

"That offer to break his legs still stands," Bart reminded his sister. "Or we could beat him to a pulp the way we took care of Robert."

"No!" Angel said.

Max rang the bell and knocked at the door.

"Ohmigod, ohmigod, ohmigod..." Angel chanted.

"Uh-oh," Joe said. "Looks like sis is all aquiver over this guy." With an exaggerated batting of his eyelashes, he laughed and his brothers followed suit.

"Be nice, boys," Jeanne admonished. Patting her hair into place and giving her hands another wipe on the apron, she crossed the room and reached for the doorknob.

"Wait! Don't answer it yet," Angel said frantically, tiptoeing back to the other side of the room to get Henry and bring him with her. "Tell Max I'm not here. Tell him I went back to the city. Tell him...*ugh!*" She covered her face with her hand and growled. "Tell him...oh, I don't care *what* you tell him, just get rid of him and, for heaven's sake, don't let him know I'm here." Henry in tow, she raced down the hall to the room she was using and closed the door, leaving it open just a crack so she could hear what was going on.

"Don't worry, sis," Brad said, cracking his knuckles. "We'll take good care of Max for you."

"Oh! No! Seriously, don't do anything to hurt him," Angel called from the bedroom. "I just want to get rid of Max, I don't want to maim him for life."

"You just leave it to us, Angel," Bart said.

She could hear her brother rubbing his hands together in gleeful anticipation—and that worried her. She never did get a chance to tell her brothers the whole story about what happened between her and Max. It wasn't *that* bad. Sure, he'd lied to her, but aside from that, well, and the fact that he was a macho sexist pig, much like her own brothers, Max was still a good man—again, much like her own brothers. And her vegetarian-pretending dog. Max really didn't deserve to face the wrath of the Brewster boys, especially after they'd each had a few beers. But Angel couldn't do anything about that now. She'd have to trust in her brothers' wisdom, judgment and sense of decorum.

The totally ludicrous thought made Angel wince.

Chapter Sixteen

The nearly two-hour drive out to the coast gave Max plenty of time to think, and Spill was a perfect listener as Max rehearsed his admission of guilt and request for forgiveness. Armed with a sheet of legal-sized paper, printed with the apology he'd struggled to compose and covered with a maze of cross-outs and scrawled lines of changed wording, he felt confident, in control, and ready to face the woman he...*loved.* Even now, a whole two days after his visit to B.J.'s office and the realization that he was in love with Angel Brewster, Max gulped. He'd never said the L word to a woman before. He wasn't entirely certain it would just slide past his lips as easily as he hoped.

He thought about the bag and its contents sitting in his trunk and snickered. "Once she gets an eyeful of that, Spill, she'll be sobbing and planting kisses all over me. I'll be in the clear. At least I'd better be after all the damned work I did." He'd felt so good last night that he was finally able to write another chapter on his manuscript. Words seemed to flow a lot easier as he projected his real life situation with Angel onto the characters of Jack Clyde and Trixie Lang...

"Jack...it's...it's you." Trixie took a long drag from the cigarette that dangled between her fingers before dropping it on the concrete outside her door and staring down as she crushed it with the pointy toe of her stiletto-heeled shoe. I recognized the gesture as a tactic to give her time to think and could almost see the sharp little gears of her mind grinding.

When she looked up again, I saw those big, pouty red lips of hers tremble as Trixie eyeballed me across the threshold, pretending not to care. Acting as if her pussy wasn't getting all juiced up as her gaze fell to the promising bulge in my pants. Yeah, the dame could play cool with those glacier glares of hers and that haughty nose stuck up in the air like one of them highfalutin broads who were always looking down their noses at guys like me. But one look at those spiky nipples poking through Trixie's sweater like a couple of pencil erasers was a dead giveaway. The doll was hot to trot. She definitely had fucking on her mind, and I was more than happy to oblige. I could almost feel my stiff dick slamming home again. It had been a long time. Too long.

"Yeah, dollface, it's me alright. You knew damn well I couldn't let you walk out of my life like that, sweetheart." My voice was even, cool, calm. I put on a damned good front, but Trixie didn't know the hands in my pockets were balled into hard knots to keep them from shaking because my nerves were all jangled. I had to do this just right. If I didn't butter up her soft, womanly, forgiving side, it would be just me and my frustrated pecker partying all alone again tonight. "Babydoll, the world caved in around me that day you left," I threw in for good measure.

Trixie gazed up at me, tears swimming in her big baby blues. "I thought I told you I never wanted to see you again," she said, just like she really meant it. But I knew better. At least I thought I did until she smacked me across the face. Hard.

197

I rubbed my paw over my cheek. "Did that make you feel better," I asked as our eyes locked like radar. "'Cause if it did, I got another one on the other side reserved just for you, babe." I turned my kisser and she smacked me again on the other cheek. Things weren't exactly going as well as I'd expected, so I figured maybe I'd better try another tactic.

"I missed you, Trixie," I said, giving her my best hangdog expression. "Real bad." She glared at me with eyes like round blue gun muzzles. "I was a real heel to lie to you, honey. I should have come clean about offing your baby brother, but I didn't know how to tell you. Every time I think about hurting you it tears me up inside, just like somebody had split my belly open with a paring knife and my guts were spilling all over the floor." She was still staring at me as if she was itching to slap me again, but then I thought I saw a crack in some of that ice, a detached sort of compassion flickering in her eyes, so I kept going. "I'm nothing without you, doll. I'm as powerless as a pawn on a chessboard." I was getting close, I could feel it. That's when I went in for the kill. I twisted my face, screwing it up like I was gonna bawl like a baby and then, in the sappiest voice I could muster, I said, "Without you, Trixie, babe, all I got is a feeling of isolation, of utter solitude and helplessness, creeping like a heavy hand over my heart." I tapped three fingers against my chest. The final coup came when I coughed up the L word, doing my best not to choke on it. "I love ya, baby."

"Aw, Jack," she said as she wrapped her arms around my neck and pressed her warm tits against me. "I shouldn't have walked out on you, but I was sore. I didn't want to believe those things you told me about my brother, but I did some checking and found out you were right, Jack. About everything." She reached up on her tiptoes and planted a kiss on my jaw. "I missed you, you big lug. I missed talking to you...I missed feeling your hands on me..." She ground her pussy against my dick and I clapped *my paws on her ass, giving a good squeeze before jerking her close. "Most of all," she whispered in my ear, "I missed feeling that big, hard dick of yours jackhammering up my tunnel like a miner who's digging for gold."*

Yeah, I knew me and Trixie were going to be okay...

Following B.J.'s directions, Max drove through the small touristy town and up into the hills where he pulled onto a long, winding gravel drive. He let out a low whistle when the log cabin structure came into view. "This place is huge," he said, putting the car into park. He saw three other vehicles there, one of which he recognized as Angel's. When he got out of the car and walked around to the trunk, he heard laughter and loud voices.

For just an instant, Max hesitated. What if she was having a party? What if she was entertaining some other guy? What if—

Shit. It didn't matter what Angel was doing or who she was doing it with. He'd just spent two hours driving out here with the express purpose of making a grand apology and making her cry and he'd be damned if he was going to turn around and go back without seeing her and clearing things up between them once and for all.

"Come on, Spill," Max said as he hauled the bag from the car's trunk. "I'm a man on a mission and I need you for backup and moral support, pal." Sucking in a deep breath, Max trudged up to the cabin, rang the bell and knocked at the door.

There was shushing and whispering. Max leaned his head closer to the door, listening. That's when the door flew open and he nearly fell over the threshold as he was greeted by a woman who had to be Angel's mother. She was the spitting image of Angel, only a somewhat older version.

"Mrs. Brewster?" Max said in a croaky voice that reminded him of a teenager picking his date up for the prom. "I'm Max Wiley. I'm here to see—"

The door swung wide and suddenly Max found himself being yanked inside and surrounded by five big, fierce-looking, muscular guys. *Uh-oh...*

"So you're the jerk that upset our little sister, huh?" one of them said, crossing his arms over his chest. The guy had to be at least ten feet tall and Max felt like a ten-year-old.

"You made her cry, and Angel *never* cries," said one of the other cavemen as he loomed over Max, scowling.

"We ought to break both your legs for hurting our baby sister," said another of the behemoths as he rolled up his shirtsleeves.

"Hold on fellas." Max raised both hands, feeling as though he'd just stumbled into a lumberjack convention by mistake as he eyed the jean-clad, plaid-flannel-shirt-wearing men. Being a big guy himself, it wasn't often he felt dwarfed. "I...uh...I came here to—" he cleared his throat and swallowed hard, "to talk to Angel. This is personal...between me and her," he somehow managed to finish with a bit of bravado, which was a miracle considering the fact that he had to fight to keep himself from whimpering like a crybaby little girl.

"Oh for heaven's sakes, boys, give the poor man some room," the woman said, squeezing between two of the monsters and taking Max by the arm. "You're scaring Dr. Wiley. I'm Jeanne Brewster, Angel's mother. How lovely of you to come all this way for a visit." She beamed a smile and looped her arm through his. "Won't you come in? There's a nice batch of freshly baked cookies and there's a pot of strong coffee, and some hot cocoa, and the boys brought plenty of beer. We'll have a nice chat and get to know one another." She dragged Max to one of the overstuffed chairs and just as he was about to say something, one of the muscle-bound giants gave his shoulder a shove, seating him in the chair with such force that Max gave an *ooph*.

"Yeah, sit down, doc. We want to talk to you," the ferocious shoulder-shover growled.

Max opened his mouth to speak again when he heard Spill barking. He started to rise, but at least four meaty ham hocks held him down. "That's my dog," Max explained. "He got left outside."

Giving Max a sneer for no good reason, one of the men walked to the door and opened it and Spill came prancing in with his slightly crooked gait. After sniffing the air and looking about, the tongue-lolling dog made a beeline for Max, planting himself at his master's feet after turning around in a circle twice.

"Hey, the little guy's only got three legs," one of the brutes said, squatting to pet Spill. "He's a real cutie."

"Yeah, well," Max said, sitting tall in his chair and doing his best to look ominous, "looks can be deceiving. Spill can get mighty fierce if he feels his master's in danger. He's been trained to clamp those steel jaws of his onto a man's limb and yank until it comes clean out of the socket, so I'd be careful if I were you."

"Hey, little buddy," another of the thugs said, sitting on the loveseat across the coffee table, "want some beer?" Popping to his feet, the fierce three-legged limb-yanker gleefully padded to the man and lapped up the spot of beer from his hand.

"He gets around real good," another of Angel's brothers, a blond, said, lavishing attention on the dog. "How'd that happen to him?"

"Some street punks used him for target practice," Max said. "It was part of an initiation to join a gang."

"Assholes," one of the dark-haired brothers said.

"Language, Bartholomew," Jeanne admonished with a chastising finger.

Shoulders slumped, the caveman dropped his head. "Sorry Mom."

"Was he a stray?" another brother asked.

"Nope. The owner didn't want him after I had to amputate Spill's leg, so I kept the scrappy little guy. That's when I signed him up for those limb-yanking lessons," Max added with a chuckle.

"There, you see, boys?" Jeanne said, bending to pet Spill. "The doctor is really a very nice young man. I want you all to be nice while I go back and finish cooking dinner." With a sharp, cautionary look to her sons and a warm smile to Max, Jeanne left the room.

"Is Angel here?" Max asked the lumberjack look-alikes. "I really do need to talk to her."

"Hey Max." One of the blond brothers extended his hand. "I'm Joe," he said, ignoring Max's question. "That's Josh, we're twins in case you hadn't noticed." In all the commotion, Max actually hadn't. Now he saw that the two men were identical, except that one wore red plaid and the other blue. "That's Bart, Ben and Brad. They're triplets."

Max nodded as he shook Joe's hand and then each of the others. Not that he usually noticed this sort of thing, being a straight guy and all, but any one of the Brewster boys was good looking enough to be a male model. As soon as the thought skimmed his consciousness, Max shook it off because guys simply didn't think that way about other guys, unless they were gay. "Nice to meet you," Max said, lowering his voice an octave to a nice, deep manly pitch. "I've, uh...heard a lot about you from Angel."

"Whatever she told you, we're really not all that bad," Ben said. "Unless," he added with a menacing look, "somebody hurts our baby sister."

"Which brings me to my question," Max said. "Is Angel here?"

"So, why don't you give us your version of what happened," Josh said, ignoring Max's question.

"There's nothing much to tell. Your sister and I were getting along real good and then I botched things up by not being honest with her."

"About what?" Brad said. "You married?" He gave Max a sinister look.

"No, I—"

"Engaged?" Bart asked through a narrow-eyed glare.

"No, I—"

"You weren't two-timing our little sister, were you, Max?" Joe said, looking as if he were ready to use Max's head for a punching bag.

"Of course not, I—"

"Because we've already had to punch out a couple of guys for doing that," Joe finished.

"You gay?" Ben said, looking rather uncertain.

"For chrissakes," Max said, "I'm a writer. I write hardboiled crime fiction and I didn't tell Angel about it."

Josh stood straight and scratched his head. "That's it? That's all? Angel's all pissed off just because you didn't tell her you're a writer?"

"She hates the kind of books I write." Max shrugged. "I knew that. I was afraid to tell her that my pen name is Frank Coleman and I—"

Joe leapt off the arm of the chair and shot bolt upright. "I *knew* you looked familiar," he said. "*Jack Clyde, Private Detective and his Crime-Busting Dog, Billy,* right?" He waved a finger toward Max who, drop-jawed, simply nodded in surprise. "I recognize you from the picture on the back of the books. Josh and I are major fans."

"Frank Coleman? No shit!" Josh said, pumping Max's hand with enthusiasm. "We've read all of your books."

"Thanks," Max said. "Now if only your sister felt the same way."

"She hates all of that sexist shit," Josh said. "No wonder she busted your balls when she found out you write books like that."

"So, you didn't actually do anything to break our little sister's heart?" Bart asked. "Other than to keep from telling her that you write that stuff, I mean."

"Well, damn," Ben said, "you mean Mom dragged all our asses up here on a Saturday for nothing? Our sister's making a federal case out of things just because you didn't tell her you're a writer?"

"Well," Max scratched his head, "I think Angel sort of got the idea from reading part of one of my books that I was doing what I had my character, Jack Clyde, doing. You know, that I was feeding her a line just so I could get her into—" He stopped abruptly, remembering that he was talking to Angel's five behemoth brothers. "Uh...what I mean is..."

"Yeah, yeah," Brad said, waving a dismissive hand, "we get it. We weren't born yesterday, you know. Our sister thinks you were buttering her up just so you could get her into the sack."

"So," Ben said, "is that what you were trying to do?"

"No!" Max said with an indignant huff. "Of course not. I have nothing but the utmost respect for your sister." He swallowed hard.

"Whoa! Maybe you were right, Ben," Bart said, snickering as he nudged Ben with his elbow. "Maybe the guy *is* gay after all."

"Trust me," Joe assured his brothers, "any guy who writes like Frank Coleman can't be gay." He studied Max. "Of course, we wouldn't be too keen on you treating our little sister the same way that Jack Clyde treats Trixie and the other *busty broads*," he hung invisible quotation marks over the words, "in those stories of yours."

Jeanne came back into the room then, flashing a bright smile. "Well, since you're a writer, Max, you and my daughter have a lot in common." She grinned wider. "Dinner should be ready in just a few minutes. Max, of course you'll be staying," she stated rather than posing it as a question.

"I'm grateful for the invitation, Mrs. Brewster, but I sure would appreciate it if somebody here could tell me where Angel is."

"Oh," Jeanne said, still brandishing a warm smile, "I'm sorry, son, but we can't do that."

"She gave us strict instructions," Joe said with an apologetic shrug.

"She said to tell you she isn't here," Josh said and Joe elbowed him, muttering *moron* under his breath.

Max groaned. "I drove a long way up here just to talk to Angel and—"

He was interrupted by a loud bark, which didn't come from Spill because he was sawing logs in a corner of the loveseat. After the second bark, Spill cocked his head and growled before answering with his own bark.

"Shhh! I told you to keep quiet, Henry," came a hushed voice from down the hall.

With a knowing smile, Max glanced from Jeanne to each of her sons, who were doing their best to pretend they hadn't heard anything.

"So, as I was saying," Max said loudly as he ambled down the long hall with Spill at his side and the Brewster clan at his heels, "I drove two hours so I could come up here and tell Angel that I'm sorry for lying to her." He stopped at the door that had just quietly snapped shut. "And so I could apologize for being a bullheaded sexist pig," he said, leaning his forehead against the door. "Even though I doubt that I'll be able to change all that much."

Henry barked again and Max heard Angel shushing him. Then Spill barked again and Henry answered him.

"Dear," Jeanne said, rapping lightly at the door, "I think Dr. Wiley knows you're in there, so you may as well come on out."

"Yeah, come out of there, brat," Josh said. "Max is an okay guy. You're making a big fuss over nothing."

"Give the guy a break, sis," Bart said.

"It takes guts to apologize," Ben said, "especially when the woman is as stubborn and pigheaded as you, Angel. Come on out of there and talk to Max."

"Go away!" Angel said. "I'm not here. And I am not pigheaded, either. How did you find me, anyway, Max? B.J. opened her big mouth, didn't she?"

"Your boss said nothing," Max said truthfully. "I made something special for you, Angel. I want to give it to you. It's in the living room."

"I'm not hungry," she answered.

"It's not food. It's something very special that I made for you with my own hands. You'll like it, I promise." His lips hiked in a grin as he imagined her bawling her eyes out and climbing all over him.

"No thank you. Now just go away, Max. I don't want to see you. We're just no good for each other. You drive me crazy and I drive you crazy. We'd probably end up killing each other."

Max lifted his head from the door and turned to the others. "She's got a point there. We're always butting heads. Any suggestions?"

Jeanne turned the doorknob. "It's locked."

"We could break it down," Brad offered," and bring her to her senses.

"You lied to me Max," Angel said, sniffling. "You flattered me, saying all those things you didn't mean, just to get me into bed."

"I meant every word I said to you," Max said. "And if I recall, I wasn't the only one eager to hop into the sack, Angel."

"Oh dear," Jeanne said, slapping her hands over her ears. "I probably shouldn't be hearing this." Then she dropped her hands and grinned. "On the other hand, I guess that means my baby's not a lesbian after all."

"Did he get you pregnant, sis? Is that what all this is about?" Joe asked, glaring at Max.

"No! Of course not," Angel said. "Other than being a liar and a smooth talker and a sexist and a male chauvinist, Max was a perfect gentleman."

"Well, that's good to hear, dear," Jeanne said. "Now why don't you come out because I'll be serving dinner in just a few minutes. We'll all have a lovely chat together."

At the word *dinner*, both Henry and Spill barked.

"I'm not hungry, Mom."

"Well, at least open the door so little Henry can come out," Jeanne coaxed. "The poor dog must be starving."

"He's not hungry either," Angel said, and right on cue, Henry let out a whimpering half-starved-dog moan.

"Angel," Max said as everyone still crowded around him, "just give me five minutes. I really do need to talk to you. Alone. It's important."

"Whatever you have to say to me you can say in front of my family," she retorted.

"Oh, man, she's cruel," Bart said, wincing.

"I can't say what I want in front of your mother and brothers," Max said. "It's private."

"Not interested," Angel said. "Please go away."

"Why the hell do you always have to make things so difficult?" Max half growled.

"Me? Is that why you drove all the way up here, Max? Just to insult me?"

"God damn," Max said, leaning his head against the door and pounding his fist on the doorjamb. "Son of a—"

Max turned when he felt an insistent poke in his back. "Language, Dr. Wiley," Jeanne said, jabbing a chastising finger under Max's nose.

"Oh, jeez, I forgot. Sorry, Mrs. Brewster." He turned back to the door, shoulders slumping. "Okay, Angel, you got it. You win. I give up. I'm leaving. And this time you won't be hearing from me again." He leaned down and gave Spill's collar a tug. "Come on Spill. We've got a long drive." He started pushing his way through the sea of Brewsters.

"Great," Bart yelled at the door, "now see what you did, brat?"

"Max?" Angel's voice sounded tiny.

He stilled but didn't turn back. "What?"

"What did you want to say to me?"

Dropping his head to his chest, Max half chuckled and half sighed. "Nothing. Forget it. It doesn't matter." He kept on walking into the living room with Joe following close behind.

"Angel's stubborn as hell, Max, but she's a good kid," Joe said as Max headed for the door. He only knew it was Joe because of the red plaid shirt. "Don't give up on her."

Blue plaid Josh dashed into the room. "Hey, you can't leave yet, Max. She'll come around. You'll see."

"Nah," Max shook his head in resignation. "I got the message loud and clear this time. Angel's right. We're just not cut out for each other. I was crazy to think she'd come around and forgive me. I knew honesty was really important to her, but I went ahead and lied to her anyway. Nothing I can say or do is going to change that." Max shook hands with the twins and they gave each other manly pats on the back. "Thanks for trying to help. You Brewster boys are all right."

Offering the brothers a friendly wink, Max left the cabin with Spill in tow.

Chapter Seventeen

"He's gone," Joe said, heading back to Angel's room. "Hope you're happy now." Angel cracked open the door an inch and her five brothers muscled their way in, with her mother bringing up the rear. "Here," Joe said, shoving Max's bag at her. "He forgot this. There's a wrapped present inside."

"How could you treat the boy like that," Jeanne said, "especially after he came all this way just to apologize to you? I'm ashamed of you, Angel."

"But, Mom—"

"Yeah," Josh cut Angel off, "the poor guy humbled himself in front of you and your whole frickin' family and you treated him like shit—sorry, Ma," he added before his mother could call him on his salty language.

Brad opened his mouth and Angel clapped a hand over it. "Okay, just hold it. I really don't want to be bombarded with criticism from each of you right now. Regardless of what you might think, this is my life, my problem, and strictly my decision to make." She gave a warning scowl to each of them.

"I just wanted to know what's in the bag, that's all," Brad said after Angel lowered her hand.

"I was wondering the same thing," Jeanne said, doing her best to peek at the bag's contents. The brothers echoed her comments.

"Did you ever think," Angel said, "that I might want some privacy?"

"Hah!" Jeanne's barking laughter cracked the air. "You've clearly forgotten this is the Brewster family, haven't you?"

Bart gingerly slipped the contents from the bag before Angel realized what he was doing. The big moose had the audacity to rip off the wrapping paper! "It looks like a photo album," he said.

"Give that back to me," Angel said, wondering why Max had given her a photo album when they'd never taken any pictures of each other. Unless Max had one of those hidden cameras in the— Oh. My. God. She lunged for the album and flew through the air, landing on her bed with the book under her.

"Tickle time!" Ben yelled and, before she knew it, Angel's poor tortured body was jerking with forced laughter.

"That is so *not* fair!" she said as the convulsions subsided and she sat up. Of course, the album was out of her possession by now and in the hands of the tormenting Brewster boys. "Thirty-some years old and you baboons are still a bunch of bullies," she said to their backs as her brothers left the room, album in hand. "What if they're pictures of me naked?"

"Don't worry," Josh called over his shoulder. "We'll observe them with a purely clinical eye." Angel groaned.

"You took naked pictures of each other? Goodness." Jeanne stiffened. "Even your father and I have never done that. The closest we came to—"

"Mom!" Angel slapped her hands over her ears. "I really don't want to hear anything about you and Dad in...in *that* way. I prefer to think of your six children being delivered by Sasquatch, just the way you told us when we were little, okay?"

211

She let her hands drop. "And, no, Max and I didn't take naked photos...well, at least none that I know about." She sank her teeth into her bottom lip.

"Come on, dear," Jeanne said, tugging her daughter from the bed. "We'd better get out there." Feeling drained and resigned, Angel complied and followed along.

"Whoa, Angel," Joe's voice rang out from the living room. "You should see this."

"Seeing as how the gift from Max is supposed to be mine," she said, rounding the corner, "that would be nice."

"She's gonna cry," Josh said with assurance.

"Oh yeah...big time," Brad concurred. "Better get the box of tissues, Ma."

Her curiosity peaked to maximum levels, Angel brushed past her mother and ran into the living room, crawling over her brothers and wedging herself between the twins so she could see what all the fuss was about.

All it took was one quick glance and Angel gasped. Then, just as predicted, the tears started. "Oh my God...Max..."

The rich, padded leather-bound album was filled with the antique Rubenesque postcards that had been scattered around her office. Artistically arranged on each page, some were secured with ornate photo corners and others peeked out of little cut paper frames. Women's quotations from her collection filled some of the space between the postcards. They weren't the scrawled, messy ones taken directly from the list hanging in her office. Each quotation had been retyped in appealing, fancy fonts, then printed out, cut and pasted in place.

Dotting the pages were tiny, gold heart-shaped trinkets, bits of ribbon and lace, and other delicate decorations. As she turned each page, the tears rolled silently down Angel's cheeks.

"Oh, he must really care about me," she mumbled.

"Well, duh," Ben answered. "Looks like that was obvious to everyone here but you, lamebrain," he said in his most helpful, sensitive manner.

Angel flipped the pages quickly, her heart pounding rapidly as she scanned the beautiful book, astonished at all the trouble Max had gone to for her. The time, effort and care that must gone into the creation of the book just boggled her mind. When she approached the end of the book, she flipped another page and gasped again, and everyone crowded in close to see why.

The last section of the album consisted of antique postcards with photographs of men, mostly from the Victorian era. Some were bodybuilders while others stood stiffly in three-piece striped suits. Most wore grand mustaches. Accompanying the postcards were quotations from men, printed in a heavier, more masculine font face.

"Look what he did," Angel said, shaking her head in wonder. "He added all of these himself."

"'On the one hand,'" Josh read aloud, "'we'll never experience childbirth. On the other hand, we can open all our own jars.' That's from Bruce Willis," he said.

"Here's one by Dave Barry," Bart said. "'If a woman has to choose between catching a fly ball and saving an infant's life, she will choose to save the infant's life without even considering if there are men on base.'"

"Ain't that the truth," Joe said with an exaggerated eyeball roll.

"'Here's all you have to know about men and women,'" Angel read aloud, "'women are crazy, men are stupid. And the main reason women are crazy is that men are stupid.'" She laughed along with her mother and brothers. "That's from George Carlin." She shook her head slowly as she marveled at the book in front of her. It was, by far, the single most romantic thing anyone had ever done for her. Hell, it was the absolute most romantic thing she'd ever heard of!

Jeanne brought her daughter a box of tissues, and Angel dabbed her leaky eyes and nose. "The boy's in love with you, dear," Jeanne said softly as she kissed the top of Angel's head.

"Hell, yeah. Any guy who would do something like this has got it really bad," Bart said.

"Either that or he's gay," Brad added with sage wisdom as he fingered a strip of lace framing one of the postcards.

"He's not gay." Angel bounded to her feet. "I have to stop him."

"Oh...I'm afraid it's too late, dear," Jeanne said. "Max is long gone by now."

Joe glanced at the time display on his cell phone. "Maybe not. He hasn't been gone all that long. I'm betting he's probably tied up in all that weekend tourist traffic in the center of town." He leapt off his chair. "If we hurry we might be able to catch him."

"Let's round up the posse, Sheriff," Josh said in a low, affected voice as he jumped to his feet, "and we'll head him off at the pass."

Soon, all the brothers were on their feet and heading out the door.

"Hey!" Angel called after them as she slipped into her shoes. "What about me?"

"And me!" Jeanne said, untying her apron and scampering toward the kitchen.

"You've got food cooking in the kitchen, Mom," Angel said as she rushed for the door. "Just stay here until we get back."

"Not on your life," Jeanne called. "Just give me a minute to take the meat out of the oven and turn off the burners under the pots. You don't honestly think I'm going to miss this, do you?"

In a matter of moments, all five brothers, Angel and her mother were crammed together in the large van and barreling down the winding gravel road.

The Brewsters were on a mission!

Chapter Eighteen

"I don't know what I was thinking when I drove up here, Spill," Max said, shaking his head. "Thank God I got out when I did is all I have to say. Even better, I managed to escape without regurgitating the L word like some big lovesick dope." He gave a humorless chuckle.

Like most of the touristy towns along the Oregon coast, Cannon Beach, with its famous Haystack Rock landmark, was littered with vacationers and teeming with cars and recreational vehicles. It seemed to Max that getting through that one small stretch of road in the shopping district was taking an eternity. As far as he was concerned, the sooner he could get back to Portland, and far away from Angel and the whole Brewster clan, the better.

"What the hell could possibly be so damned interesting," Max said as he observed a horde of people streaming in and out of the tiny shops, art galleries and restaurants. "How many seashells with painted scenes of Cannon Beach does one person really need?" He marveled as he noticed the happy, spellbound expressions on the women and the vacant-eyed zombie-like expressions on the men. "That would be me, Spill," Max said, gesturing to one of the walking dead. "That's what my life would be like if I hooked up with Angel...or any other dame, for that matter. Nope. Uh-uh. From now on it's strictly the bachelor life for us guys, right, buddy?" He reached over and messed Spill's fur. "We don't need all that relationship grief or those rings through the nose, or any of the other crap that comes with letting a woman wheedle her way into your life."

Tsking as the traffic crawled, Max looked into his rearview mirror when he heard a honking racket behind him. "Probably another poor shmoe that's eager as hell to get away from a woman," Max said, chuckling. "Hang on there, pal," he said, tapping the horn in return. "I'm first."

The honking grew more persistent and Max strained to see what was going on. That's when he spotted the van, which looked a helluva lot like the same one he saw parked at the Brewster cabin, but it couldn't be. The vehicle seemed to come out of nowhere. Most likely some local who'd taken a short cut through the back roads. Max kept returning his gaze to the rearview mirror and the honking van, stuck in traffic behind him now.

And then Max saw her. Angel.

And all of her brothers.

And her mother.

And Henry.

They'd all tumbled out of the van and were running toward him, shouting and calling for Max to stop. He slammed on his brakes, causing a screech of tires and a chorus of angry honking and colorful language from the row of cars and their occupants behind him.

He rolled down his window and popped his head out. Spill, the ever-brave three-legged beagle, suddenly mistook himself for Wonder Dog as he leapt from the car's open window and raced toward the advancing Brewsters.

"Max! Max!" Angel cried as she ran toward him. "Wait. Please. You can't go."

God damn if she didn't look beautiful with her cheeks all rosy and her flaxen hair waving in the wind behind her as she ran. Just like that avenging angel he'd seen the first night they met.

"Get your ass back here, Wiley," Joe shouted. "Angel's got something to say."

"Language, Joseph!" Jeanne barked breathlessly as she scampered along, doing her best to keep up with the rest of her brood.

"Hey, buddy," one of the drivers behind him yelled to Max, "get that piece of shit car of yours off the road so the rest of us can get out of here."

"Language, mister!" Jeanne admonished as she waved a chastising finger and slapped a hand on the car's hood before scooting past it.

His hands on the steering wheel, Max dropped his head against his arms and laughed. "Oh, Lord, what have I gotten myself into?" With nowhere to park or to pull over, Max shrugged, said, "Aw, what the hell," and just put his car in park in the middle of the street. In the next instant he was running through traffic to meet Angel.

By this time people had poured out of the shops and gathered on the street to see what all the commotion was about. The last thing in the world Max wanted right now was an audience.

"Max! I'm sorry," Angel called as she maneuvered around some of the motionless cars. "I saw the album you made. It's the most beautiful, sweetest, wonderful, most romantic thing I've ever seen in my life. I love it so much it made me cry, Max. And I love *you*, too!"

A whoop went up from the Brewster boys at Angel's public statement of affection, but the loudest howl of joy came from her mother. Max had to admit that it felt mighty damn good to hear those words skip past Angel's lips. He had to hand it to Dominick Spinelli. The old guy sure knew plenty about women.

Max zipped through the remaining cars between them like a maze until he reached Angel. As soon as he was close enough, he caught her into his arms and kissed her.

"I love you, too," he said quietly against her ear. "That's what I drove up here to tell you."

"Oh, Max." Beaming a bright, happy smile, Angel reached up on her tiptoes and kissed him.

"What was that?" Josh said, closing the distance.

"Yeah, we didn't hear you, Max," Ben called from just behind Josh.

"I said I love her," Max said, exceedingly conscious that a street full of curious onlookers were listening and watching his every move. He felt like he was the featured attraction on the evening news. *Man says the L word at eleven...*

"Sorry, can't hear you, doc," Brad shouted as he cupped his hand to his ear and smirked. Echoing his words, the rest of the Brewster boys mimicked the ear-cupping as they all stood a mere car's length from Max and Angel.

"Aw, damn..." Max looked at the strangers who'd gathered, and then at the eager faces of the Brewster boys, and then at Angel's mother, who practically glowed with expectant delight. Then he looked into the beautiful face of the woman he loved.

"Angel Brewster," Max shouted loud enough for everyone to hear, "I love you." Angel squealed with delight at his proclamation. "With every fiber of my being, dollface," he blared like a stage actor projecting his voice to the last row, "I love you."

With the abruptness of a flash flood, the Brewsters and a throng of jovial strangers crushed against them, laughing, clapping and belting out cheers. In the midst of it all, Max heard Spill and Henry getting into the act, barking their fool heads off.

"Hey, that was real sweet, pal," the driver who'd yelled to Max about moving his piece of shit car said, patting Max on the back. "Now, if the show's over, lover boy, do you think you could move your car so the rest of us can get out of here?"

With the cars in front of his gone, Max was able to pull over far enough to let those behind him get by. All smiley and weepy and bubbling with more excitement than anyone else present, Jeanne had already asked Max...no, make that *ordered* him, to come back to the cabin for dinner.

Following a filling, celebratory meal, after which Jeanne insisted on doing the cleanup herself, she came back into the dining room with a bottle of champagne and two glasses that she set before Max and Angel. "Boys," she addressed her sons, "get your coats and gear because we're going home now." She punctuated her statement with an exaggerated wink. Angel groaned and Max chuckled.

After a couple of smacking kisses and lung-squeezing hugs from Jeanne and a hearty round of pats and buddy-hugs from the Brewster boys, everyone left and Max and Angel were alone.

"I like your family," he said. "They're down to earth and real. Your brothers are crazy about you, and your mom's a real doll."

"My brothers are a royal pain in the ass, but I love the big dopes. And Mom is great. She's the original Susie Homemaker— a true domestic goddess who lives for keeping her family happy." Angel shook her head. "One of these days I'll make her see the light."

"She did a fine job raising her daughter," Max said, nuzzling Angel's neck before popping the cork on the champagne bottle and pouring them each a glass. "I like the way she hustled her brood out of here so you and I could be alone."

"Me too."

"To your mother's sage wisdom," Max said, holding his filled glass aloft in a toast.

"And to this crazy thing called love," Angel responded with a come-hither smile. They clinked glasses and sipped.

They'd just finished their first glass of champagne when Angel glided a finger beneath Max's chin as she poured him a second glass.

"Hey," he said, grasping the bottle, "that's my job."

Angel held the bottle tight and filled her glass. "Here I was just about to tell you that since you've been a very good boy, I'd let you in through the backdoor tonight." She stood and turned her backside to Max, clapping her hands on her ass and gyrating. Then she picked up her champagne and strolled from the room with a smooth, seductive sway.

"Damn...I've got to use the L word more often," Max said, his gaze transfixed on Angel's swiveling hips as he took his champagne and followed her into her room.

Chapter Nineteen

Angel wrapped her arms around Max's neck as soon as he'd stripped off his clothes. She swooped her tongue across his naked chest. "I'd forgotten just how good a certified prime sexist tastes." She gave a throaty chuckle before nibbling one of his nipples. "I just love the way your dark chest hair tapers off into a long, thin line down your body. All the way to your great big macho cock." Her teasing fingers tiptoed down the fine trail to Max's three-piece package.

He sucked in a breath when Angel's cool fingers wrapped around his dick. squeezing. She brought her head up, licked her lips and purred. Max's gaze zeroed in on her puckered nipples. Those sweet little berries stood at attention, just begging for his mouth. "Do all feminists have tits this gorgeous?" He clamped his teeth on a nipple, tugging hard. He loved the way she shivered in his arms and moaned at the sensation.

"Don't call them tits," she said breathlessly. "It's crude."

"Can't help it...I'm just a crude, sexist pig," Max said, taking the other rigid peak into his mouth and teasing it with his teeth. This time Angel went weak at the knees. Max groaned a satisfied chuckle as he supported her wavering frame. "In any case, dollface, you've got the best damn tits, boobs, knockers, bazooms, maracas, or whatever you want to call them, I've ever seen." He went back to nibbling and tugging.

"Breasts will do just fine," she said, swallowing a long, hard moan. "And you, doc, have got the best damn cock, dick, boner, pecker, schlong, or whatever you want to call it, *I've* ever seen." She held his cock firm against her thigh as it jerked in gleeful anticipation, squeezing and then rolling it against her soft flesh. Her dripping pussy juices glided across its head, baptizing it with her wetness.

"I don't care what you call it, doll. A dick by any other name is just as happy." He started to pull away. Angel clutched him.

"Where do you think you're going?" she said.

"Over to my jeans to get one of those nice long strips of condoms I brought with me." He kissed the tip of her nose but she held tight. "Then I'm throwing you on that bed and having my way with you."

"No...it's okay. I'm on the pill. Don't wear a condom, Max," she said, grinding against him as she gazed into his eyes with those big baby blues of hers. "Let me feel you...the warmth of your flesh as it throbs and pulses and you empty yourself deep inside me."

"Oh Jesus..." Max said, concentrating hard so he wouldn't come all over her leg and hand.

"Come on, Macho Man," she said in a gutsy voice. "Fuck me. Show me what Jack Clyde would do to Trixie Lang."

With a low, guttural growl, Max grabbed Angel by the waist, lifting her from the floor. Carrying her a few feet to the nearest log wall, he plastered her there with his body. "He'd fuck her brains out, just like this," Max said, spreading her legs as he supported Angel's weight. Angel gave a gasp of surprise as they locked gazes. With a fierce swiftness born of half-crazed lust and passion, Max impaled Angel on his marble-hard cock.

"Oh, dear God!" She screamed, throwing her head back against the logs as he shoved into her fast and hard. "Max!"

"Tell me again that you love me, dollface," he said as Angel wrapped her legs around his waist.

"I do." She swallowed hard. "God help me, I love every miserable, unreasonable sexist bone in your body, Max Wiley."

Max discovered a position deep inside Angel's hot, juicy cunt that felt supreme. Perfect. "I wish I could stay here forever, buried in the center of your feminist flesh," he managed just before the familiar tingle took hold of his balls. Crying out her name, he shot his semen into her.

Angel's pussy muscles clenched and unclenched around him as she cried out her release. For that brief instant in time the lovers embodied Jack and Trixie as well as Max and Angel as their fluids mixed and their bodies shuddered together in a gripping climax.

"I've...I've never done it standing up before," Angel panted as Max slowly moved them to the bed, hoping she had no idea just how shaky his legs felt at that moment.

"That makes two of us, dollface," he said with a chuckle as he set her down on the edge of the bed. He collapsed next to her, wrapping her in his arms as they fell back against the pillows, spent and satisfied.

"Well, I'm very impressed," she said, kissing his shoulder.

"Yeah...me too. I'm damn good."

"A regular macho stud." Laughing, Angel gave his arm a playful whack. "So that's how Jack Clyde fucks his women, hmm? Maybe I'll have to start reading your books." She paused a moment and then crinkled her nose. "Nah." She giggled.

"Actually, Clyde hasn't done that up to now, but you can better believe he'll be doing it in a future book. Now that I know such a feat is really possible. Frankly, I had my doubts." Max brushed his lips across hers.

As soon as he had the strength to sit up, he reached for the two glasses of champagne, handing one to Angel. "We'd better finish these before they go completely flat," he said, downing his in three big gulps.

Not to be outdone, Max noticed, Angel followed suit, gulping hers down. "I just hope the alcohol doesn't keep you from getting it up again, hot shot," she said, smirking as she flipped his half-erect cock.

"You don't have to worry about that, doll. All I have to do is think about taking you doggy-style." Max braced himself for the onslaught of pillow-whapping from Angel. "Now all that pillow abuse, on the other hand," he said, grabbing the pillow and planting it under his head as he reclined against the headboard, "just might impede my recuperative powers. Now be a good little doll and play nice if you want little Maxie to come out and play again."

"Ugh, honestly." Closing her eyes, Angel tsked and shook her head. "You are so terminally, hopelessly sexist, Max. What am I ever going to do with you, hmm?" She grabbed his face in her hands, planting a loud smack on his lips.

"There's only one thing I can think of," Max said. And then he did something he swore he'd never do in his entire life. Ever. He slid off the bed and got down on one knee before Angel. God knows, it wasn't something he'd planned. It was purely an intuitive sort of thing that just spilled out from the pit of his gut. Nothing had ever felt so goddamn scary or so right in his life.

"Marry me, dollface."

Angel screamed—actually screamed, which had both Spill and Henry barking like mad as they raced into the room and vaulted onto the bed.

Max felt like screaming or barking or both, right along with them. Did those ring-in-the-nose, ball-and-chain commitment words really just spurt from his mouth? Was he crazy? Was he insane? Had he lost every ounce of the sound male logic that had convinced him he was born to be a carefree, unattached bachelor?

Max sighed. Yes, definitely. All of the above. Clearly, that's what happens to a guy when he falls in love.

"Are you serious?" Angel said, fending off dual face licks from the dogs.

Max couldn't help but laugh at her question. "Trust me, sweetheart. Marriage proposals are something no single man in his right mind jokes about to a woman."

"But..." Angel started and then paused, worrying her bottom lip. "Aren't you afraid we won't get along?"

"Hell yes. I'd be amazed if we did, but we'll have a helluva good time trying."

"Aren't you worried we'll have next to nothing in common?" Angel added.

"Absolutely. Especially now that we won't have that business about our parents thinking we're gay in common anymore." He got back up on the bed. Taking Angel into his arms, he kissed her tenderly as Spill and Henry did their best to join in the fun. "At least life with my feisty little feminist will never be boring," he said, gently pushing the dogs away. "So, what do you say? Do you think you can bring yourself to marry a deep-rooted sexist?"

"Anybody can change," Angel said with a bright, hopeful smile.

Max eyed her skeptically. "Meaning you or me, babe?"

"Why...both of us, of course." With an amused look, Angel hugged him tight. "Oh, yes, Max. Yes, I'll marry you!"

Seeing as how his mouth went dry and he went numb from the top of his head to the tips of his toes, Max figured he was either extremely happy or scared shitless. Maybe it was both. Yeah. Definitely both.

"Max?" Angel shook his arm as he just sat there for a moment silently. "Are you okay?"

"Probably not," he mumbled, and then, with a deep breath, he shook himself out of it. After all, it wouldn't be good for his future wife to think he was a big wuss. He had to look on the bright side. Before long he'd be a married man, which meant he'd have unlimited tit, cunt and ass privileges. Frequent access to Angel's numerous carnal attributes made the whole commitment thing a lot easier to swallow.

"You have no idea how much I love you, Angel." He covered her mouth with his, plunging his tongue into the silky recesses. "Life with you is going to be my greatest adventure."

"I love you, too, Max." She could barely get close to him with the dogs crawling all over them.

"Okay, you two," Max said, taking Spill and Henry by their collars and leading them off the bed. "It's time to make yourselves busy elsewhere." The tongue-lolling furry duo happily pranced along as Max led them out of the room. Then Max decided to have a bit of fun.

"I'll be supporting us once we get married," he said to Angel, looking over his shoulder with a solemn expression. "Once you quit your job and become the little apron-wearing woman of the house," he continued, with dogs in tow as he took them to the living room, "I'm sure your mom would be thrilled to teach you how to do all sorts of nice housewifey things for me like she does for you and your brothers." Max had to bite the inside of his cheek to keep from laughing when he imagined Angel's incredulous, outraged expression.

"I beg your pardon?" she yelled after him, her voice almost a squawk. "Is that what you're picturing in that tiny male brain of yours? Your idea of marital bliss?"

God, she was easy.

"Yeah. It'll be great, Angel." Preparing a dog-drooling feast, Max dribbled some beer into a couple of bowls and added some scraps of leftover pork roast. "Just what I always planned. You'll start the day making me a nice big breakfast and a pot of coffee before I leave for work." He placed the dishes on the fireplace hearth, patted both dogs on the head and returned to the bedroom, closing the door to prevent further canine visitations. "Then," he continued, "you'll bustle around the house vacuuming and doing laundry and picking up after me for the next couple of hours."

Angel's eyes and mouth formed Os. Before she could say a word, Max went on. "You'll take a lunch break to watch some game shows or the soaps," he said. "Then you'll spend the rest of the day in the kitchen while I'm at the clinic or when I'm working on my manuscripts, baking all sorts of cookies and desserts and whipping up multi-course dinners for me and my buddies before you usher me into the family room so I can snack on beef sticks, chips and beer in front of the TV while you clean everything up."

Climbing back onto the bed next to Angel, Max nuzzled her neck and pulled her into a hug. "Aw, dollface...we'll have the perfect life together, won't we?"

"Hah! Dream on, Max." Angel squirmed out of his embrace, scrambling off the bed so fast it seemed as though she'd been zapped with electric current.

In two seconds Max had her back on the bed, flat on her back. He held her fists tight in place as he looked down at her. "Just like a dame," he said, shaking his head. "All furious, feisty and flummoxed."

"What!?" Angel gasped. "You're teasing me? You think that was funny? That's your idea of being sweet, loving and romantic after asking me to marry you and spend the rest of my life with you?" She continued to fight, but Max held her firm. "Forget it. I take it back. I have no intention of marrying you, Max Wiley."

"No. My idea of being sweet, loving and romantic," Max said, going for the jugular and heaping on the guilt, "was taking more than two days to shop and clip and type and print and glue just to make that big album of postcards and quotations for you, dollface. All because I love you."

Angel stopped struggling and became soft, sweet and submissive. "Oh...that's right. You did do that for me, didn't you?" She looked up at him with those big watery eyes and he melted. "Okay, Max, because it was the best thing I've ever had any man ever do for me, I'll change my mind. I'll go ahead and marry you." She beamed a smile up at him and he bent down to kiss her. "Besides...I knew you were joking all the time."

"You little minx!" Max tickled her until she screamed, begging for mercy.

"No, that's not fair," she said, catching her breath. "That's what my brothers do to control me, and I hate it!"

"Damn. I knew there was a reason I liked those Brewster boys so much."

Chapter Twenty

"Remember the compound in Africa I told you about? The one my friends own?" Max asked as he tossed Angel this way and that until he had her on her knees with her butt positioned high in the air.

"First of all, yes, I remember," Angel said with a tuneful sigh. She'd certainly have her work cut out for her trying to de-macho Max Wiley. "Second, Max, you really do need to get over this notion that I'm your personal rag doll to be tossed about whenever and however you like, okay?"

"Sorry, dollface, it's just that I want to fuck my brand new fiancée so bad that I've got to fight not to come just looking at her sweet, succulent body."

Max had a way with words, she'd give him that.

He trailed a path of damp kisses from her mid-spine down to her butt crack, with each touch of his lips turning her on even more.

"After all, when we were in the dining room sipping champagne," he reminded her, "you did say I could do it doggy-style." Max's hands stilled when Angel went stiff. "Oops. Sorry, doll. Forgot how you dislike that term."

"Yeah, right."

"It's true," Max said in all innocence. "What I mean to say was *backwards*. In the backdoor, or however the hell you want me to say it."

"You're incorrigible, Max."

"Which is why you love me so much."

"Just remember," Angel said with conviction, "next time, I get to be on top."

"I hope you don't honestly expect me to take issue with that, sweetheart."

"Good. Because I'm looking forward to the ride of my life." She wiggled her backside at him.

"So how about taking our honeymoon in Africa?" Max suggested and Angel looked over her shoulder to catch his gaze hot-glued to her jiggling ass. Kneeling behind her, he groaned with pleasure as he smoothed his hands over the surface of her cheeks, pressing his fingers into her flesh and trailing his thumb up and down the length of her crack. "Just you and me and all those wild animals under the stars."

"Mmm...like Tarzan and Jane," Angel said, envisioning the two of them running around half-naked and fucking like lions in heat. "How romantic. I imagine Africa's probably a vegetarian's paradise. While we're there I can see what I can do about making some social reforms."

Max became stone-still. "What?"

"They're still performing clitorectomies in parts of Africa," Angel said. "Can you believe that? They actually cut off the—"

"Angel," Max said slowly, "I know what it is. And I know it's wrong. But—"

"Good, then maybe the two of us can work together to—"

"Dollface, are you crazy? Do you want to get us both killed? On our honeymoon? You just can't traipse off to foreign countries and start meddling in their business."

"But, Max— Ow!"

"Sorry, sweetheart," Max said, smoothing his hand over the place on her butt where he'd just pinched her. "I had no choice but to resort to brute force to bring my little activist fiancée to her senses and back to the issue at hand."

"Which is?" Her butt hiked a bit higher as Max's thumb slipped deeper into her crack. "Ooh, yeah...now I remember. That feels so good, Max. I like your idea. Let's do it."

No sooner were those words out of Angel's mouth than Max thrust his stiff-as-steel cock up into her cunt, eliciting a surprised yelp from Angel.

"Max! What are you doing?"

"You mean you can't tell?" he said with a hoarse chuckle before pummeling into her depths again. "You said *let's do it*, and so, humble servant that I am, I obeyed your directive immediately."

Angel wiggled her ass and let out a throaty chuckle. "I meant let's go to Africa, Max."

"Oh."

"Don't worry. I'm certainly not sorry that you misconstrued my meaning. Mmm...lordy, you feel so good inside me, Max. I missed you—and all those wonderful, amazing things you do with that cock of yours—so much when we weren't talking."

"I missed you, too, baby," Max said. "If we hadn't gotten back together I never would have had a chance to watch the beautiful sight of my cock entering and exiting your pretty, dripping pussy." He reached forward to play with her breasts. "Oh yeah, I can picture myself doing this with you for years to come. There's no way I'd ever get tired of having your slick pussy suck my cock inside while I watch." He cupped one of her breasts, kneading it as he seated his cock again. "It feels good to be home, dollface" he said slipping out and shoving into her again fast and hard. "Right where I belong."

Angel loved the way he groaned just then. She grasped him from behind, searching for his sac. When she made contact, she squeezed his balls with gentle pressure as Max gave her nipple a vigorous pinch and twist. "If we get along half as well out of bed as we do making love," she said, "we'll be okay."

"Don't move a muscle," Max said, slipping out of her depths as he reached over to the nightstand.

"What are you doing?"

"Condom."

"But..."

"Feeling adventurous?" Max asked, rolling on the condom and then taking his place behind her again.

"Well...I don't know. That depends."

"That's okay," Max said, "never mind. I keep forgetting that women don't possess the same spirit of adventure that men do."

"You're trying to goad me again, Max."

"Is it working?"

"If you're game, then so am I," Angel answered, wondering what Max had up his sleeve.

She gave a little cry when he spread her cheeks and then slicked his tongue up the crevice. "Oh...now *that* is definitely a new adventure," she whispered.

"You've got a gorgeous ass, Angel," he said, kneading her flesh. "I'd like to explore it deeper if you'll let me."

"You mean..."

"Have you ever done it that way before?"

"No," Angel said. "I guess you have, huh?"

"Uh...actually, no, but Jack Clyde has. I did the research and wrote it into one of my books."

"Well...that's handy. Gee, hardboiled crime has come a long way since Mickey Spillane, hasn't it? I don't remember Humphrey Bogart doing it in the ass in any of those old detective flicks." She chuckled, stopping abruptly as the head of Max's cock nestled into the crack of her ass.

"So, are you game, doll?"

Angel only hesitated briefly. "I can take whatever you dish out," she said with false bravado. "I love you and I trust you, Max. Just be patient with me, okay? I'm not quite sure what to expect."

"We'll take it slow and easy. Only part way in the first time until you get used to accepting my cock there, okay?" Angel nodded. "I need some cream or oil or something," Max said. "Something for lubrication."

"I have no idea what's here in the cabin," Angel said. "We'll have to look around."

Nearly ten minutes later they were both back on the bed, giggling while Max rolled on another condom.

"I'm going to feel like a basted turkey, Max," Angel said as she watched him slather softened butter on his sheathed cock.

"I love turkey," he said, jiggling his eyebrows."

"I've always been quite fond of stuffing," she retorted, still eyeing his buttered cock.

Behind her again, Max massaged butter on the outside of her anus and slipped a buttered finger inside to lubricate her. It was an odd and curious feeling, having a finger up her ass for purely carnal purposes. At first she didn't like it and squirmed, but as Max's finger continued to move inside her gently, she found the sensation to be quite pleasurable.

"Now just relax, sweetheart," Max said. "Don't tighten up. It'll be easier that way for both of us. You have such a pretty little rosebud here." The buttered head of his shaft replaced his finger at her small opening. "Every part of your body is beautiful to me, Angel," he said softly. "I want to love every inch of the woman I love." He kissed each of her ass cheeks.

If she absolutely had to do something as lamebrained as marrying a diehard sexist, Max Wiley was definitely the man. This brand new sexual experience they shared, along with the thoughtful, romantic album he created for her, showed Angel that her hardheaded tough guy could be perfectly sweet, gentle, caring and sensitive when necessary.

Max nudged his buttered cock forward until it met with resistance from the muscles ringing her anus. Angel felt her buttocks tense involuntarily beneath his splayed palms.

"Just let me know if you need me to go slower or stop." Max advanced his cock gently. "There will probably be some discomfort at first, dollface, and after that it should feel damned good."

"Okay." After a moment she added, "We're butt virgins, Max." And she giggled. Angel had no idea why that ludicrous statement came out of her mouth at that moment, other than because she was nervous.

While she was relaxed and still giggling, Max exerted more pressure. "That's it, sweetheart, just let yourself relax and have fun with this." With another gentle thrust, Angel's muscles eased, allowing Max entrance.

"Oh! Oh...*ooh...*"

"Are you okay, my little butt virgin?" Max asked, chuckling as he tenderly eased more of his cock into her anus.

"Yes. It's...well, it's kind of weird. Different. But I like it. It's... Mmm... Yeah, that feels good, Max."

"Goddamn right it does, dollface." He groaned. "What a great sensation. Incredible. Jesus, you're so tight."

"Does it feel better than what you expected after doing your important butt-fuck research?" Her voice was tinged with humor.

"Hell yes," Max groaned, barely able to get the words out.

Angel started to giggle. It was cut off as she heard a heated moan rise in her throat while Max moved ever so gently inside her. "I want more Max. Give me more."

Instead of moving his cock deeper inside her, Max reached forward, jamming two or three of his fingers up her pussy. The delicious sensation of fullness almost sent her over the edge as Max moved inside her ass and her cunt.

"You feel amazing, dollface," he said, finding her clit with his thumb and abrading it. "Believe me, I want to thrust all the way into you as much as you want me to, sweetheart, but we've got to take it nice and easy. I don't want you to get too sore the first time." His voice caught. "Jesus Christ, Angel, you feel so fucking good I could die a happy man right now without a single regret."

"Oh God...I'm going to come, Max."

"Not yet, sweetheart," he said, withdrawing his fingers from her pussy. "I want to keep this going for both of us as long as I can. It feels too damn good to stop."

"Exquisite," Angel said, panting.

Max massaged her ass cheeks as he slipped just a tiny bit further inside her. "I can't hold out much longer," he said through labored breathing. "It's showtime, sweetheart. Ready to see stars?"

"Fuck, yes," Angel nearly screamed as she swirled her hips.

Max reached beneath her again, shoving his hand up her dripping cunt while his thumb flicked rapidly over her engorged clit.

Angel heard an otherworldly growl of pleasure erupt from deep within her lungs as Max finger-fucked her. The new dual-filled sensation of pleasure was so extreme, so intense that Angel wished she could be suspended in time, right at the split second before she shattered.

Max grunted, sounding almost like a wild animal. "Angel...dollface!" he flat-out roared as he came, clutching her writhing hips as she screamed her own release.

By the time they were finished, Max and Angel were utterly spent. Breathing loud, satisfied sighs, they buckled into an exhausted, contented mass of tangled limbs.

"Thank you," Max said, "for making me the happiest man on the face of the planet."

"Because I gave up my butt virginity to you, you mean?" Angel laughed.

"No, smart ass." Max's laugh sounded as weak and tired as hers. "For loving me."

"God damn it, Max." Angel sniveled.

"What's the matter?"

"You made me cry again." She slapped a tired hand on his chest, rubbing her fingers over the sculpted planes of his pecs. "I love you and your ugly mug and your big stiff dick, you big lug."

"Hey!" With visible effort, Max dragged himself up on one elbow and grinned. "You read my book, didn't you?"

"Yup. When I first came up here to the cabin." Angel pulled herself toward the edge of the bed and opened the nightstand drawer, retrieving the book. "Clichéd. Sexist. Bigoted. Full of the kind of impossible scenarios that can only come from a typical, twisted male brain. Aside from all the things that inherently made me hate it, I sort of liked it. It was entertaining and hilarious."

"Hilarious?"

"Oh...I guess the humor must have been unintentional, huh?"

Max shrugged in response as he disposed of the condom.

Angel patted his thigh. "Sorry. It doesn't matter. You're a good writer, Max. I can see why you have a strong following."

"Thanks. That means a lot to me. Honest. I read some of your stuff when I went to your office a few days ago. You're really good too. Some very funny stuff." He chuckled.

Angel laughed. "Not intentionally."

"Oh," Max said. "Sorry."

"Hey...what do you think about me helping you to add a feminist slant to your Trixie character? We could collaborate, Max. It might be fun." Angel sat up, eagerly anticipating Max's response.

Clearly alarmed, Max opened his mouth to retort and then snapped it shut. "Sure," he said after a pause, "if you let me help you write your feminist articles for *Women's Wit and Wisdom* magazine. You know, input a man's perspective. Maybe I'll talk to B.J. about it. I could have my own column. She could run it right alongside yours."

"Uh-uh." Angel wrinkled her nose. "Maybe we should just agree to steer clear of each other's writing. What do you say?" She extended her hand. "Deal?"

"Deal." Max looked at Angel thoughtfully. "Hey, what's going to happen when we have kids?"

"You want them?"

"Yeah. You?"

Angel smiled. "I have no choice. My mother will hound me forever if I'm married and don't provide her with at least one drooling grandchild suitable for knee-bouncing. But, yeah, I really would like to have kids. Maybe one or two. What did you mean when you asked what's going to happen?"

"I was wondering about the likelihood of twins or triplets."

"Who knows? We could have one, two, three or God knows how many all at once." Angel laughed when she saw Max's dazed expression. Before the future father of her children knew what hit him, she sat atop Max, straddling his groin.

"Oh, sweetheart," he said. "I can't recoup that fast."

"What a wuss." Angel grinned at his surprised expression when she flipped his depleted cock. "Well then, this feisty feminist will just have to do something to bring her big macho lover's cock back to life. Are you up to the challenge, stud?"

Max looked down to see his burgeoning cock already answering for him. "I can take whatever you got, baby. Let me have it."

Angel slithered up and down Max's hard body, tickling him with her breasts and teasing his cock and balls. She sat upright and cupped her breasts, eliciting a promising groan from Max. "Wanna see me play with myself?" she said, plucking at her nipples, pinching them into rigid peaks. "Ooh, you have no idea how good this feels. It's like these wonderful little zigzagging shocks of pleasure shooting clear down to my pussy. See?" Angel dropped her hand. She slid it between her and Max, watching his eyes bulge as her fingers disappeared. She happily noticed that his recuperative powers were far more miraculous than Max had imagined.

"You're killing me, Angel. I'll never make it through the night."

"Damn. We haven't even made out our joint will yet," she teased in return. "Try not to die on me just yet, Max. I'd miss your colossal cock way too much." After testing him again with her hand, she found her future husband perfectly primed for action. Angel beamed a smile, raised her hips and slid her pussy onto his hard shaft.

"I love watching you play with yourself," Max said, his gaze on Angel's fingers as she rubbed her clit.

"Mmm, good." Her eyelids fluttered closed and she concentrated on not coming too quickly. "Next time you can put on a show for me, okay? I'd love to see you masturbate."

"What a dame."

"What a guy." She dropped on him again, twisting before she began to sway left and right. "I love you, Max," Angel said softly as tears filled her eyes. "I think you're my missing half."

"Together we make one helluva great whole," he said as he moved his hips beneath her.

"Get ready to come now, Max," she said matter-of-factly.

Max chuckled. "Oh? Who made you boss, missy?"

"Get used to it, buster. I'm a woman, Max. A dame. I know what makes men tick."

"Oh, you do, do you?" He gave her a slow, appreciative appraisal.

"Honey, this busty-broad knows exactly how to rock your world," she assured him. "How to make it spin right out of this galaxy. So get ready to see stars." With a throaty chuckle, Angel removed her fingers from her pussy. She licked them slowly, purring and tightening her inner muscles to squeeze his cock as she did. The silly grin left Max's face as his eyes widened and his breathing quickened. With a wicked smile, Angel lifted her breast and lowered her head, swirling her tongue at its tip. Max's growl was damned near primeval.

It was when she put her nipple between her teeth, closed her eyes and moaned that he screamed out, "Jesus H. Christ!" and climaxed with such force he banged his head on the headboard.

"Max Wiley, you are *so* easy." Angel's satisfied chuckle lasted merely an instant before her head tipped back and a husky cry tore from her throat. Screaming out Max's name, she collapsed against the man she loved.

The ballsy guy and his feisty dame fell asleep in each other's arms, fulfilled, blissfully fatigued, well-fucked, and supremely loved...

Chapter Twenty-One

The day before the wedding me and Trixie had a nice, quiet dinner at our favorite little Italian joint where we knew the owners and they treated us real square.

All I could think about as I sat there eyeballing my old lady, my sexy little Trixie while I slurped up the last of my pasta fagioli, was how much fun we were gonna have once I got her alone so we could play cops and robbers. We took turns being the cop. Trixie insisted. By now I'd learned it was better to just go along with her women's lib gibberish instead of fight it. As long as it ends up with me shoving my dick up her hole, who cares who's the cop and who's the robber, right?

And anyway, I liked the way she paraded around wearing just the jacket of her police uniform, with her bare ass sticking out, flashing her badge and her big twin maracas, and toting a water pistol filled with bourbon. Seeing how screwy dames can get, I put the kibosh on letting her tote her loaded gun around when we were having sex. I'm kinky, but not crazy.

Over the three-cheese ravioli she licked those pouty, cherry-red lips of hers and then I felt her toes creeping up my leg and settling on my dick, teasing it until it took notice. She was getting me all hot and bothered and we hadn't even had our spumoni yet. What a dame!

I must have had a shit-eating grin on my ugly mug because she laughed when she looked up at me as I tried to keep my composure and avoid shooting my load all over my pants right there in the restaurant. Trixie had a bouncy, tit-jiggling way of laughing that made men want to sell their souls. It was a bright, silvery sound like ice clinking in a glass.

When I finally figured out that I couldn't live without the dame, it was like getting bashed over the skull with a baseball bat repeatedly until my brain had been pounded into mush. A torture that multiplied itself every moment when I thought about being shackled to a ball-and-chain. But then, the more I thought about me and the doll hooking up for life, I had to admit getting outfitted for that ring through my nose was a whizbang of an idea.

"I love you, you big lug," she said, curling those magic little tootsies of hers over my balls.

"I love you, too, dollface." Yeah, that's right. I was even saying the L word now without doubling over in pain. Me, Jack Clyde, Private Detective. Who knew I'd turn out to be a regular sap one day, just like all the rest of those hapless guys being led around like a pooch on a leash. My plan to remain a bachelor was shot full of holes, busted to hell. So what? Life goes on.

Sure, things may get rocky and there might be some days when Trixie gets into a shit fit and starts clawing at my eyes with the unleashed fury of some jungle cat until I feel like clobbering her, but as long as me and dollface got each other...as long as I can feel her slip into my arms each night after we fuck our brains out, Jack Clyde is a happy guy.

Daisy Dexter Dobbs

Imagine frantically trying to file your way out of a locked bathroom door with a teeny nail file, dressed in nothing but a too-small towel while you're waiting for a real estate agent and a family with three small kids to arrive for a showing of your house.

Okay, now picture the contents of a box of just-delivered sex toys (purely for research purposes, you understand) strewn on the bed just outside the same locked bathroom door.

Welcome to the madcap real world of award-winning author Daisy Dexter Dobbs.

With her works hailed as the best in screwball romantic comedy, Daisy firmly believes in the healing power of love and laughter, although she's quick to disavow any notion that the often hilarious foibles and mishaps in her life have any connection whatsoever with the zany predicaments of the characters in her romantic comedy novels.

Uh-huh. Right.

A Chicago native, Daisy now lives in the Pacific Northwest. She is happily married to her high school sweetheart, and has one child.

Learn more about Daisy and her books by visiting her website at http://DaisyDexterDobbs.com, or stop by her blog to join in all the fun at http://daisydexterdobbs.blogspot.com/.

Samhain Publishing, Ltd.

It's all about the story...

Action/Adventure
Fantasy
Historical
Horror
Mainstream
Mystery/Suspense
Non-Fiction
Paranormal
Red Hots!
Romance
Science Fiction
Western
Young Adult

http://www.samhainpublishing.com

Printed in the United States
55295LVS00001BB/121-1008